Becoming Strangers

Becoming Strangers is Louise Dean's first novel, and the winnner of the Betty Trask Prize, 2004. Louise Dean lives in France with her husband and three children.

Becoming Strangers

Louise Dean

Scribner

First published in Great Britain by Scribner, 2004
This edition published by Scribner, 2004
An imprint of Simon & Schuster UK Ltd
A Viacom Company

7 9 10 8 6

Simon & Schuster UK Ltd
Africa House
64–78 Kingsway
London WC2B 6AH

www.simonsays.co.uk

Simon & Schuster Australia
Sydney

A CIP catalogue record for this book is available from the British Library

ISBN 0-7432-4000-6

Typeset by SX Composing DTP, Rayleigh, Essex
Printed and bound in Great Britain by
Cox & Wyman Ltd, Reading, Berkshire

In memory of
Edward George Waller
1914–1999
&
Gwendoline Dorothy Waller
1916–2001

'This is the great private problem of man; death as the loss of self. But what is the self? It is the sum of everything we remember. Thus what terrifies us about death is not the loss of the future but the loss of the past. Forgetting is a form of death ever present within life.'

Milan Kundera

1

Before he'd had cancer he'd been bored with life. Since he'd taken dying seriously, he'd been busy; he was occupied with understanding the disease and training his body to resist it. How hardy he was, physically. Six years of operations and excisions, starting with his chest, then the cancerous cells had metastasized to his lungs and on to his liver. A suite of initial excisions revealed each encampment to be partially malignant. He'd insisted on warfare. Each time the doctors told him and his family the chances of recovery were poor and the recurrence of cancer a likelihood. Year after year a fresh crop of cells emerged, excisions followed and he lived. The knife-and-forking of his body seemed to give a perverse impetus to his will to survive.

His tenacious hold on life was partly begotten by the conviction that his life *must* have accrued some value over time. What about all the sights and sounds recorded, all those thoughts tracked? They must be worth something. They must add up to some meaning. Billions of words over the years ordered into a handful of simple notions. His mother! His country! Right and wrong!

He gave up work. He took to reading. Politics, philosophy, biographies.

An exploratory probe of his pancreas had revealed further metastasis just two weeks previously. They could not operate again, they said. He shook the doctor's right hand with both of his hands and nodded. Later that evening, he overheard his wife sharing the news over the phone, from the study, door closed. 'He's ridden with it. They can't do anything for him now,' Annemieke said.

About three days later, their two adult sons had come by with the tickets for two weeks in paradise, a hotel spa resort on a Caribbean island. Very exclusive. Very final. He'd shaken their hands with both of his and nodded. Annemieke had kissed them.

'He's getting weak,' she had said, looking at her husband, 'the travelling won't be so easy. But I am strong enough for us both,' she'd added, then excused herself to answer the phone.

He had sat with his boys, holding the gift card between his fingers, pursing his lips, stroking his moustache, murmuring in bass tones, weighing reason as he listened to their news. The older boy was running his own Europe-wide Internet search business, the other finishing a PhD in philosophy at the University of Brussels. He tried to see them as real people.

Meanwhile, he could hear snatches of his wife's excitable conversation in the other room.

'Afterwards,' she was saying repeatedly and with emphasis.

He read the gift card again. The instruction was, '*Vermaak jullie!*' ('Enjoy yourselves!'), the implication that once that was done, he could come back and die properly.

This was going to be their last holiday. They had had a few last holidays previously, but this was going to be truly final. His wife's way of confirming this was to remind him now, on the aeroplane, that they had had some good times during their thirty-one years of marriage. She sighed from time to time as she turned the pages of her magazine before setting it aside.

'So many things,' she said to him, resting her jaw on her palm and looking into his face, 'and so empty, so meaningless.'

He agreed without looking at her.

'Very nice, very well made, but next year it is finished and if you are going to spend so much on something . . . oh, it just drives me crazy.'

Removing peanut matter from a back tooth, mindful of her lipstick – she was an attractive woman – and taking a last swig of her gin and tonic, she told him that she had calculated they had had over forty holidays during their marriage. She handed the plastic glass, small bottle and tonic can to the flight attendant. The peanut packet she had rolled up and inserted into the can's opening.

He thought of paperbacks, triangular-heaped, wet and spineless by poolsides and of shellfish detritus left on dinner plates, pink and drying. He thought of the night-time efforts to kick away tucked-in white sheets. Hotels, hospitals; both had required from him a degree of submission. His wife did not submit. Her chin was hard. She used it to conclude her sentences. Her eyes sparkled. If she was pragmatic then she had reason to be. Initially he'd been given six months to live, he'd taken six years so far. It had caused her to be severe.

'Six, nearly seven years of lucidity,' Jan thought, catching her eye and looking quickly away, 'clarity come upon me like the word of God.'

'Excuse me,' he said, as his elbow knocked hers off the central armrest by mistake. He had confirmed his belief, hospital stay after hospital stay, that human relations were best conducted courteously; he was thankful for good manners. The existence of love, unconditional love, he doubted. He even wondered about his children. He had no idea whether he was ready to die; it didn't come in degrees after all, allowing one to get accustomed to it. Death was a binary affair, not cumulative. On/off. The starter pistol fired not a second before it fired.

Now, with the 'fasten seatbelts' lights illuminated and his wife tucking a spare miniature vodka into the pouch in front of her, he reminded himself of his resolve to make it up to her.

He barely knew her and he had gone to a great deal of trouble to know her less in the last few years. It was reasonable to think that neither of them was entirely to blame and it was possible, even now, that they might quit each other as friends. That was what he hoped this holiday was for; he hadn't told her as much, but he assumed she felt the same way. Given that he was, in fact, dying now.

To his left, he saw a segment of fellow Northern Europeans squinting and wincing at the sudden sheath of equatorial sunlight. He reached across his wife and with a neat action, using his forefinger and thumb, raised the shade over their window.

2

Annemieke's pleasure increased as the elevator rose. Her face pronounced a smile as the light illuminated the characters 'PH'. Her boys had not let her down. The room conformed to her standards in luxury; thick white towels, high thread-count sheets, stainless steel and lustrous wood – these were the things she had been persuaded were right.

In the bedroom her husband sat down with a book, adjusting his mouth and glasses with every turn of the page and dropping his shoulders, occasionally giving his neck a little shake.

'I thought reading was supposed to relax you,' she said, not for the first time.

She had gone to freshen up, ready to take a turn about the place, to see what it had to offer, but her husband had settled into the book. He settled, she moved. This was how they had always been; his illness had simply developed the difference between them as light develops photographic film.

She went off to see the spa. Everything was in order and above all else clean. She was accustomed to thanking God out loud for the cleanliness of any encounter she made. Restaurants, friends' homes, schools, and of course, in particular, toilets.

'I can tell a lot about a place when I go to the toilet,' she had declared to a variety of audiences, causing Jan to smile and say quietly, '*Summa summarium*.'

On her return to their room she described with careful bird-like hand movements the high ceilings, wooden fans, long glass windows on to an azure swimming pool with an adjacent marble Jacuzzi. She had an eye for detail. The swimming pool was half covered by a Tuscan-effect palazzo roof, surrounded by a tiled veranda that looked out over a cliff on to the tumbling Atlantic Ocean. 'And, Jan, these are the same tiles that Leni and Eric are having in their shower room. But here they are on the outside. Leni likes to think that no one else puts outdoor tiles on the inside but I have seen it before, when we were on holiday in the Charente. I told her that.'

She had seen a group of men lounging around the pool, holding their stomachs in. Their women were in the Jacuzzi, talking sideways, keeping their faces to the sun.

Down a tree-lined pathway, there was a roofed bar, she told him, like an Italian outhouse with some thirty high stools against a brick-finished counter. In the centre there was a pizza oven and the smell of baked rosemary and hot wet Parmesan had made her hungry. Three young women, in robes from the spa, had been sharing a large flat pizza, their glasses were refilled with red-coloured cocktail from an ice-sweating jug. Through gardens with wide-leafed grass and plump blossoms, sprinkler-fat, she had come to a lawn with a small round pool in the middle and behind it a courtyard with access to some ground-floor rooms and a whitewashed stairway that led to the main hotel. On the first floor were two restaurants, one casual in the style of a French bistro, all heavy wood and aluminium, and the other furnished with candelabra and high-backed chairs, presenting themselves to large empty round tables. Some staff sat at one table and talked in earnest. She had stood for a moment at the door, watching them. The manager – the only one who wore casual clothes, the only one who was white – laid his suntanned forearms on the table and held out his handwritten notes so that the staff could see them. He seemed an agreeable young man, with an expressive and animated face. Handsome, she said, making a small leap of judgement. Here she paused.

Jan had picked up his book again.

'Good, good,' he said, 'it sounds your sort of place.'

She had seen a young couple in swimsuits kissing in the doorway to their room. They could quite easily have kissed in their room, but they needed to kiss there and then. The Spanish-looking girl had long ringlets of dark hair and the man was young enough to be smooth-skinned, hairless. How soft their skin must have felt as they pressed together. So young, so clean from the pool, clean all over. She wondered whether they were able to forgive each other when they argued. Perhaps they didn't argue. Perhaps the need to touch each other overwhelmed every discontent.

Jan was nodding at the book. It was not mute to him, it spoke, he listened and responded even as she stood there before him, hot behind the eyes, breathing little shallow breaths and looking at herself in the mirror. She did not look her age – forty-nine – but soon she would and then it would all be over for her. She had said her goodbyes in many different ways, tenderly and angrily. He hadn't heard them, either way.

She left the room and made for reception where she waited a long time for the young girl there to answer her questions regarding the horse riding.

She had spotted the Bible at home, among his books. 'I will not be alive like a dead person', she said to herself, 'waiting to live in the afterlife!' She could not stop herself from thinking such things. She lay awake at night reasoning the resentment into righteousness.

She gathered some leaflets now, he could look through them if he wanted to go off and do any of his tourism things. He could help himself. She was going to have a holiday that suited her. She would make the most of the spa. Her own health deserved some attention. Hadn't the doctors said that it's so often the carer's wellbeing that gets completely neglected? She held the spa brochure at arm's length. Usually she borrowed Jan's glasses.

A revolting man was checking in, hot and bothered. She glanced at the signet ring on his right pinkie, the sweaty tendrils beneath his Panama hat and the shield of sweat emblazoned on his back. He said he was from South Africa but his accent was Irish with a self-assured rolling comedy of inflection. She waited for him to notice her, which he did.

'Well, hello,' he said to her with a grin. 'Nice weather isn't it? I think I've single-handedly raised the temperature in this wee room about five degrees.'

When she got back to the room, she gave Jan the pamphlets that were of 'cultural interest'. She had chosen those she considered the most ridiculous, a historical tour of the plantations and an afternoon of beadwork.

'These look like your sort of thing,' she said. 'There was a vulgar South African checking in downstairs. He made a pass at me. Perhaps he thinks he is at Club Med.'

Jan looked at his wife now that she was opposite him, perched on the side of a chair, studying her reflection in the long mirror. He could picture the scene at reception. She would have used her left elbow to prop herself as she leaned against the counter, leaving a delicate deliberate space between the counter and her breast. Her long fingers would have played with her necklace and when the man turned towards her she would have given him that same slow smile which she was giving the mirror now, a look that causes a man to look twice.

3

The next morning Annemieke called reception to ascertain whether there were any vacancies for a full body massage that day. Just one. She could come now. Jan was already awake, reading, making some notes in a small jotter he'd bought, sat on the balcony with a coffee and a cigarette. She had to smile, looking at Jan out there with his book of grievances. She had looked at it once or twice when he was absent. It was full of semi-philosophical notes and remarks, occasioned by his readings, a few of which dealt with human virtue, some were quotations neatly referenced, some seemed to be his own reflections. She could read into them plenty of criticism of herself, she was more than likely the 'middle class', the 'bourgeois', the hedonist, the materialist to whom he referred. When we die, everything dies, she said to herself, even the blame. The children wouldn't want his books and notes and jottings.

'I thought we might make an excursion,' he said pleasantly. 'We could hire a car. Have a look round the island.'

'I'm not a sightseer, Jan,' she said, 'as you know.'

She gave herself a good wash; she wanted to feel just right when she lay down on that massage couch. These indulgences were fraught in so many ways. Money and time ticking away while you tried to feel good. An indifferent masseur or beautician, an unpleasant manner, a painfully deep rub or treatment, thin towels, or the sight of herself, under bright lights in a full-length mirror: any of these could ruin it.

He was standing when she left.

'We might have lunch together,' he said.

'You look after yourself, I shouldn't want to hold you up.'

Naked under a robe, waiting with a cup of lemon tea outside the massage room, she became increasingly nervous at the selection of music being piped over the speakers. It was young music, all pulse and beat and gravel and urgency. She would not be able to relax to it.

With the usual command given, to undress and lie under the single white sheet while the masseuse stepped out of the room, she felt more at ease. The lights were dimmed, the music lowered. When the masseuse returned, she asked Annemieke questions in a monotonous voice of Eastern European accent, interspersing them with notes about the oils she was using, varying neither the cadence nor the metre of her speech.

'So you have come here with husband. This is a neroli, orange and bergamot oil very good to stimulate the senses and invigorate your spirits. They are older, your children, then. They have left home.'

'How old do you think I am?' said Annemieke.

'Forty something,' she said, 'early forties.'

Annemieke was reminded of the option to tip the masseuse. This gave her an anxiety like heartburn. She started to wonder how much time had passed and how much remained. Opening her eyes and turning her neck slightly to find the clock, she cricked her neck and exclaimed. The masseuse spoke gently.

'You hurt your neck. You have very stressful life.'

Already twenty minutes had passed.

'Yes,' Annemieke said and snapped her jaws and eyelids shut.

The masseuse put her fingertips to Annemieke's temples and rubbed in small circles, softly but with growing pressure. In her mind's eye, Annemieke saw Jan's face, protuberant with his own sorrow. The masseuse finished with deep strokes of her thumbs against the sole of one of Annemieke's soft feet, clasping the foot like a prize, pressing the toes to her collarbone.

Standing in her robe, at the spa reception, Annemieke signed the chit quickly, looking at the counter, not at the girl. She did not leave a tip.

Only a homosexual or a has-been wears *short* shorts, thought Annemieke, standing still in front of the man. The South African pulled his short shorts back up from around his ankles and positioned his genitals gamely inside the fishing-net interior. They were dark blue nylon with a white-bordered slit up either side.

Annemieke had gone into the wrong changing room after her massage, deliberately. She had observed that it was the men's room and loosened her robe slightly to affect a deeper V before she entered. The day before, as she waited for the elevator back to their room, she had heard the South African arrange a midday massage – or a 'rub-down', as he called it – and as chance would have it, there they both were, in a small stark white changing room, her robe slipping.

A man such as he was not going to refuse.

'I must be in the wrong place,' she said, a shoulder exposed, and she could see by his expression that he remembered her and from the goofy turning of his mouth that he was rapidly putting two and two together and coming up with an erection.

She locked the door behind them with the simple depression of a round button on the handle. She approached him and put her hand inside the short shorts, unleashing her catch from the net. And all the time he smiled like a son of a bitch. Expressionless, she gave the hot and hairy handful a few pulls in order to make sense of the mess. Humbly and warily he placed his hands on her breasts, as if waiting for the next steps to be communicated.

She drew the line at giving such a man a blow job. She guided his apish right hand between her legs.

'Okay,' he said with a friendly smile, a thumb either side of his waist, levering the shorts over his plumpness. With a gamin flourish of his hips, he let them drop down to his knees. One further shake and they were about his ankles and that seemed as far as he was able to dismiss them. She sat down, robe about her hips, her hands behind her, her back arched, then she slowly began to walk her hands backwards.

He knelt down above her, steadying himself with one hand, giving his old friend a stroke and seeing to the task of fucking a middle-aged woman in a grandiose lavatory just before lunch on a Monday.

4

Seeing such a bitter-looking old man, all jowls, flushed from the heat, Jan took his seat at the bar well outside what he presumed was the old boy's limited range of hearing. In the last six years he had spent a great deal of time at a great many bars, even though he was not a heavy drinker. He liked public privacy. He liked to take an occasional modest respite from his life, to enjoy civilized refreshment and an altered perspective.

The old man scowled when Jan was brought a large bottle of San Pellegrino with a long thin glass and a lime wedge. He leaned sideways; making a great and ungainly effort to see better what Jan was wearing.

Catching each other's look, they smiled slightly.

'Bit hot,' the old man said loudly, shaking his collar.

Jan looked noncommittal, raising his eyebrows and steering his lack of opinion with his ears, left and right.

'Oh, so-so.'

The old fellow nodded and said nothing, then, apparently reconsidering, moved a seat closer to Jan. 'Can't hear you, mate. What did you say?'

'Yes, it is. Hot.'

'Been here before, then?'

'No, this is my first time.'

'On your own?' asked the man, showing his canines.

'No, no. With my wife. I'm waiting for her now,' Jan returned, looking down at his glass so that the man would not see his thoughts. He resented the intrusion. He had a lot to think about and not much time. Was it possible for such an old man to be a practising homosexual? It was possible, he had a moustache, but usually they were writers or artists. This man did not look like either. He was English or perhaps Australian, the accent was coarse.

'Same here.'

Jan hoped that the conversation would end here. He was ready to stand up and make a polite farewell, to dash off a signature, to leave the two-thirds of his bottle that remained.

'I say,' said the man, aspirating his words as if speaking to an Officer and leaning over the bar with his eyebrows pumping up and down, 'did you happen to remark that the ladies go topless here?' His blue eyes flashed.

Jan smiled stiffly. 'No, I haven't been to the pool yet. I'm not much of a swimmer.'

'Nah,' he said, 'blow the swimming. But from where I'm sitting, you can get what they call a bird's-eye view. An eyeful.'

Jan closed his eyes and took a breath through his nose. He had made a deal with himself, when the illness first struck, to be plain with people. He didn't have enough time to indulge them. He turned on his stool to face the man and opened his eyes slowly ready to reveal a stern expression. The old man was putting his eyebrows through a series of elevations and the back of his head was jostling his forehead. He remembered the English films of the 1950s and 1960s, the Carry On films. He laughed.

'What are you drinking?' the man said, pushing his glass of water aside.

'Well, if you insist, a lager top,' the man said with pleasure, sitting back in his seat and taking a good look at his new friend. 'Are you buying?'

'Certainly.'

He winked, cocking his head, 'Then I'll have a whisky chaser with mine.'

5

George Davis had been sitting out by the pool with his trousers
rolled up, thinking. He and his wife, Dorothy, had been up
since six. He had never slept much, now he slept hardly at all.
He'd had plenty of time to think about the past since he retired
at seventy, but it seemed a bottomless well. There were so
many different ways of looking at the same thing. By eleven
o'clock, George was standing at the Hibiscus Bar, taking swigs
from a ginger ale in a short glass. He was dissatisfied, on
account of his normal preference for a drop of whisky along
with the ginger ale. His eyes were fixed on the clock opposite.
It was an old railway clock, oak rimmed and he could discern
the year on it – 1856. He was waiting for midday , for decency's
sake.

He'd not had many holidays to speak of. His first had been
with Tubby Haynes down at Brighton. They'd gone there on
motorbikes, kipped the night on a bench. Glorious days, plenty
of girls. It was exciting just to walk past a group of them – arm
in arm they always were, keeping what they had to themselves
and he and Tubby raised their hats like real gentlemen. With
his oiled red hair and twirly moustache, a tall man, he cut quite
a figure. He and Tubby would take a couple of girls, and
sometimes their mothers, for an ice cream on the front.
Sixpence a cone and Tubby going through his pockets at a
slight remove, looking for coins. George always came up with
the brass. He worked hard and he was careful. And his old
man gave him what he could, when he could.

Shielding his eyes he looked straight out at the ocean, then he turned and looked back at the hotel. Between its two main buildings, the Caribbean sun was hand on hips, staring back at him, square and brazen.

'He loved me, the old boy did. No questions asked.'

The British Telecom phone directory had had no listing for Thomas Haynes in the London region. He'd gone to call him a few weeks ago. He thought about Tubby Haynes and the others in their old gang of mates nearly every day. All dead, he supposed, since he couldn't track down Tubby. The lot of them. And he was the last, still alive, with the memories to himself.

The wife would say, just to egg him on, 'Whenever you get a phone call these days it's to say old so-and-so has passed on, makes me glad I gave up my friends years ago, when I married you.'

'Nobody asked you to give up your friends when you married me.'

'Well, we moved to the country, didn't we?'

'After the war,' he'd tell her. 'You had the chance for plenty of friendship during the war when I was away.'

She'd not look him in the face then. 'Well, we left London and I never did see Glenys Guthrie again. Nor any of the other girls from the paper mill.'

It provoked him, so he'd stop her from what she was doing and stand in front of her to have it out.

'You wanted to raise the kids in the country, fresh air, you said, and it was me what made it happen with the idea for the nursery. In thirty-odd years I couldn't make anything of it but I stuck with it because it was what you'd said you wanted.'

'I never asked you to stick at it!' she'd cry, getting shrill like she had a whistle stuck in her throat.

They always argued about the past, they couldn't seem to share it.

He could feel his heart pumping just thinking about it. Why did it all matter so much now when it was all too late? As if he was arguing for his life.

'You married a man that stuck at things. Tough luck. Couldn't you have written letters to bleeding Glenys Guthrie?'

'I did,' she'd falter, her bottom lip giving way.

'AN' ... SHE ... NEVVAH ... WROTE ... BACK ... TO ... YUH,' his voice went all London when he was at the end of his rope.

'I forgot to put the address in.'

'She'd got other things to think about. We all did. There's me breaking my back in that bloody mud, pulling lettuces no bigger than weeds out the ground hoping to make some money and one thing after another going wrong, and this and that needing fixing or buying new ... Look at me, what have I got out of life?' He'd see that she was about to subside, and then he'd say it again, just to con the both of them that there was something left to fight over. 'Well, what have I got?'

'You've only got yourself to blame!' she'd say, dying down as soon as she'd said it.

Because she'd start with the friends business regularly now, they were at each other's throats nearly every week. He didn't know what was wrong with her, harping on about the same thing. He ought to be able to let it drop, seeing she didn't seem to hear anything he said, but sure enough she'd start up the next week with 'Of course I had to drop my friends.'

'You're losing your marbles,' he said.

'And you're going deaf, so that makes us even,' she retorted and her teeth got in the way of her lips, so quick and so pleased was she with her reply, like when she'd got a word with an 'x' in it when they used to play Scrabble.

The week before they came away, he wouldn't talk to her for three days. Then their younger daughter came by to take some cuttings from the geraniums. What with the others coming for photos and medals and bits of crockery, relics, it was like a museum with a takeaway, he said to his friend Norman.

Nigh on sixty years together and they'd had their share of love, in a practical sort of way, but there'd been hate too. You couldn't tell him that there was any marriage that wasn't equal measures love and hate. That was the way it was and it killed you off in bits and pieces, got you ready for the end, like stewing meat for the pot.

'Put that in your pipe and smoke it,' she'd said and that was one thing he'd noticed lately she did she didn't do before. She was getting spiteful and triumphant with it. She wasn't content to have the last word; she had to have it twice. That was why he'd headed off to the bar, he'd told her he was going out for a spot of fresh air and some normal company.

'Go on then,' she'd said, 'see if I care. Even if you find someone to talk to, you won't hear them.'

So he'd left her in the room and as soon as he put his foot outside the door he'd felt bad about it, angry with himself and with her, sick of it all. He ought to have turned about and made it up with her, but it was too late for all of that. Their bad habits would go with them to the grave now.

'She wasn't keen to come, the missus,' he admitted to Jan. 'She's a stay-at-home sort. She's sitting in the room now. Blimey, we might as well be at home. She's got her book and a cup of tea, she's all right. I've always had to drag her along with me to whatever we did. She wasn't always a homebody but she's got worse lately, likes to sit on her arse all day; thinking she says she is, or reading,' he raised his eyebrows and sighed. 'Always seems as if she's on the same page.'

'I suppose my wife feels that way about me,' Jan said, finishing his drink.

'Oh yes?'

'Sure. I also like my own company.'

'I'm not sure that's the case with the old girl. Sometimes it's hard to get through to someone even if you've known them your whole life. The years seem to make it harder, as a matter of fact. Like you've found thousands of ways to get around them, detours, you know, road closed, follow diversion. Do you know what I mean?'

'Yes, I do.'

'Shall we have another?'

Jan looked at the clock. It was one-thirty. Annemieke would not still be in the spa, she must have decided against joining him. Perhaps she'd found her own lunch.

6

Dorothy Davis was rubbing her toes through her stocking, perched on the edge of the bed, her bag beside her.

'I don't feel like eating a big dinner now. I had some scraps for lunch. No thanks to you. Got them sent up. Still, if you've made an arrangement we shall have to go and that's that. I'd prefer to have a sandwich in the room. But there's no point in making a fuss then, is there?'

'You won't give in to it, will you,' said George, taking his shirt off and wiping his armpits with it. He laid it beside her on the king-sized hotel bed.

'Open the suitcase, George, you'll find the dirty clothes bag at the top,' she said.

'We're on holiday,' he said, dropping a sweet wrapper into the ashtray on the side table and opening the doors that led on to the balcony, examining the mechanism as he did so. Nice work. He'd helped himself to a handful of the boiled sweets on the reception desk.

'I see from the notes here that everything excepting alcoholic beverages is included in the payment for your stay,' the chignon-haired woman down at reception had told him. Like a doctor's nurse. He'd loosened his grip on the sweets.

Their granddaughter had sprung this holiday on them. She was a thirty-year-old banker who earned a fortune. She sent them gifts from time to time, with incomprehensible notes, like 'Just because' or 'Happy Tuesday'. Now the grand-daughter had provided for them their first and last luxury holiday. Left with the brochure between them on the coffee table in their front room, George had trailed a single finger down through the sample buffet menu descriptions. With the gas fire at full tilt and the rain lashing against the windows, he'd read aloud to her from it.

'Fresh oysters, crab, shell-on tiger prawns, filet mignon, seared tuna steaks, a selection of braised root vegetables, herb salads, and organic fresh-picked garden vegetables – these are some of the items you'd expect to find at our buffet bar.'

She'd shivered. 'A goose just walked over my grave,' she'd said, putting her library book aside.

'No goose,' he'd said, deadpan, not looking up, 'but listen to this; typical dishes from our chef Jean Martin's à la carte menu include, boeuf bourgignon, slow-roasted guinea fowl and duck à l'orange. Do they peel the Jaffas before they stuff them up their back passages, do you think?'

'It's a sauce.'

'I know that,' he'd said, sighing and shifting his bad leg off the spring-loaded footstool deftly, to avoid the jack-in-the-box retaliation, the smacking of the back of his calf. She'd heard him rattling around in the pantry, purposefully making noises that were bound to alarm her, and on cue – she had fifty-five years' worth of being on cue – she followed him out to the kitchen to help him make his tea.

'Call her,' she'd said to him there, her head round the pantry door, 'give her a ring and say we can't go, on account of your arthritis. She won't have paid for it yet.'

He didn't turn from the shelves, but took his reading glasses from his top pocket to squint at the label on a jar of piccalilli. 'She has. All we got to do is show up.' He handed her the jar and she set it on the side and went to get the cold ham from the fridge. There was nothing more to be said.

And now they were sat here, in this white room with its soft white rugs on a pale stone floor, billowing curtains, and a balcony that overlooked the sea. Strangers to the place, strangers to themselves. With no crossword to do, no post to bring in, no tea to get on, none of the regimented procession of news programming on radio and TV – seven a.m., eleven a.m., one p.m., five p.m., nine p.m. news; the same stories served different ways all day until they were stone-cold, what were they to do?

'See if there's an iron, George,' she asked her husband who was standing, clad in vest and corduroy trousers on the balcony, looking down at the pool below.

'Topless,' he said grimly. She raised her eyebrows.

'And what can you do about it, at your age,' she said, 'you're not the man you were.'

He went into the bathroom with her following. He gave the shower the scrutiny he usually gave to faulty radiators and used cars, checked the head on it and pronounced it safe for her to use if she wanted but he'd just have a quick wash and brush-up, a quick wipe-over. Dorothy looked in the mirror at the bristle over her permanently puckered mouth. 'Oh Lord,' she said and felt around her cosmetics bag for the lipstick.

There was a knock at the door and a black woman came in, wearing a smart green frock with a pinafore over it, and told them she was going to turn their bed down for the evening. Coming out of the bathroom, Dorothy went over to George, and both of them stood hands at their sides, backs to the wall, waiting for her to finish. They nodded and thanked her, and each noticed the accent of the other move up a tremor or two, posher.

'She's left a couple of chocolates on the pillow,' said George, going to get one. 'They're cold,' he unwrapped one and bit it, 'minty tasting. Do you want yours?'

She shook her head and he went back out to the balcony, leaving her to finish her face.

They got to the bar on the dot of six-thirty, taking a turn round the gardens at twenty past. They found they were pretty much alone apart from the barman. It was George's way to engage staff, anywhere, in chitchat. But the man would not be engaged, neither would he look them in the eye. Dorothy felt her cashmere throw – a birthday gift from the granddaughter – weigh upon her like an ermine mantle in the still heat.

George handed her the special welcome cocktail and removed the tiny paper parasol for her when she poked it up her nostril for the second time. After draining his glass, he gritted his teeth and frowned, looking out to the sea. He'd been likened to Montgomery, physically.

As other people arrived, couples mostly, Dorothy and George stepped aside to allow them to get to the bar and then stepped back into the same space afterwards. When it was seven exactly, they went to the restaurant.

7

When the waiter came to take their drinks order, Dorothy was buttering a bread roll and hadn't a clue what to ask for. George pressed her with impatience, thirsty himself.

'Come on, dear, ladies first,' he said heavily, rolling his eyes in the direction of the Caribbean waiter. The fans were spinning and the jazz music was loud, she felt rushed. She'd been thinking of the effort in laying the tables. She gave the buffet the same scrutiny a sportsman gives a game he himself plays. She saw it all in terms of the hours worked as if it were her own arms that were doused in pineapple juice, as if there were cheese under her fingernails, flour on her slippers.

'A sherry,' she said hastily, wishing she could think of the name of a cold drink she liked.

'A beer, thank you,' said George with a courteous but clipped smile. She knew he was afraid of waiters. To him, it might have been Saint Peter standing there, judging him.

'You look nice,' he told her.

She was wearing a long-sleeved, long-skirted dress she'd bought for their fiftieth wedding anniversary.

'Oh, this. You remember this. Bought it in Eastbourne with the girls. It's washed up all right, hasn't it,' she smiled, adding, 'you look all poshed up yourself.'

He had his polka-dot braces on over a brown checked shirt and was wearing a lightweight beige jacket he'd needed to get dry-cleaned before they came. He was drumming his fingers on the table, making the fragile vase of flowers skip a little, and craning his head at the double doors.

'I wonder if I should give their room a call,' he said, looking at his watch.

'It's only just gone seven.'

'He wanted to eat at eight, see. But I said, the wife and I prefer to get going at seven if that suits. And he said, all right, but you never know if they've understood do you?'

'Doesn't he speak English then?' said Dorothy, her lip trembling.

'Oh, yes. He's got a proper accent too, none of the old "zis" and "zat" nonsense.'

'How about his wife?'

'I don't know, haven't met her. She was getting herself a treatment at the spa, he said.'

'Is she young then?'

'He didn't say.'

'Well, how old is he?'

'Don't know. Middle-aged, I suppose.'

'Oh.'

Jan and Annemieke rounded the double doors, side by side, Annemieke placing her hand on his arm as if to guide him. The Belgian man was wearing a sports jacket and chino-type pants, and his wife a waisted dress with beads at the hem and a low-cut flounced neckline. She had been at her make-up palette with fury, put green on her eyelids, dark brown over the sockets of her eyes, a shimmer blush along her pronounced cheekbones. She wore a tawny glittery lipstick, like marmalade congealing.

'An old woman!' thought Annemieke, taking a look at Dorothy and turning her face to Jan, hoping to catch his eye so that she could let him know she was not impressed. If she wanted to have supper with old ladies on her holiday she could have gone to see her own mother. 'This is my holiday,' she started to say to herself, preparing a conversation she would be having later.

George was delighted, and stood to pull a chair back for his friend's wife, at the same time nodding at the waiter to come over.

'Drink,' he was saying, making a cup shape with his hand and raising it to his lip, 'thirsty . . . .'

'Campari and soda,' said Annemieke, quick as a flash, resting her face on a manicured hand.

'Now that's a drink,' said George, widening his eyes and nodding at their waiter.

The room was a large clean arena, pillared and marble-floored with heavy round tables, draped with three tablecloths each and large matching napkins. There were three glasses at each place. The paned glass windows reflected the glare of too many table lamps and hanging chandeliers, but in places there were empty dark spaces where the windows were open. It was to these spaces that one's eyes wandered for comfort. At a table by an open window there was a woman in her sixties, sat opposite a young black man. He wiped his mouth delicately, and his eyes moved like white doves startled by unexpected noise. But she brought them back with her big soft hands moving in the air. The old girl, with badly shaved chins and sagging breasts, was pushing bits and pieces on to his plate with her knife and fork, and shaking her head with insistence. Feeding him up.

The waiter came and indicated the seafood buffet, pink and bulbous, glistening, intermingled with scrunched lettuce offerings on trays of ice cubes scattered with wedges of lemon. George swallowed hard and led the way, applying himself single-mindedly to each silver platter and composing a heap of food on his plate, which he set about as soon as he had placed it on the table. He ate fast and did not speak.

Annemieke sat back from her own plate and waited a moment before raising her glass and saying, 'Santé.' George looked up at her; the few bristles that were his moustache were wet. 'Good health,' he said.

'Eat up, dear,' George placed a hand on Dorothy's elbow. She looked at the plate to which she'd helped herself and turned her fork over on the tablecloth, once or twice.

'The oysters are wonderful, Dorothy, did you have some?' asked Annemieke.

'No.'

'What did you take?'

'I don't know.'

Each of them looked up from their dinner and at her. George said quickly, his voice moving over the rough edge of anger.

''Course you bloody well know what you got.'

'I can't think of it, though, the word. The name,' she said, and her fork was trembling in her hand so much that she put it back down.

'They're prawns, your favourite, what we get down at the seafront, every week,' he sighed loudly and exclaimed, 'Gordon Bennett!'

'I'm getting old.'

Annemieke looked at her husband, but failing to catch his eyes, she dabbed her mouth and said to Dorothy, 'So, this is your first time in the Caribbean?'

'Yes.'

'And for us, no. We have been in the region many times. The Florida Keys, Mexico, and we've been to St Martin and to Trinidad too, before it was so popular, before any of them were, well, what they are now . . . package deal places . . . we take a long-haul holiday every year, sometimes twice, besides of course the short stays in Europe. But, yes, we like to go to upscale resorts as it's only for a week or so. I think we have deserved those few weeks. I wish we had done so much more, seen more. But Jan's work has taken first place. He sees himself as contributing to the good of mankind. I say to him, it's car rentals, my dear. My boys have seen the world and I see the difference in them. I think that it is good for one, morally, to travel.'

'How's that?' asked George.

Annemieke paused and took a sip of her wine.

'It expands the senses, the intellect and, well, culturally, borders and so on.'

Jan topped up all of their glasses and nodded.

'I wouldn't know,' said George, 'we're homebodies. I like my own sort as a rule and I think it'd be better for us all if we stayed put, kept to our kind.'

Annemieke looked at her husband again but Jan, feeling her eyes on him, kept his face lowered and began to chew a new mouthful with steadfast rhythm.

'Mind you,' George went on, 'I had a terrific time in Italy during the war. But that was special circumstances. The usual rules didn't apply.'

'Oh, for a world without usual rules,' said Annemieke.

'There must be rules, dear; even when there aren't rules, there are rules, and then it's just the more confusing. Better to be straight. Honest.'

'There are rules, but you can choose whether you want to follow them or not . . .' started Dorothy. She was amazed to see that the Belgian woman flushed, her rouged cheeks rose like dough, her mouth fell slack and spare as a large man approached the table and bade her 'Good evening'. He turned to all of them with a nod and a smile.

'Hello there,' said Annemieke, 'nice to see you again. Jan, this is . . . I'm sorry, I've forgotten your name.'

'Bill Moloney.' The man extended a hand to Jan and raised it next in a salute to both George and Dorothy. 'Well, I'll not hold you up,' he added.

He sat at a single table, at a remove from them, and signalled his salute again as Annemieke looked over, then later, catching Annemieke's awkward glance, he raised his glass and in a loud voice said, 'Your health!'

The men responded eagerly.

'It's his own he ought to worry about. I met him at reception. Remember I mentioned him to you, Jan? I think he's interested in me. Sorry,' she said with a small shrug.

'Sex. All about you. It's the sex,' said Dorothy, mumbling, but loud enough for them all to hear. Jan stared at her, his mouth open for just a moment, his fork poised to enter it. George cleared his throat and drank noisily from his glass.

'We came here on account of our granddaughter giving us the tickets as a present. Took us by surprise. We've never been on this sort of a caper. You can't complain, though,' he said, rearing a little with the gas in his system.

'By us it is also the case,' said Jan, 'a gift to come here. From our sons.'

'But we could have come all the same, Jan!' Annemieke reproached him, 'this kind of holiday is normal for us. But our oldest son, he is doing so well with his business. He has bought a big town house in Brussels; it was something like one point two million euros. A friend of ours, a stockbroker, he tells us it is a very good investment. He likes to spoil his mother; he spends too much on me. But then, this is a special case, you see. A last holiday. My husband is very ill. With cancer.'

Jan laid his knife and fork side by side on his plate and closed his eyes momentarily.

Dorothy wished she had a dustpan and brush to sweep up after the Belgian woman. She noticed that the woman was dropping little bits and pieces of bread as she twisted the bread roll in her hands, turning in her seat, looking over her shoulder at Mr Moloney and then looking back at her husband and at them.

8

Jan had had plenty to drink at the bar with George that night, the women left them to it, but still sleep eluded him. It was the drugs.

Night after night, he lay awake, plucking his past. The bald facts were what remained. His business partner, his one-time friend, André De Vries had cheated on Jan in these last years, when Jan was forced into retirement through his illness, divesting him of the profitable parts of their company – and also his wife and children. Off they went for trips here and there, sunshine days in the rain, while he sat inside, sheltered.

'He likes to laugh. I like to laugh. The children, they must also laugh,' Annemieke said in explanation, the first time she and the boys had gone off with him for a Sunday lunch in Brugge. She wore a multi-coloured sweater, tight over her bust, and a long military-style skirt with straps. He had grabbed her by the arm.

'This is the man that has stolen from me, and from me means from us, Annemieke.'

'He has an explanation. I wish you'd listen to him. He means to capitalize on, well, what is it, the capital, the liquid assets, that's it, the cash and then he will turn them into assets, property and so forth, he will expand the franchise and then, he will give us our share and in this way you need not work, Jan. You must see it is the best thing. Don't be paranoid. We all care about you. You need to rest.' All of this she had delivered at pace. He had wondered whether she had done so from emotion or because they were running late. She had not been at all concerned about his hand around her upper arm. 'I must go, Jan. You will not listen to him, will you, you won't give him a chance? It's not André's fault that you have cancer. You have a persecution complex.'

'You look cheap,' he had told her. 'You are cheap.'

'Stop it,' she said, 'stop it. You are demeaning yourself.' Her reply, delivered calmly, had caused him to let her arm drop instantly. To them, he must look like a fool, to his sons. They thought he was going mad; perhaps it was true. Perhaps he misunderstood De Vries. They had worked together for years, been friends.

Then one of the boys had knocked on the door to the study, 'Mother?' he'd said without coming in and she had left. When he heard the kitchen door close, he called out, in a cowardly sort of way, 'Your mother's a whore and yet you love her.' Then he called out, 'What about me?' and was so ashamed of himself he lay on the sofa and wept.

Often, when he was finally about to go to sleep, he saw the optimistic set of De Vries's eyebrows hunching over immediate and easy ambitions. He had a horrible feeling that when he was dying, this man's face was what he would see. He'd have to make an effort to push him aside, to see behind him, further back, the happiest time of his life; his childhood, modest and rural, as bland and good as rice pudding, milk-fat and rain-fed. Days of comfort, meadows baking under a soft light, a mother warm and tender, ready with his clothes warm from the stand in front of the fire, the smell of cow shit, long walks and a father dead in the war. What boy could have asked for more? Her to protect him and he her.

If only his memory could rest easy, but no, it paced up and down, goose-stepping into the near-past, seizing at the photographic images of the holidays they had taken before he was ill. The four of them; André and he and the wives, in expensive white places with cheap black labour; the Maldives, Mauritius, holidays which had started when the children were at boarding school, about ten years before. Their second wind, supposedly. Annemieke, discovering sex again, but not with him, bartering for wood carvings as if she were bartering for life itself, triumphant over pennies, rubbing anti-cellulite lotions into her body with the door to the bathroom locked. He recalled too André's wife, Lucie, sat at dinner table after dinner table with nothing to say, her eyes occasionally meeting his as they let the other two have their sway. Together, they conjugated the drinking; I drink. You drink. He, she and it drinks. We all drink. After the diagnosis, he stopped drinking for a while, when he was a believer in the medical establishment. They said his body needed to be given a chance. He was to find other ways to relax. He thought it would make him less bitter but it made him worse, being both sober and resentful. It was the resentment he had to kick, not the drinking. This was why he couldn't sleep.

When he lay awake with all of this in his mind, he went back further to find better things. The children. Two boys, growing up with the purpose of becoming strong of mind and body but then suddenly a new regime adhered to, one prescribed by their friends. The speedy loss of moral weight. The loss of opinion or conviction. They both found cynicism an easy way out. A generation thing he was told. Sitting in their rooms with headphones on and feet up on the wall. Euphoric briefly when they returned with a new pair of sneakers from Brugge. Doors shut. To everything they said, 'I don't give a shit.' How can you argue with that? He couldn't. He was envious of them.

He had to hold firm, to go back further. As little kids they had thrilled him. Tired him out at weekends and after work and thrilled him. The euphoria of falling in love, daily. At times he came close to crying with thanks for the chance to look at the world through their eyes. Ben in the car, four years old or so, listing the reasons he was happy that day. Marcus, so mischievous, making Papa hide under the bed and Jan staying there unaware the boy was having his supper downstairs. Those boys, they could have been . . . he didn't know what. He used to nod quick and hard at them when he said good night, to get out of the bedroom fast so as to avoid being run down by the feelings he had for them.

Before that there was Annemieke. But she became a prisoner of his faults, according to her. She was a professional hostage. She grew up in Antwerp after the war – with her mother's self-aggrandising stories, tales of the Jewish community being dragged away despite her noble efforts. Her mother told her that they themselves had some Jewish blood. It could have been them on the trains! She said it was a miracle they were alive. The father denied this. 'You exaggerate,' he said every time that Jan saw them together. His wife's earliest memories, she told him once, were of night-time stories that drifted into unwarranted confessions and secrets. (Her mother told her that she despised the father, that her life was over the day they got married.) 'What use is a life without love?' she had moaned, 'God forbid that you should suffer such a thing. Love is everything,' she had impressed upon her daughter.

Jan thought as little of the mother as she did of him. Sunday afternoon visits, once a month, were odious to him. The father spent the time in his greenhouses, leaving Annemieke, Jan and the children to listen to the mad old woman hold forth on the latest roundup of nonsense she had read the week before in the newspapers and magazines that printed the bad news. The mother was the sort of person who read enough to be a menace. She had scientific terminology to excuse each one of her hatreds. Jan wished she'd knit instead. When the father was dead and buried, the old woman moved

into a retirement complex up on the coast, just thirty
kilometres away. It soon became every Sunday afternoon that
the two women sat in the old woman's seaside apartment, the
children drinking fizzy drinks, and discussed the 'emotional
climate' of Annemieke's childhood home as if this was all
that endured. Jan watched them from the balcony, over-
looking the sea, where he went to smoke a cigar. He was a
non-smoker at the time, but a cigar took time and he
persuaded himself that this was some sort of compensation
for the visit. With books and tapes passing between them
every weekend, the mother supplied Annemieke's growing
attachment to various self-help fads. Their ideas fed a
nostalgia for an imagined brutality, they spoke of bruises and
scars with conspiratorial smiles and sighs.

Tired of it all, Jan asked Annemieke, in front of the children
and the mother, whether the father had in fact battered them.
The mother spoke up.

'There is physical damage and there is emotional damage
that can be done, Jan, and who is to say which is the worst?'

'But did he actually hit you?' said Jan on the way home in
their BMW.

'Oh, mother exaggerates,' said Annemieke; and then, slipping blithely into her father's personality, she would complain
about her mother.

Jan suggested she get a job, but she couldn't, it was all so
stupid, so meaningless. She couldn't be like him, moving
vehicles around the country for profit. She was busy with the
children, the home, the mother, and her various women's
groups. At these groups, on weekday nights, she gleaned the
cant of several philosophies that suited her, from Freud to
feminism, she swallowed them whole. She said things like,
'Woman is the nigger of the world.'

As a young woman, when they met, she had been agile in

every way – funny more often than not. As she grew older her humours hardened and were broken only by small compliments. Not from him, for those were discredited immediately, but from others.

Some nights, before he became ill, especially after dinner parties for some reason, he considered shooting every one of them in the beds where they lay.

Your cancer is wish fulfilment, Annemieke had told him.

It was a second-hand idea. André had shared the thought with Jan at work; five days later his wife repeated her lover's hypothesis.

9

George was parched when he woke, on account of the three or four glasses of Scotch he'd had with Jan at the bar, after the ladies had retired for the evening. Dorothy was moving about the room, her nightgown like a blancmange on guy-ropes, creeping and bending and sighing. She was attending to the boiling jug kettle and making them both a cup of tea. They had a small jug of milk in their refrigerator; it was changed every day. 'Where are the cows?' he'd asked the girl who did their room and she had looked at him blankly. He'd mooed once or twice and made the hand gesture of milking a cow. She'd backed out of the room shaking her head and muttering.

They sat together on the balcony supping their tea, strong and astringent as the new light. He sighed in deference to the tea.

'Could get used to it here,' he added. His wife said nothing. He told himself she was getting hard of hearing, but really she liked to keep herself to herself as much as she could. He pressed her for an answer.

'I say, could get used to it here.'

'Well, there's not much point in that, is there?'

'It's just a turn of phrase.'

She was silent.

After a while he spoke again, 'Nice fellow, that Jan. We had a talk last night, must have been talking more than an hour or so . . .'

'Chewed his ear off, did you?'

George drained his tea and studied the sea view.

'Well, luckily not everyone shares your bad opinion of me.'

He rose to put his teacup inside and stopped as he went through the double doors to say, 'More tea?'

She shook her head for too long a time. She seemed to be struggling with her mouth to get her teeth in a comfortable position. She was right, she was getting old. He could see it in her, but not in himself, thankfully. He raised his eyebrows at his reflection in the mirror over the sideboard and left the teacup where she could easily find it to rinse it out.

He'd barely been able to sleep for thinking about the conversation he'd had with Jan. Poor chap, on his way out and yet, as George had pointed out, he himself might kick the bucket first. But he hadn't really believed it and Jan had said as much, 'You look like you're indestructible, George, men like you go on forever.'

'I don't worry, you see,' he'd said, 'not about my life. I worry about the family but if you was to ask me whether it had been a good life I'd say yes it had. Mostly on account of the war. I feel privileged to have been a part of something like that. No matter which way you look at it, it was *right* what we did. How many people can say as much?'

He took his cap and told Dorothy he was going out for a turn around the grounds before breakfast. She could wait or she could go on ahead, he said.

'I'm not hungry,' she said, 'I'll wait till lunch and see if I can manage something then. Maybe a slice of quiche or something light.'

'That's good of you, dear,' he said, raising his eyebrows. Much of what he said and did was for his own benefit nowadays. He didn't kiss her, but let himself out with a feeling of pleasure.

Strolling out through the main staircase, past the restaurants and on to the pathway, he saw the staff dotted about the place

tending to it all. A man in a straw hat frowned as he attempted
to fasten a rose tree to a long stake. George stopped to watch
until the man took off his hat and wiped his forehead, and
turned to look at George.

'Hard to keep 'em going in this heat,' George said.

The man laughed, 'H'every day is same,' he said, 'this not
Piccadilly, rainy old London town.'

George laughed too, 'I was in Africa during the war,' he
said, 'that was hot.'

The man looked serious again and said nothing. Even
though he looked old, George realized suddenly that he was
probably too young to have been alive during the war. Jan had
been polite. For who, now, was there just 'the war'?

He wandered past the outside pool and pressed his face
against the cool glass windows of the spa. They might have
their massages today. The South African chap with the Irish
accent had been at the bar, quite a jolly fellow, and he'd said
he'd had a good one. A 'rub-down,' he called it. Funny chap,
nervy, a bit of a boozer.

There was an annex being built on to the side of the spa,
they were in mid-construction, the area was roped off.
George was surprised to see a solitary figure on his knees in
the middle of a half-tiled floor, bare-backed, fingers splayed
over the black and white tiles he'd just laid. He was tanned,
with hair in a ponytail and a cap on backwards. On his
back was a tattoo, an elephant with many hands and a crown
on its head. George peered closely. The window was open
and he could hear the man talking to himself, sounds of
reassurance.

'Not a bad job,' George ventured.

The man turned around, he was all sinew, a young fellow.
He cracked a broad grin.

'Cheers,' said the young man.

'For a beginner.'

'Can you tell?'

'Well, you've got 'em a little bit skew because your pug's not even. What you got there, a cement mix is it?'

'Yeah, it's got the acrylic in with it. Floor's not even underneath.'

'Your job is to make it even, see, to correct it. Use the cement. I did a spot of tiling once or twice; I'm no expert but I'll give you a hand if you like.'

The young man looked about them, 'I don't think it would go down too well with the management.'

George nodded.

'I'm supposed to have this done by ten.'

George shook his head. 'You'll never do it. You've got about twenty square foot still to cover.'

'Well, come on then!'

George slipped his shoes off. He entered the new room by a side door and crept around the edges, then got down on his hands and knees and crawled to the middle, wincing and exclaiming a couple of times.

'All right?' asked the fellow.

'Yes, until I get up,' said George, 'I'm seventy-nine, you know. Aches and pains are something shocking, but there's life in me yet.' He offered the young man his hand, 'George Davis.'

'Adam,' said the young man.

'From London are you?'

'Hackney, born and bred.'

'Right, then you might know a thing or two about hard work. We're all right in the middle here but it's the cutting the tiles to go round the edges that's the bugger, right? That's what's going to take the time. You want to get to the cutting, my eyesight's not marvellous, and I'll get you straightened out in the middle here.'

'Sounds good,' said the fellow and they went to their work. By ten they were more than half the way through.

'We'll have it done by eleven if my back holds,' George had said, straightening himself with a great moan. Through the windows he saw Jan's wife in the Jacuzzi and he gave her a wave. She didn't see him. She was busy talking to Mr Moloney. She looked angry.

10

As Bill Moloney got into the Jacuzzi, the waters leapt up like the slops from a bucket, and splashed over the side of the pool, leaving a semicircle of dark grey on the surrounding paving. He moved to sit next to Annemieke. He couldn't have been less appealing to her, as he sauced himself with the water, the same highly antiseptic water that was so detrimental to her dermatological moisture balance. He sluiced underneath his armpits, then he put his hands up behind his head, showing the strands of wet hair that hung like seaweed from those discoloured diamond shapes.

'I've been keeping an eye out for you,' he said.

She considered leaving, but was not inclined to make a display of her thighs and bottom as she exited the pool. Her sarong was over at her pool-chair; there had been next to nobody there when she and Jan had come down. She gave a small hard laugh, like a cat coughing up a fur ball.

'Really?' she said, touching the thick golden crossbar of her sunglasses.

'You've heard about the mating pandas at the zoo, now? The sign outside the male's cage, well, it got the panda ladies enraged, it said, "Eats shoots and leaves". Now I didn't want you to think I was that sort of an animal.'

She closed her eyes. 'Fine.'

'Would you like to join me for lunch?'

'No, thank you.'

'Ah, come on now . . .'

She lifted her sunglasses quickly and her eyes hurt in the glare of the sun. 'Look,' she said, 'you have surely seen last night that I am here with my husband.'

'Oh, yes. Looks like a nice fellow. Don't worry, I'm a very subtle man in my own way, it's hush-hush as far as I'm concerned.'

'No. It's not hush-hush. It's just nothing. Nothing at all.'

'Nothing?'

'To me, it was nothing.'

'Well, it didn't feel like nothing to me.'

'Are you going to let the matter drop or are you going to become a problem?'

'Well, there's no need to get yourself all flatulent over it,' he said. And then, just as she thought he was at last taking offence, his moon-like face – half of it bathed in a red allergic reaction, to the pool, to the sun, to his drink, she did not know what – broke into a warm smile.

'My husband is terminally ill,' she said, 'he is dying of cancer. I don't want him upset.'

'It seems like you're the one who's upset, now.'

'Well, think what you like. It's really not important to me.'

He put his hands into the water to rest them on his knees and looked squarely at her, 'I'm an innocent, so I am, but a lovely lady like you, going about doing things that you're unhappy over, now why would you?'

They were in precisely the right place for this conversation, she thought, in hot water, up to their necks in it and though she wanted to get out into the neutral air or better still bathe in the cool waters of the pool, she was stuck there, like a lobster in a pot.

'Look, I'm not the sort who goes around shagging willy-nilly like that,' he smiled, squeezed his eyes shut as if to erase those words and started again, 'What I mean to say is, I know what it is to struggle with the earthly appetites. Well, just look at me; you can see who's on the winning side. It's not my iron will, now is it? We're just two people, you see, we don't know each other. It happened,' he held up his hand to stop her saying anything, 'it did happen, so it did, we can't undo it, and I'll accept it when you say it wasn't for you. But I'll also say I don't believe it. Ach, what I wanted to say was, don't feel bad about what happened. It doesn't make you a bad person. Well, not entirely.'

'I know that, thank you.'

'Having sex with a stranger, I mean.'

'Please . . .'

'When you're married. And your husband's poorly.' He grinned quickly and followed it with an apologetic stretch of his lower lip to either side of his chin. 'There are worse things. I know. I'm a terrible sack of shite myself.'

'Please, Mr Moloney,' she said, slowly, attempting a false smile and finding that her lips weren't as crafty as they had once been, 'just leave me alone.'

He raised both hands. 'I will,' he said, 'but I'll be saying to myself, she's suffering, that fine woman, and it's a terrible sad thing in a place like this, which is like paradise. It makes you think,' he added, portentously raising a finger, 'where is heaven and where is hell? Are they inside or are they outside?'

'Unbelievable,' she said, shaking her head.

She went to get out, and slipped in her urgency. She raised one leg again and in stretching caused her bikini bottoms to gather indelicately in the cleft of her bum. Overheated and aware she was now showing all of her red-veined backside, she swore.

'Can I give you a hand there?' he asked, standing up suddenly, and she felt the shadow of his bulk between her and the sun.

She shook her head and this time made it out of the pool and over to her sarong, which she used to bandage herself quickly, her wet hair over her face.

11

When Jan got to the bar, George and his new comrade, Adam, were sitting before glistening glasses of beer and a half-empty plate of pizza. It could only have been midday but there was a small crowd assembled, dipping cigarettes in and out of ashtrays, and beyond them, on the other side of the bar, a group of Americans facing determinedly away from the smokers, minding their accessories. One of their women was moving across them offering them sachets of artificial sweetener from a basket. She explained that she had had to go and get it from the restaurant.

'They never have it here at the bar.' The others agreed that it was indeed bizarre. 'I asked them yesterday to keep some here, but they took it back up to the restaurant.'

'More ice if you don't mind,' said one young tanned American male, pushing his long glass across the bar, and five of his friends fell back a footstep, exchanging looks and suppressing laughter as the barman handed him a single ice cube between tongs.

'Yeah, you go easy on that frozen water stuff, young fellow,' quipped another man, aside.

George and Jan were at the helm of the bar between the two factions.

'Americans don't like second-hand smoke,' Adam had said, making his point with a nod of his head in their direction.

'Everything's got to be new with them,' sighed George, wiping his brow with the barman's tea towel. He was pleased to see Jan, standing up briefly and moving a little to make space for Jan to stand alongside them. He explained to him their morning's work with a great deal of nudging whispering, casting suspicious looks at the barman and the other residents.

'Don't want to blow the whistle on the young fellow,' he said to Jan in a heavy whisper, 'had to help him out or he'd have never got the job done, see?'

Pink-faced and happy, George raised his eyebrows in mock indignation as Adam regaled them with his disbelief at seeing the old fellow whip his shoes off and take to the job.

'I couldn't keep up with him,' he laughed, 'and I'm thinking to myself all the while, this old boy, he must be at least sixty!'

'Oh, very good, son,' said George wiping the back of his mouth with his hand, 'you'll go far. But not in tiling. Whose round is it?' he asked. Jan ordered in another three beers and they clinked glasses.

'Cheers.'

'Good health.'

'Your health.'

'And have you also come on a working holiday, Jan?' the young man asked, squinting at the sun.

With his blond hair over one eyebrow and a slightly self-congratulatory expression playing around his mouth, he reminded Jan of their younger son. Jan shook his head and smiled, having already forgotten what he had been asked.

''Cos they want me to do a bit of work in one of the bathrooms this afternoon and I thought I might get you fine gentlemen to pitch in.'

George shook his head, 'See, I'm really more your leader type than your worker. You've got the knack of it now, anyways. And as for Jan, well, he is strictly white collar.'

'Excuse me?'

'Office. Management.'

Jan flushed and blew air on to the front of his cheeks,

shaking his head gravely, 'No, no, no. Not at all. I grew up on a farm and then my business is car hire, so in the early days I did a lot of the mechanical work, the repairs, myself. The last fifteen years, I've been behind a desk, sure, but not always.'

He noticed that George looked pleased with this answer, turning his red face from one acquaintance to the next, the common factor.

'And how do you come to be working here?' Jan asked Adam, leaning forward, resting his forearms on the wet counter top. His expression was so grave that for a moment Adam had the impression of being on an interview. He sat back on his stool and held his lower leg across his lap.

'I went to university. A pretty crap one. Did Business Studies. I can't think why, the old man, I suppose. But I just couldn't get any enthusiasm up for a corporate job, you know. I went and interviewed with lots of companies, but I'd always blow it at some point. Some of the interviews were a couple of days, with a sort of spoof business situation, like a contest. I'd end up taking the mick, having a laugh, being a bit rude. I suppose you got to respect that it's important to the people there but I was just turning up for the old man. So I thought, fuck it, I've got to get out and do some thinking, and that's what I've been doing for the last couple of years. In Asia, in Africa, and now here. I'm going on to Central America next.'

'Sounds bloody good to me,' said George, 'I wasn't so different from yourself. Had the wanderlust. Used to bugger off on the bike down to Brighton or up to Yarmouth. But we never had the chance to do anything like your world travel, though with the war you could see a bit of the world. But we had responsibilities to go home to, most of us were married or engaged, had kids.' He added with a sour grimace, 'No pill back then.'

'But what will you do? Where is your thinking taking you?' asked Jan.

Adam shook his head. 'I'm in the middle of it right now. Hard to say.'

'How do you know it's the middle?'

'Because it's not the end.'

'But what's the point?'

Adam looked at him with still blue eyes and, smiling, took a long draught of his beer. He sighed as he drained the glass.

'Wine, women and song. Now that hit the spot,' he said, 'got to get off, lads, work to do.' He shook hands with both of them, putting a second hand on their arm as he did so. 'Cheers, George,' he said, 'very much. I owe you. And for the bevvie. Top man.'

George nodded.

Both men watched him walk slowly up the path to the main hotel, his feet half out of his trodden-down sneakers, untying the green staff shirt from around his waist and putting it on before he reached the door.

'It's a different world, today,' said Jan, seeing George's admiration plain in his face.

'It is, but people don't change, do they? I look at a lad like that and I see myself, Jan. Not the ponytail and tattoos, granted, but the attitude. Good laugh. I always wanted to have a boy. A chip off the old block they used to call me, and to see the old boy smile at that! He used to say, that's my wealth that is, pointing at me, that's what makes me richer than a rich man. It ain't things what carry you on, is it, it's your kids. I'd have liked a son.'

Jan slid the menu towards George who took a quick look and they chose another pizza, taking account of each of the topping options. George sanctified Jan's suggestions sombrely.

'Sausage is good. Peppers is good but they do repeat on you. Mushrooms. Good.'

Jan ordered a bottle of the house white wine. He could

recognize several of the people at the bar now that they had been there a couple of days and he nodded if his eye was caught.

With the pizza shared equitably, George belched and pushed the remaining slice to Jan, 'It's yours, mate, fair's fair. I've had my half.' When Jan hesitated, he ate the last piece himself rather than let it waste.

'Shame to chuck it.'

They agreed that although it was nice to come away with the ladies, it was a bit of luck to find some quiet time like this, time for a bite to eat and a drink and some 'cordial conversation' as George put it.

'See, I've had to ask myself, over the years, whether it wouldn't have been better if we'd got ourselves divorced, would we have been happier like?' George said in a quiet voice. 'People like us didn't do it. Not like nowadays. I remember in our village, people would whisper to each other about a certain lady, "Look, there goes Mrs So-and-so, she's divorced." Funny ain't it, the way things are now? My eldest daughter's gone and got divorced and is thinking about getting remarried. Didn't you ever think about it?'

Jan was silent.

'Beg pardon, didn't mean to pry.'

'We are Catholic. There is that, you see. But I was just thinking that it must be something else also as I have not observed my religion in many years. I think the example was set before me. Although my own father was killed in the war, those families I respected, their parents were married all their lives. Well, they worked together, as business partners you could say on a farm or at a shop, I think it made a difference.'

'Too right. It was different in them days. The family was the business, wasn't it. My mum was the boss. Lord above, didn't she mind the pennies, counting out of my father's wages for this and that and mine too when I got older, putting some by, here and there. It wasn't about religion then either really, we didn't go to church much. I've never been much of a religious man. I believe what I believe, more and more as I get older, but I've done a few things I ought to be ashamed of, that's the truth of it. Don't feel right going into church and doing the mumbo jumbo.'

'We've all done such things.'

'Yes, but,' George leaned forward, close to Jan so that Jan could smell a mixture of the white wine, garlic and beer, 'I've been ambidextrous. Had affairs.' A small burp released the smell of sausage into the mixture.

'Oh,' said Jan.

'There's the things I did and the things I thought about. The things I didn't do. Sometimes I wonder if the regret ain't the worst. First of all, right from the beginning, Dorothy was second best. That's the truth of it. There was a woman before her, Millicent, her name was. Millie. Lovely. She was a dancer. Not professional but she loved to dance. She said to me one time, "George, come dancing with me, do a few lessons and get yourself up to scratch, will you?" And I says no. I sat home thinking well, if she likes me enough, she'll come round, give up the dancing. Me old mum told me she would. Never happened. Five years later or more I got this letter from her, she got my address through an old friend. She went to some trouble to get it because this friend of mine, Arthur, his family had moved twice on account of the bombing. "You don't fancy having another go at the dancing do you," she asked. "I'll stand you the lessons." It blew me away. 'Course I was hitched then. Kids too. It was after the war. I've often thought about that. I used to think, well if she still thought of me after five years, then it would be all right to write after five years, ten years. Even now, I sometimes think of writing to her and it's more than fifty years later.'

He touched the bridge of his spectacles lightly. 'Probably dead now. I never did write back. No point. But I've often thought about her. I won't say every day. Some days you wake up with misery on you and I never thought about her like that, not to make things worse for myself, but I'd daydream, us in Europe, drinking beers out of mugs. That sort of thing.'

Jan smiled. 'This is nothing to give yourself a hard time about, George.'

'No, no, I know. I mean, I did right by Dorothy and the girls. There was a woman in the village I had a bit of a thing with. She was a widow. We saw each other on and off, for the fun and games really. Such as they was. She was bit grim, on account of raising three kids on a widow's pension I suppose. Would never take her top off. I used to say, what you got, three of them? I can't say I ever thought much of her, truthfully.'

Bill Moloney stood on the other side of the bar, with a towel round his neck. He raised a full glass in their direction briefly before turning towards a Chinese woman who stood a foot or two back from the bar going through her wallet.

12

Fingertips that smelt of sun lotion placed themselves over George's eyes.

'Well, it ain't the missus,' he said, 'but I can feel a ring tapping on my specs. It's someone's missus. Is it yours, Jan?'

'Yes,' said Annemieke, making a face at Jan, 'that's me.'

'Hello,' Jan said, feeling slightly dazed after sitting in the sun through three beers and his share of two bottles of wine.

'Join us for a drink then,' said George, signalling to the barman who raised an eyebrow and wordlessly attended them. Despite George's best efforts, he remained distant.

'Haven't you had enough?' asked Annemieke and George winced visibly, and looked at Jan.

'Well, yes and no,' he replied with a cheeky smile. His eyes were brimming with the alcohol, plump and viscous.

Annemieke spoke to Jan in her own language and George closed one eye and swayed slightly on his bar stool, wondering if he would have to get acquainted with someone else at the bar, in order to carry on drinking, or whether he should go up to the room. Dorothy would be wondering what had happened to him. He'd best see if she'd had some lunch.

The young fellow, Adam, passed by the bar and stopped to tap George on the shoulder, lightly but nearly causing the old man to fall off his stool. George regained his balance wildly, holding on to the bar counter with two hands and putting his feet out in front of him.

'Easy,' he said.

'Bloody hell, George, have you been here all this time?'

George turned to his assailant, 'I've been shanghaied by this here gentleman. How's the tiling going? Need a hand?'

'No thanks. You all right?'

'Marvellous.'

'All right then, take it easy. I'm off for a siesta. Cheers.' And raising one arm in a salute that lasted until he was out of sight, Adam dipped down below the terrace towards the seashore.

'Who was that?' said Annemieke, accepting a glass of wine.

'A young man working here, doing some tiling. A Brit. His compatriot lent him a hand this morning.'

'Really? I wouldn't have thought you were still up to it at your age, George.'

'Oh you'd be surprised what I can still get up to, my dear,' said George, with a sly nod of his head and a smile at Jan. 'Or at least,' he went on, 'where there's life there's hope.' And the three of them laughed while Jan finished the bottle of wine between their glasses.

'Let's drink to that,' he said.

George finished his glass in one draught. 'A siesta, the lad said. I think I'll nip back to the room for forty winks. Enjoy yourselves, you two.'

The drugs that he was taking for the cancer made it almost impossible for Jan to drink. The combination dealt instant nausea. He had stopped taking them that morning. It was a waste of time. He would take the morphine when he needed it but from now on he would drink. The desire for alcohol had wrapped itself around the ancient feelings that he'd suppressed during the illness – love and hope and stupidity. He was going to be silly, he had made his decision. He was sick of being ill, it had been a dead-end profession. It was not too late to be an idiot. George was a fine companion for that.

The wine was burning a hole in his sadness like the sun on his back.

'You are going to burn if you don't put your shirt back on,' said Annemieke, recognizing with slight jealousy that his upper body was beautiful in a way, lean and supple still. She had been surprised to see him sitting there like a manual worker with his shirt off, his shoulders rounded for once, a drunken smile on his face.

'Are you having a nice time?' Jan asked his wife, putting his hand around her waist, nodding at the waiter and pointing at the wine list.

Annemieke readjusted her sarong and gave her bikini top a tweak behind her neck. Her breasts were the soft dropping consistency of batter. She gave him one of her bright and anonymous smiles.

'Well, as you like to say, yes and no.'

'This is your version of paradise, though.'

'What do you mean by that?'

'You like this sort of thing. Elegant society.'

'If you think it's much fun for me to come away for the last time, again, then you're mistaken. It was the boys' idea, not mine.'

'You sound bitter. But it's me who has to do the dying.'

She pushed her wineglass away from her.

'Don't I know that!'

He looked down at his body. It was very bad form to die slowly, he had learned.

'I am sorry.'

'Oh, don't say things like that, Jan. It makes it worse.'

He meant it though. He swallowed and looked hard at the barman, signalling for a whisky to go with the wine, then changing his mind and ordering two. She did not disagree.

'We need to talk,' he explained as the drinks were served. He was waiting for the right moment. He would take her hands in his and he would say, let's go all the way back to the beginning, let's be two people without this past we have made, let us be friends. Let us do something silly together, now while there is time.

But the barman was taking a long time and his wife was looking at the other people around them, so he started to speak, quickly.

'Do you know, I haven't been so drunk in a long time.'

'No, that's true.'

'I owe you an apology. As you know, I didn't choose for this to happen to me, but I should not have let it win so completely.'

She took a breath and reached for her drink.

'You did not choose it. Neither did I, nor the children. But it was given to us and we have had to deal with it.'

'I am ashamed, Annemieke,' now he took her hands in his, 'I wish I were a better, stronger man. Dying does not make you good. Nothing makes you good, not even the life we want can do that, not even success.' He looked over at the Americans. A man was checking his watch against the time on the bar clock, his wife was running her fingertip around the inside of the rim of her eye. He looked beyond them, saw the flowers nodding, the shapes blurring and blending in his confused distant vision.

'Will you sit down?' he asked her. She shook her head.

'I have been bad company these last years. I am sorry.'

She did not want him to say sorry. It would require her to say the same, surely, that was why people said it, and she felt incapable of that.

'Don't worry,' she said.

But, like Bill Moloney, he wanted something from her it seemed, he pressed her.

'I am not worrying. I have decided not to worry, that is the point, you see I'm going to loosen up.'

Bill Moloney presented himself at the other side of the bar, elbowing one of the Americans aside, gently and with apologies.

She laughed with her head back. 'You have drunk too much, Jan-tche, you will be back to your usual self tomorrow!'

He was hurt by the way she scoffed at him. He said angrily, 'Ah, yes, I forgot, you know how to live.'

'I make no excuses for myself, I don't pretend to be what I am not.'

Across the bar, Jan noticed the Moloney fellow withdraw abruptly and he felt sure that they had been observed. He felt it was disgraceful, even though plenty of people did it, to bring such misery on holiday. And then he hated the holiday too.

'Not so loud,' he said. He noticed she had finished her drink and was passing the empty glass over to the waiter.

'Not so loud,' she mimicked, 'not so loud. This is all we have heard in the house. You have become so obsessed with your life in a technical sense that you have not lived it at all.'

'Happily, the same cannot be said of you. Have you sent De Vries a postcard?'

She turned towards him and put her hands on his shoulders. She bent her head to get her eyes squared with his. 'Look, Jan, what do you want? It's been a lousy end to a lousy marriage. Do you want me to say something else? Just because you are dying I am supposed to change, to be noble? For six years? I feel young inside. I feel like an eighteen-year-old. I am not dying. You have robbed me of too many years and yes, I resent it and I've had enough. I have always been honest with you.'

He had heard this before, this last part. It was not the right place, there were people watching and yet she had dashed his hope from him, she judged and categorized his life and now she would do the same with his death. He would speak.

'Annemieke, your honesty is miserable. It is rude. This honesty of yours does not uncover any truth, it allows you to do as you please.' He stopped because his anger was getting ahead of him, and then he slammed his hand down on the bar making their drinks jump and he said, 'It is convenient!'

'I'm not a philosopher. How lucky for you that you are capable of seeing the truth. Add another note to your book.'

He felt outclassed by her, and yet he was still sure even after all these years that good was on his side. He took his glass in his hands and supped the whisky like a mug of soup.

'This is . . . terrible,' he said. He had bags under his eyes; to her he looked both doleful and importunate.

The very sight of him annoyed her.

'You know,' he said, 'when I think of you in the early days, I miss you, Annemieke. I knew from the beginning we had our difficulties, our differences. But you were a friend once. Now it seems as if there is nothing, no safe place. I thought . . .' He put his empty glass down on the counter and it slipped in the wet until he steadied it. Then he closed his mouth and was silent.

She held her glass between her breasts and looked away. She was thinking about the days after his death, the quiet house, the boxes on the floor, the boys making coffee in the kitchen, touching her back as she knelt, the sudden heart-starting sound of the phone ringing.

He went on, clearing his throat, muttering miserably, 'Nobody needs to win. Nobody needs to be right. Nobody cares about us, who's winning. I had an idea, you see, how to do it.'

She heard his voice crack and looked quickly at him, and she saw her younger son, Ben, saw the way he looked after admitting to her he had an overdraft again. In spite of her cold and hard mind, her mother's heart arched like a swallow making a circle of the sky, turning south for the winter.

13

George slipped the plastic card into the slot of the key mechanism on their door three times but each time was too impatient, shoving the handle before the lights turned green. He knocked and called out.

'I say, Dorothy, it's me, let us in, I'm having no joy with this card thing.' He waited, licked his lips, he was dry, dry as a bone. When he thought of Dorothy he thought of a nice cup of tea waiting for him. He kicked the door softly, 'Come on dear, pull yourself together, get a move on.'

He tried the card once more, took his time and stumbled into the room that was being blown by the rapidly turning fans. There were loose papers from the hotel brochures all over the floor. He called her name again and stepped on to the balcony. She wasn't there. Probably she'd popped out for a spot of lunch. His watch showed three. The beds were made, tidy as a stack of fresh lumber. He'd just have a little lie-down while he waited for her, rest his eyes.

14

The little old lady – her daughters called her 'Mrs Tiggy-Winkle' – attracted only a little attention as she left the main gates of the resort. Perhaps one or two of the staff were surprised to see that she wore a coat in the blazing heat. Nobody noticed her stand opposite the gates for a quarter of an hour or so as if she were a passing stranger considering it as a subject for a little sketch. She began to walk on the right-hand side of the road. She was pleased to discover that there was no traffic.

Over the years, a few times, Dorothy had gone to the door, picked up her bag and her hat and coat and buttoned up to leave them all. The buttoning had seemed to take forever, her jaw moving all the while, grinding grievance. Once or twice she'd gone to the end of the road and stood at the bus stop, blinking, her chest heaving with the phlegm caught in her lungs. Each time, the bus came and went and she'd let it go on its way and gone back home. It was no easier to go back than to leave.

Now, she was faced with a long slow incline, a hill that promised to reach a plateau. Ahead of her she saw the swishing sugar canes, shaking shaggy haircuts. The heat was intense. She had no idea what the time was as she'd left her watch behind. The walk was slow and tiring, so soon. She was old and useless, just like they all told her, but there was no point in getting upset over that. When she reached the plateau and saw the sugar fields stretching golden and righteous ahead of her and to her left and right and beyond them at the sides a blue which might be both land and sea, she took her coat off, folded it neatly, then popped it under a tall hedgerow. She took a swig from the little bottle of water she'd brought, swilling it around her dry mouth, up in front of her teeth, feeling it loosen her gums. She pulled the fabric under her arms away from the skin and stepped onwards.

She had had to warn them, the girls and George, about herself, without really saying anything; she didn't want anyone to panic. She knew it was coming on before the doctor did, whatever it was they called it. The bloody wicked thing was she couldn't remember the name of it! You had to laugh. She wasn't stupid, she'd been a bright young thing, read everything she got her hands on, always in the library, before George. She could remember that place in such detail, all the different smells, the listed rules, the little catalogue cards in dark blue, titles in capitals, author in small letters, the dank promising smell between the shelves, then the yeasty smell of the books themselves and the Lily of the Valley on the Head Librarian when you went to get your library card stamped. She used to think that the gate to heaven would be like that, kindly but official with the smell of flowers. All of that she could bring to mind, and much of her childhood with it, but she couldn't remember the name of her own illness! There were lots of words that had just gone, disappeared. Her world was closing down. Every time she got to the place in her mind, which took her a long time to get to, there was a sign before it, 'Closed'. Before they'd come away, there had been a day when she couldn't think what day of the week it was.

She'd decided to speak to George about it. He'd been down in the tool shed and she'd gone down and stood in the doorway, and he'd said, 'Still in your nightgown? Not going to Madge's today then?' And there she was, wood shavings all over her slippers, her long nightie picking up wood dust too and she had

what she'd prepared to say right on the tip of her tongue.
'Look,' she'd wanted to say, 'something's happening in my
head, I'm not right, but please just put up with me, don't get
the doctors involved and don't tell the girls. Please just look
after me, please.' But she'd said instead, 'Who's Madge?' and
she'd felt like she ought to ask, as a matter of urgency, because
she had the horrible feeling that it was someone she knew
really well, maybe it was a niece or a sister or even one of her
own children. 'Don't come that with me,' he'd said, 'go and get
yourself dressed and I'll take you in the car, you'll have missed
the bus by now.' She'd touched his arm, the hairs were like
electric fuse wires, always ginger there and he'd shaken her off
without looking at her, 'Go on,' he'd said roughly. His voice
went hoarse the same way when their oldest daughter told
them she'd lost the baby.

'Who's Madge?' she'd said, stepping back into the garden,
feeling like springs under her feet the planed-off wood curls
that he'd swept outside. She watched him hobble down to the
runner beans and the compost heap but he hadn't heard, he
hadn't answered her and so she'd gone back up to the house.
When he came in later and found her sitting in the front room
he didn't mention getting the car out.

So all she said to him and to the girls, was, 'I shall be quite
happy when it's my time to go.' And they teased her, 'Oh,
when's that then, Mum, let us in on the secret, will you?' It was
all she could do. At least they knew she wasn't suffering.

Coming down the hill the other side of the plateau, she could
see a small hamlet, a cluster of makeshift houses, each slightly
elevated with four stumpy wooden legs. When she got there,
she would have another sip of water. A long chicken-wire-
fenced area to the left of the road led to the first of the
dwellings. Inside the run were chickens and monkeys. On the
steps of the home a surly-faced woman stood with her hair in

rag curlers, a baby at her hip and glamorous if well-worn slippers on her feet. She looked sternly at Dorothy. Underneath her legs a long pale yellow mongrel dog was curled and he raised his head to look, then went back to sleep. The woman nodded and so Dorothy returned her nod and said, 'Good day.'

The woman cracked a smile.

'How's it going there?' she asked.

Dorothy nodded quickly.

'Fine, thank you. Lovely day.'

'If you say so.' Her voice was deep and singsong. Then she sat down, shaking her head over the baby, and laughing with real amusement.

In front of another house, a boy stood up on the pedals of his bike, balancing it with his legs tense, ready for the unexpected. Seeing her, he grinned and called his friends, and a group of children came out to watch her, their mothers stood in the doorways that were hung with lace moving lazily in the slight breeze. A couple of old men, sitting smoking with their backs against used tyres, called out to her and raised their hands in salute. She felt like the head of a carnival parade and quite naturally raised her hand to return their greetings. No one approached her; they let her go on her way, a fleeting oddity.

Two teenage girls, also with their hair in rags, sat knees-together on the steps of a blue-painted tin-roofed house. In their pink and yellow dresses, they looked quite a pretty picture. If this was poverty then it had colour to it, she thought, and a slow easiness that did not suggest hunger. It must have been early evening, the people relaxed without the need for entertainment. They all seemed to be perched as if watching but there was nothing to watch.

'How lovely,' she said.

She was able to peep inside quite a few of the houses and see into them. Each of them had lace at the windows and many of them had frippery, fabric and lace over the chairs and tables. The houses were painted the colours you found in a box of chalks, solid blues, reds, oranges, pinks and yellow. Inside, the furniture was useful; she saw the very things her own children laughed at her generation for, plastic homewares and useful coverings. She spied the ends of legs or a portion of a back, a head turning, an arm reaching as the lacy curtains blew this way and that. She wished for herself the life that was lived inside them.

Poor! she thought, spitting out the word. They have no televisions, that's it! She tutted and tusked. 'Now don't go thinking that these people are good, Dorothy,' she warned herself, 'no people is either good or bad, no matter what they have or don't have . . .' But wasn't it easier to be good when you didn't have so much to worry about, wasn't it just easier? Hadn't people been better once? With their front doors open, small things to celebrate. The girls told her it was rose-tinted nonsense.

'There was still crime back then, Mother,' they told her. The granddaughter would explain to Dorothy how media this-and-that and how the police forces this-and-the-other and how it was all different and yet all the same.

'I wish I could get myself kidnapped,' she said, stopping to rummage around the bottom of her bag for a lone Murray Mint. She found one and stood, sucking on her sweet like a duck gobbling bread.

15

Jan was awake. It was the evening, they had gone to bed drunk, before the sunset, agreeing to rise for dinner. His wife slept, silent and solid beside him, the fan causing a small ripple of white sheet to flicker over a freckled shoulder. He had his head on the pillow, but was lying on his side so that he could feel, quite palpably, the pulsing of an artery in his neck. He could hear it too. It sounded like a clock ticking. It did more for him than a solitary thought could do and so he waited there until he had what he needed from it, then he turned and looked at his wife. A small trickle of saliva lay across her cheek and he knew the smell of it, the dead breath creeping out under cover of liquid.

He really did want an armistice. He had called her, in their time together, fraud, coward, liar, and he knew that these might apply to him also. It was no good calling her these things, when the fact was that he was lying there beside her. They were complicit. He'd spent each day with her amassing evidence to prove himself better than her and dying had served him up another way to be better, to be more right. That was the truth of it. He was a fool.

He got up to smoke a cigarette on the balcony. He had taken up smoking again in the last month. He took a beer from the fridge and sat in the dull black heat of their balcony with the door open, careless of the air conditioning seeping out and the warm air stealing in. He wanted her to smell the smoke; he wanted her to mind him.

He had seen at dinner that George was impressed with Annemieke. As she aged Annemieke's face was decked with excessive emotion, like an old maid's Christmas tree, loaded, angry, ready to let something tumble. Her eyes were strained, mascara weighed heavily on lashes, but she still looked good. She looked better without make-up. Her eyes were the grey of the North Sea she had looked at many times from her mother's apartment in Blankenberge. They used to make him think of a drop of ink on to watercolour paper, dark at first, fading outwards.

Of course, old George liked the way she looked. Men liked her because she looked like she would provide the entertainment. Her fellow Dutch or Belgian women chose to wear stern, forbidding, expensive brands in dark green, brown leather and navy. Annemieke hoarded a mass of clothes, bobbled and baubled, which refused folding and rioted in the wardrobes. From the shelves a sleeve here or there stretched down towards the clothes hanger, dripping with crocheted cherries, too many zips and cuff buttons shaped like anchors or hearts.

He had thought at first that her wearing eye make-up in bed was charming, acquired from some magazine advice column typical in the 1960s – or it might be some slatternly laziness, and this thought appealed to him perhaps more. One evening, in the early days, before the children, he spotted that the colour of the eye shadow had changed from green to a pearlized white shimmer, which matched her nightdress. He had felt cornered. Yet when she ceased to wear it in bed, he was dejected. Accidentally, he found the tubes of cosmetics in her drawer; she kept them still and he became jealous. By then he'd become merely a tenant of her bed-tent, profiteer of her capable circulatory system in wintertime.

Looking into the room, he saw her turn a little, kicking at the sheets. Her feet suffered too, along with her eyes. She stuffed them into too tight too high heels, put plasters over blisters and sloughed away red patches to leave raw patches.

Finding the dry skin razor in their bathroom, the foot carpaccio in the bidet, had turned his stomach. She could not abide sheets over her feet, so those red paddles of pain turned in the night-time air.

He extinguished his cigarette and went back into the room. He put on the lamp by his side of the bed and picked up his book. He had known the light would wake her. She was roused and frowned at him, lifting her head.

'It smells of smoke in here.'

'Sorry.'

'Can't you sleep?'

'No. Insomnia.'

'Why don't you take something?'

She turned and nestled her head once more into the pillow and he saw her shoulders slacken. Before she was quite asleep again, he put his lips between her shoulder blades and kissed her there.

The phone rang. It was George.

16

It was the manager's first serious hotel. Steve Burns was thirty-five, he was single; he was committed to his new job. The resort was one of a chain of luxury resorts that were marketing themselves as 'taste and refinement in unexpected locations'. 'Taste and refinement' meant dark teakwood and uniformly white furnishings. The 'unexpected locations' were a result of the prime real estate in any popular resort area having been long since snapped up.

The manager's job description was rather alternative, rather New Age. In bold letters he was instructed to 'deliver an experience that enables our customers to reconnect with his or her inner self in luxurious surroundings'. He was, however, from Manchester. Steve Burns. Down to earth. He'd laughed about the job title; 'Total Experience Manager'. He'd shown it to his friends down at the local that lunchtime after it came in the post, red-cheeked no longer from pride, but from the several beers and the stuffy public bar on the solitary hot day of the year. His friends quizzed him. He'd been a hotel manager, but now he was to be a guru, it was a promotion, surely. Like going from baker to bishop.

'Look,' he said, 'you park seventy-odd middle class fat-arses round a swimming pool in the blazing heat, you get them up to pour booze down their necks and then you drag them off to sweat it out on the massage table and they'll find their selves all right. I don't doubt they'll find that their true self, their inner child, is just what it was before they left home; a right greedy bast'd.'

'Half your chance,' his friends had moaned and gone on to ask him about discount rates. Time to leave.

Now he was sat, in khaki trousers and a white shirt, a silver chain round his neck, hairy ankles peeping out of brown leather boat shoes, on the corner of the big dark wood desk he'd been given. A dark wood fan, brass details, a colonial era reproduction, turned above him. Here he was presented as part Werner Erhard, part Ernest Hemingway. And essentially, he was perfect for all of it, the clammy-handed Mancunian grateful for the chance to rub shoulders with the moneyed classes.

He'd already had his daily team briefing with senior members of staff and now, last job at nine in the evening, he was running through one or two of the same points with Abner and Emma, the Catering Manager and Domestic Staff Manager. He found the Caribbean staff quite proper in a way, he'd expected more of the rum-swigging, pot-smoking, '*Here com' de Lilt', mon*,' stereotype. But this particular island was one of the most religious places on the earth. It was almost impossible to get staffing for Sunday mornings. In a cunning pact with the forces of darkness, he held a weekly Saturday Night Fever party, dedicated to fond memories of school discos, and he worked the crowd hard to make sure there'd be no early risers. That way breakfast would be less of an issue and lunch an eggs-and-potato-settle-my-stomach-before-I-shit-myself sort of affair which could be managed by a line of just two or three in the kitchen.

He was explaining to Abner and Emma that their jobs emanated from his own, which under his interpretation meant that they were 'alcohol facilitators'.

'They're no trouble when they're passed out round the pool, are they?' he was saying. But Emma had been to college and was talking about increasing their captive spending – spa packages, tours – and even tipping.

'Your Brits won't tip,' he said, matter-of-factly, turning over her other suggestions in his mind. He liked to present himself as someone on the side of the common man – and his drinking. He liked a pint himself. He persuaded himself that it was best not to milk the customers, but to make sure they came back.

There was a small commotion outside the frosted glass double doors to his office and an old man burst in, wearing a string vest, trousers and braces.

'Hello-hello, mate,' he said, 'can I help you, Sir?'

'I've lost my wife,' the old man said.

'Not entirely bad news, then,' he said, smiling broadly. Abner and Emma looked at him, both shocked and afraid. (Oh, the old girl would turn up; she'd be in the spa more than likely.)

'Mr Davis, isn't it?' he said. He did his homework; he read the names and profiles of all his guests for the week. He'd remembered this couple, on account of their ages. He might have known there would be 'issues'. In his experience the geriatric punter was more hassle than he was worth. That and the new parent, terrible pains in the arse, expected everyone else to suffer along with them, couldn't get over their indignation that God or Biology had done this to them, inflicted them with rheumatoid arthritis/a kid.

'So, when did you last see Mrs Davis?'

George was rubbing his jowls left and right with his big hand, 'Not since the morning.'

'Did she go off for the day then, off on a tour or something?'

'No,' said George and his face was suddenly wretched, 'I left her in the room and I got a bit carried away with the day's events, sat out having lunch with a new acquaintance, had a few drinks, went back to the room in the afternoon, late, and I must have fallen asleep.'

Steve checked his watch again; it was just after nine-thirty.

'I just woke up,' said the old fellow.

'Right. That's quite a while she could have been missing, then, Sir,' said Steve.

'Yes. That's what I've been saying to your receptionist and the bellboys. Have they seen her, I've been asking them, and they keep telling me to come and see you. Why can't they just answer me?'

The entire staffing shift had changed at five, thought Steve. He'd have to call some people. Lots of people. But first they should check the premises.

'Now you're not to worry, Sir, we're going to sort this out, we're going to make a full search and concurrently,' he paused over the word, hesitant for a moment, but it held good, 'we'll make inquiries of all the staff here today.' Abner and Emma remained open-mouthed in shock and fear.

'How old is she?' Emma asked George, turning in her seat.

'Eighty-two.'

Emma shook her head and made a moaning sound, 'So old and it's been so hot today.'

'Thank you, Emma,' said Steve. 'Now, Mr Davis, let's get on with the plan of action. I think it would be best if you waited by the bar, had some supper, a bowl of soup or something.'

'Don't manage me, son. Just get your arse in gear and make sure you get the police called in right away.'

17

It was Adam who put his hand on Jan's shoulder in the dining room. The Belgian couple sat at a table for four, on their own, near the door. Seeing Adam's eyes alert and quick about the room, Jan wiped his lips and put his napkin on his plate, pushing it aside. Annemieke laid her knife and fork to rest and put her hands to her face as Adam explained that he'd just heard George's wife had gone missing.

'Yes, George, he has told me this already.'

Adam shook his head. 'Poor old boy, he's got to be worried sick. I thought maybe you and I could see if we could help him.'

'But of course,' said Jan pushing his chair back from the table, 'I am waiting for him to meet me here after he has seen the manager. He has been some time now.'

'Terrible!' said Annemieke with a loud voice. One or two of the other guests looked over at the group. 'She is an old woman. It's already the evening! It's getting late! They need to find her.'

Jan put his finger to his lips.

'But the more people who know, the more can help look for her,' she said, looking about her.

Adam looked at Annemieke and shrugged. Jan stood up.

'Let me go and find out what we can do.'

'I'll wait for you both at the bar,' she said, rising also.

There was something comic about the members of the kitchen staff, wandering around the grounds of the hotel, looking in places that a human being could quite plainly not

be, saying in stage whispers, 'Mrs Davis, are you there?'
They had been advised not to alarm the other guests. A
group of three of them came out of the sauna and one of
them, in chef's pants, turned the key in the lock as they
exited, shaking his head and pointing out the tool sheds for
their next inspection.

George was standing by the poolside, surveying the troops in
action, a finger pushing his lower lip into his mouth, chewing.

When Jan and Adam came up alongside him, he shook his
head and said, 'Where the hell is she?'

'Have they searched the beach?' asked Jan.

'They're down there now,' said George, 'I've been down
myself. They're looking everywhere but there's a limit to how
far she could have got, she was no walker, her feet hurt just
going down to the bus stop.'

'Does she drive?' asked Adam.

George shook his head.

'Could she have gone out on a tour?'

'She would have told me, but there's no note in the room,
nothing.'

'You ought to tell reception to put any calls for you through
to the manager,' said Jan. George nodded but without
conviction.

'She wouldn't know how to use a phone.'

'No, but other people do.'

'Yes, someone might call for money. She might have been
kidnapped, I can't help thinking, terrible things, I shouldn't
have left her alone . . .'

'No, no, I mean some friendly help, someone might call on
her behalf.'

George shook his head.

'She's gone and I don't know where. It must be the first time
in fifty-odd years I don't know where she is. It's peculiar.'

Adam put his hand on George's arm as the manager and a group of men came into view from the direction of the beach. The manager was out of breath. He leaned forward with his hands on his hips and then raised his head and shook it, looking at George. Small drips of sweat fell from the sides of his face into the cotton of his shirt. He used his sleeve on his forehead.

'What about the police?' said George.

The manager looked at Adam and Jan, standing either side of George, for a moment.

'That's our next step.'

'Next step? I asked you to do it when we were back in your office.' George looked at Jan, 'That was an hour ago.'

'There's not much they can do, though; they're not a very organized crew down there. I didn't want to overreact, till we'd had a good look about the place, you see.'

'When an elderly woman is missing, there is no such thing as an overreaction,' said Jan.

Now the Mancunian saw that all the buttons on the man's shirt were done up and he heard that his clipped accent was Northern European, Dutch or German, and he disliked him. He knew he would prove a thorn in his side. 'All right, Hans,' he thought to himself.

'Believe me, we're leaving no stone unturned, Sir. Right now, my staff are still out looking in the grounds and I will make sure to extend the search to the local area. We are making phone calls. You need to understand the way a community of this sort operates, Sir, in order to understand that the police might not be the first choice. It's a word of mouth type place.'

'I think that this is bullshit,' said Jan, 'you are protecting yourself. You don't want bad publicity, that is it.'

George looked wildly between the two men. Adam, with his

hand still on George's arm, spoke up, 'Let's just call the police, it can't do any harm.'

The manager assented, 'Of course. No one's trying to protect themselves.' He shot a look at Adam.

18

The last of the hummingbirds was finishing its work for the day, inserting its perfect proboscis into the vase-like sheath of a hibiscus, hovering, quivering with pleasure. The air was murky with the scent of the aristocratic flowers that know only the satisfaction of drenched soils. The sprinklers twitched and twittered and rained silken droplets on to the petals of the flowers. It was as if the brazen red hibiscus flowers prostrated themselves to get wet — tongues out, shameless.

Annemieke went to the bar with her Chinese shawl, red and black and gold, draped over one shoulder and one arm. Her steps down the pathway sounded brittle in her heels and her haste.

There was a crowd there who had not yet gone in to supper. They had become a group over the last few days, she noticed, establishing a sort of gentry at the place. They were the people who wore Rolex watches and left Cartier accessories around the pool, sunglasses and bags. If one of them went to the bar he would certainly ask the others if they wanted anything, and such courteous acts persuaded them of each other's decency. She had been asked herself, that morning, by one of them whether she needed a drink. She had looked up from her book, and declined with a long smile, looking across at the man's wife, a blonde woman with a slightly hooked nose who liked to play fast and loose with her bikini top. (She whisked it away when she was tanning her back and replaced its twin triangles over her fried-egg breasts when she tanned her front. She fastened it only when she was on the move.)

Now the same man and woman were 'hosting' a group of three couples, all in their forties, to which an English couple were attempting to adhere. She and Jan had met these two, Harry and Maxine from Surrey, the night before at the bar. Now they waved her into the circle, asserting something more than their right to belong by bringing her in, saying with excessive familiarity, 'Annie love, gin and tonic, am I right?'

'A glass of white, thank you,' she said, turning as if she had just noticed them all, standing there in their white and gold with aftershave fighting perfume tooth and nail for air space. She bid the group all a good evening.

'Jason Ryder,' said the American man who had offered her the drink that morning. 'Missy Ryder,' he added, stepping aside to reveal his wife.

'How's the grub tonight?' Harry asked her, looking winningly at hook-nose's husband, giving him a wink in reference, one assumed, to some previous discussion of theirs.

'I'm sure it's not up to New York standards again,' said Maxine, 'but you've got it all there, haven't you? Lucky.' The man called Jason demurred, looked noncommittal and put his hand down the back of his wife's dress.

Annemieke spoke, 'I could not eat actually, Harry.' Immediately, the women turned towards her. A certain class of women, as she knew, fall over themselves to be the nicest person at any gathering. 'One of the ladies staying at the resort has gone missing. Possibly kidnapped, possibly abducted. It's been twenty-four hours now and they're not holding out much hope.'

There was a level of surprise that was exceeded by its demonstration.

'You're joking me,' said Harry.

'I don't believe it,' said his wife, looking at him with wide eyes. He put his arm around her shoulders and pulled her towards him. Their eyes were fixed on Annemieke. She was trying not to smile. Sometimes she got a little carried away.

'I thought I should warn you all to be careful. I'm afraid one has to be prepared for the worst news.'

The American couple looked at each other.

'What are they doing about it? The management,' asked Jason Ryder.

'Is it that lady who eats supper with the young . . . ?' his wife began.

'No, not her, actually it happens to be the wife of a friend of ours, which is why I'm so upset by it, they're good people, so . . .' she looked about her, 'decent, simple people.'

The women shook their heads.

'That elderly couple,' Jason's wife said, nodding, 'I saw you dining with them. Such a genuine couple.'

'They must be in their eighties,' said the other man.

'Well, we must see what we can do,' said Jason, turning to his American friends.

The night had closed in on the bar and the barman was appointing it with several candles in jars as he'd been instructed by the manager. 'Think experience,' he'd been told, candlelight was tasteful, as opposed to dimmer switch operated lighting which was crass and could be operated wilfully. 'Think *romance*.' The previous barman had been very quick on the switch, going from dim to glare according to his own whims. The new barman would not make the same mistake. The guests stood with their backs to the bar to look at the illuminated blue water of the man-made pool, sipping on their drinks, murmuring to each other. Annemieke alone kept her face angled towards the gardens behind the bar. Her features were touched by candlelight. One could see that her brow was troubled, but otherwise she was as still as the flowers that settled, untroubled by bee, butterfly or humming bird.

19

Jan took George to the bar for coffee, one black, one milky, and stood apart from the group. They were waiting for the manager to come and tell them what news he had. He had said he would meet them there at ten.

Annemieke excused herself and went over to the two men. 'Any news?'

The men shook their heads. Jan explained that George had given a full statement to a police chief who'd come out with two other policemen.

'They appear to be taking it very seriously.' He said this for George's benefit, recalling that the chief had been forced to press hard on his triplicate pad as he took down the main details and that the purpose of the other men with him seemed to have been to express concern over the state of his Biro. The chief had offered George his assurance that they would do their best.

'This is a small island, Sir,' he'd said to George, 'everybody know everybody.'

'Well, it sounds like they'll do what they can,' said Annemieke, touching George's hand briefly.

George was grinding his teeth and looking into the gloom of the gardens, through and beyond the bar. He nodded.

'Where's Adam?' she asked Jan.

'He's gone back to his apartment.'

Annemieke raised her eyebrows and clucked loudly.

'To find out whether we can use his landlord's car tonight.'

'Why, what are you planning?'

'Well, we're going to go and look for her.'

'Is that smart?'

'We need to do something,' said Jan quietly. 'Put yourself in his place.'

'I'm just thinking that we don't want to lose two more people. You're old men,' she whispered, looking askance as if it was a secret.

'Don't be ridiculous.'

The Americans, who had moved closer to the three of them and stood patiently by in recognition of their fellows' proximity to the epicentre of the events, now began to agitate.

'Excuse me,' Jason said, 'but we understand you may have a situation and we would like to offer to help.'

Jan turned to him and shook his head. With his heavy upper lip and hangdog solemnity he looked like an old and sickly cow refusing a handful of grain, Annemieke thought.

'It's very good of you,' she said, and, turning to Jan, 'I explained to Mr Ryder and his friends what was happening. I thought we could use all the help we could get.'

George did not seem to be listening; his hands were splayed on the bar, supporting his upper body with his wrists.

Jason started to explain that the American Consulate on the island might be of use to them, it was bound to have access to superior assistance. 'They'll see that the American citizens here are affected by this and they'll act, I can assure you.'

Jan looked pointedly aside.

'Let's be frank, this situation affects the community of this resort. It's potentially serious. For all of us. Our wives. We ought to have been advised of it by the management already. We're all involved,' Jason said, frowning. Jan remained expressionless, immovable. George did not turn around. Annemieke was nodding with sympathetic eyes, her eyebrows together.

'I'm not impressed with the management here. It's totally hands-off if you get my drift. Where is the guy when you need him? Talk about a permanent vacation. I think we could put a little heat on. I play golf, back home, with the chairman of the group that owns these hotels.'

'Well, I think that would be a great help,' said Annemieke.

Jason took his cellphone from his pocket and walked away a few steps saying, 'Sure, we'll get on to it.'

At that moment Bill Moloney, his sunburn obvious even in the near dark, came up to the group and stood on its edges, waiting. He looked as though he was about to say something but seeing Jan with his back to them all, a hand now on George's shoulder, he withdrew. Annemieke was pleased. She said to herself, 'So much he cares, the great idiot.'

Standing aside gazing towards the uniform black of sea and land and sky, George was saying to Jan, 'She'll have to be scared witless, mate, now that it's dark. What does she know of the dark, we're always in bed asleep by nine these days. She'll be tired.'

'Someone will be helping her to get back here.'

'What if she has been kidnapped? I heard them American women saying that's what they thought too.'

'Oh nonsense, how often does that happen?'

'I don't know.'

'Well, it does not. These islands live and breathe tourism; every single person here makes their living through it. It's too small, George.'

'But we was warned. That group were saying that first night not to go out the hotel. They must have been here a few times.'

'Well, so have I, in the region at least, and I know this is nonsense.'

'Do you think she's still alive, Jan?' he said, looking at his hands and exhaling through his nose.

'Yes, I do. Of course I do.'

He felt a hand on his back and became irritable thinking that it boded more offers from Annemieke's American friends. He turned round to see Adam standing behind him, his shoulder-length hair tied back.

'Ready when you are, chaps,' he said, showing them a bunch of keys.

'Good man,' said George.

'My landlord was using his van, but that big fellow who's staying here, what is he, Irish, he lent me his hire car. Just heard me asking reception if there was a car I could have to take you two about and he gave me these. Says it's got a full tank.'

'No news,' said Burns, approaching the bar.

'Then we go out in the car, now,' said Jan.

'Do you know your way around? I'd come with you but it's best I stay here to field any information or calls.'

'Sure. We have a guide,' Jan looked at Adam, 'and we have a car.'

'Oh good. I'd give you one of our vans but our drivers are off duty and it's not insured . . .'

'At last the great man himself arrives.' Jason interrupted, stepping forward. 'Mr Burns, I want to be assured, I want to have your word, that your company is doing everything it can to resolve this situation. I'm a personal friend of your chairman, Mr Cohen, and I know he'd want you to be going to the greatest personal lengths to find this lady. There are a lot of eyes on you here,' he added.

'Important ones,' put in the brown-haired man.

'I am doing my best, Sir,' said Steve. 'There's a woman missing here. That gets all of my attention.'

Later he would think of many other things he could have said, things that would have better asserted his own dignity. He couldn't forget that he'd used the word 'Sir' and he kicked himself for it. It was fine used with an Englishman who would know its inherent sarcasm, but an American would take it literally. If each of us has his or her own special conceit, that lie which allows us to do our job, Steve Burns's was that he was not a flunky, not a corporate brown-noser, he was his own man.

20

The island's villages were spaced at about ten minutes' drive from each other. One home would become ten and then thirty, right on top of each other, and at the centre of each was a corrugated iron roof with a few tables at which men sat about, drinking. At a fishing village, a group of men were washing down the wooden blocks that they used to gut the fish they brought in, and women were sitting dangling their legs from tables that had been cleaned earlier. Jan watched from the open car window. Women wandered in and out between their homes and the central shelter. Bottled beer was drunk and often a board game was played, lit by the paraffin lamps or single bulb that swung from a beam. They heard music and laughter and much banter, loud accusations and ripostes that followed at a higher pitch. They were forced to slow down as men in the cars in front of them slapped hands with passers-by or stopped without warning to talk to a friend.

From a bar, some men recognized a driver in one of the cars that was ahead of theirs and they were jeering at him, calling him 'a fucking idiot', and the man's responses caused them to laugh uproariously and redouble their cries.

The three men sat and waited.

Adam was driving, and George was alongside him, with Jan in the rear. Adam would stop the car and lope off into a bar, hailing the men there with an easy-going 'How you doing?' Although he was a stranger, they smiled at him. It was the long hair, thought Jan. The tattoos. A man could go about the world nowadays and be universally liked, that way. When he was young, there'd been the brief fling with hippydom, and then it was romp all the way to the grave wearing better clothes than one's parents. Nowadays, adolescence need never end. But his sons' clothes were certainly more expensive than his. Evolution care of Armani. He smiled.

Now Adam was accepting a beer, conveying with his body language thanks and the time pressure of his task. His own button-down collared shirt felt like a shroud about his neck. He put two fingers to it and pulled the opening.

Adam sat down on a stool with the men, wide-kneed, explaining where he worked and what he was doing; when he had them on his side, smoking one of their cigarettes, he explained the situation. Necks craned as the group in the bar looked towards the car. George and Jan sat there watching. Jan felt the weight of his face, long and serious.

'I wish I hadn't said what I did earlier today, if you recall,' said George. As he was sat in front of Jan, in the dark, Jan could not see his face, only the glint of his glasses in the driving mirror.

'What? Oh, about the other women?'

'Yes. I feel bad about it. Meanwhile Dorothy was going missing.'

'George . . .' he said as a soft and comforting reproof, having nothing of substance to support it.

'You get confused. You get everything out of order until something forces you to get things *in* order.'

'Yes.'

'Something happens to make you see clear.'

'Yes.'

'You must have thought, what a bloody old fool! I bet you see clear, don't you, Jan? With the cancer on your mind and all. At my age I ought to. Didn't I? Pray God I don't have to lose her to make me see clear. Be no good to me then.'

Jan said nothing. They were quiet for a while, together in the warmth of the night. Slightly tired, Jan felt himself grow comfortable and almost forget why they were there until Adam came back and jumped into the driving seat, slamming the door behind him.

'Nope,' he said, 'let's go on. I left them the number of the hotel. They'll keep their ears and eyes open. Seemed like good folks. Think they'll do some asking about.'

He started the car.

21

It was just past midnight when they reached the capital of the island, a city of some two hundred thousand inhabitants, with a small hub of maybe eight or nine buildings over ten storeys. The city followed an inlet from the sea for a couple of miles and then lost interest in itself. Around the commercial centre were settled the town's main activities – duty free sales and twenty-four-hour amusement arcades – and the centre of its history: a small parliamentary building from the 1700s with a lean-to church. Beside the arcades, small dark rooms were the main bars and Adam proposed to take a wander down two or three side streets. Any lingering tourists were going home to resorts or cruise ships, vaguely disappointed, and residents were settling back down, having indifferently served these folk with food and drink.

Jan suggested he and George take a street.

'Stay where you are,' said Adam, 'with him. I can whip round the area pretty fast on my own.'

George sat still, his left arm outstretched, looking at his wedding band in the lamplight from above the car.

'When I was young, no one wore wedding rings, not men. Never thought I would but she went and bought me one for an anniversary present, years after we were married, and I've always worn it. Thirty-odd years I should think.'

His shoulders sagged. He couldn't seem to take his eyes from his hand.

'Back as soon as I can,' said Adam, leaning through the car window and giving the roof a double bang as he turned away.

'Sure,' said Jan.

'Her hands have always been so dry, the wife's. She uses a hand cream. It's purple and perfumed, smears it over her wedding ring, she's been using it for years, it's made the gold go dull. I can see her now wringing her hands together to get the full benefit. Like she's keeping her tools in good nick, that's all. She's not vain. If there's any lotion left over, it gets dragged up to her elbows.' He laughed. 'I suppose it's got animal fat in it or something. She's not what you call delicate. She was busty when I met her with the body underneath turned nice. Now she's a bit doddery, her body's propped up with this and that. Bloody corsets! That's her age group, you see. But she can be nimble. Hotfoots it up to the gate to greet the postman. She can make it up the garden in a half run when the phone rings. Actually it's a bit of a game between us, you get into them, don't you, when you've been together for years, I always try and beat her to it. She gives me the evils if I do, I can tell you.'

He was quiet for a while, watching a group of teenage boys kicking a can around under the lamplight of the small park outside the parliament buildings. A whoop went up as one of the boys, with the can between his ankles, jumped sideways, let the can into the air and then kicked it towards the rubbish bin that they'd placed central to them all.

'I don't suppose it's been an easy life for her. We've always worked long hours all of our years, the both of us.'

Jan felt for his own wedding ring; for a hard thing it was soft, worn by time.

'She's a marvel with the cooking.'

'Oh yes?'

'Yes.'

The boys were exchanging high fives and picking up nylon tracksuit tops and T-shirts and parting ways. As an after-thought, one of them quickly hopped back into the park to put the rubbish bin back underneath a lamp and he balanced the can on top of the refuse.

'Yes. Good English cooking.'

'Is that possible?'

'Bloody right. Steak and kidney? Cottage pie? Shepherd's Pie? Lasagne?'

'That's Italian, lasagne.'

'No it's not.'

'Sure it is.'

'It ain't.' George was adamant.

They were quiet again.

'I never ate it in Italy,' said George, 'not like Dorothy can turn it out. She's a good person, Jan.'

Jan was quiet.

'Do you know what I mean?'

'Actually, George, I think it is a failing in me I don't often see the good in others. Perhaps because I think everyone is like me.' Jan gave a curt laugh.

George turned around in his seat, it was quite an effort as his back was set from sitting there, and he looked Jan right in the face.

'What a load of rubbish, mate. Who else but you would be sat here in the back seat of a hire car listening to an old man drivel on like a silly old bugger in the middle of the night?'

As George raised his head in the half-light, Jan saw the loose flesh under the man's eyes, cheeks and chin. He blinked and swallowed.

'You will have her back, your Dorothy.'

'Yes, but will I? See, see . . .' Jan heard his teeth grind.

'What do you mean?'

'There's more to it than I've let on, mate. I'll never get her back in a way. She's gone for good. Listen. The wife, she's not really with it, in a manner of speaking, not all the time. She slips in and out. Behaves strangely. She's always been a bit on the sneaky side so I never thought nothing of it. She was always closing things up when I went in the room. She's secretive, over nothing.'

'Well, so am I. Aren't you? As we get older . . .'

'The other day I saw her shoving something under the seat of the sofa one time, so I said to myself, what the devil has she got to hide from me, I'll get her out the room and have a look. So I tell her that Mrs H. from up the street is at the gate and she pops out and while she's gone I look and blow me, it's a bleeding pack of crisps. Now why would she be hiding that?'

'Maybe she thought you'd eat them.'

'No. Don't like them, they get under my dentures. She'd been forgetful for years, we'd teased her about it, it's got worse and worse and she gets her words muddled up or forgets them and has these funny little panics about it. She can't remember the simplest things and she gets all angry with us when we try and help her. Starts shouting, nasty stuff, terrible some of it, the things she brings up from the past and sort of turns them . . . Well, I spoke to the doctor about it when I went for my own check-up and he said, bring her in. I told him, she wouldn't go, so he said, tell her just for a general, as I need to get my records up-to-date. 'Course, she wouldn't go. He calls me up a few weeks later, he's a good sort, asks how it is and I said, well it's funny you should call because we've had a terrible day. She went up to the shops to get the pensions, same as she always does on a Thursday but then she was gone for hours. The old bloke that runs the post office saw her sitting on a bench and she said to him she was ever so embarrassed but she'd forgotten which way to go home. Fifteen years she's made that walk. "George," he said, "I'll tell you straight, it sounds like Alzheimer's." And he sent me a few pamphlets, which I read and gave to her. She put them aside, somewhere and Lord knows where, I asked her for them as I meant to show the girls, but she'd forgotten where they were. Bloody Nora. She keeps saying, I'm just getting old. Let me get old in peace won't you? So I have done. And now this.'

'George, I am sorry.'

'I didn't want to face it, Jan, see, because then something would have to be done. Things would never be the same again.'

'Yes,' said Jan, 'I see that.'

Adam came back to the car and leaned through the open window.

'Man in the last bar I went to says his cousin told him she'd met a nice old English lady who seemed a bit confused. Gave me her address. Said the police had also been by, his brother's a policeman, he'd told him the same thing.'

They exchanged looks. Adam's eyes were large and clear and his head was ducked so that he could see them and they him; the lighting cast a halo over the blond ratty hair that had come loose from its elastic band during the drive. He turned his rueful smile on them. It occurred to Jan that for Adam human beings were ultimately harmless and one could afford to be widely affectionate. Jan himself was his opposite, he realized, as off-putting as the young man was winning, a stranger everywhere, whereas this young man was at home abroad, anywhere.

'He asked us to pop by the woman's house first thing, rather than now, as she's got four young kids,' said Adam.

'Is Dorothy with her?'

'Seems so. He didn't know much except that his cousin, her name's Charlotte, had asked her brother to go to the police but they came to his house, first, as it happened. They told him to let her know they'd pop round first thing. Here's the address.' He held out the piece of paper and George took it.

'Where is it, then?'

'About five miles from the hotel, inland. Not even a village, just a few homes together. A hamlet you call it.'

'She must have walked,' said George. 'She bloody did as well. She walked off.'

'Cheer up,' said Adam, 'we'll have her back with you soon enough. We should head back towards the hotel, then pop round to see this lady, Charlotte. What do you think, Jan?' he asked, putting his right hand behind George's seat as he reversed back.

'Ya, ya,' said Jan, 'good idea. When it's daytime, first thing.'

He rolled up his window and peered through the glass as they passed through the villages and towns that were now barely lit.

He was reviewing a scene in his mind. There was him, standing just outside his bedroom, holding the door ajar, dressed in his pyjamas, shouting at the top of his voice to make himself heard over heavy metal music. It must have been more than four years ago, before he took any of his trips away.

'Turn the music down,' he had been shouting, over and over again, until finally the music just stopped altogether as if the power button had been pressed and his youngest son stepped out of the living room.

'What's your problem?'

'I'm trying to sleep.'

'It's four in the afternoon.'

'I said, I'm trying to sleep. I am dying here!' he'd shouted.

Annemieke had tutted as she went past him and he'd reached up to the bookshelves and grabbed a book and thrown it after her. The bookmark fell out, it was a Polaroid photo taken in the 1970s on holiday in Spain. He'd put it away when he saw what it was.

In it Annemieke was lying on the hotel bed in her bikini with the boys' toy cars and tractors parked all over her body.

He'd come in the door, spotted them, driving the little plastic-tyred vehicles up and down her and said, 'Wait, I want to play,' but first he'd dipped the tractor into an iced drink and driven it over her tummy, then dipped it again and driven it up the inside of her leg. They'd shared a heavy and certain look and he'd raised his eyebrows, quickly looking down at his crotch. She'd covered her mouth with her hand so as not to laugh out loud. 'Can't they go and play in the road?' he'd moaned and fallen on the bed atop her, whispering into her ear, 'I'll be an old man when I get the chance to have you in the afternoon.'

22

It was her habit to take a single cup of very good coffee in the morning, with sugar if she needed it, but this morning she had had three. Jan had called her before seven to let her know that the couple were reunited and they were all on their way home. By eight, her mouth was dry from talking. Missy and the brown-haired American woman, Beverly, were either side of her. Their husbands were by the outer doors, on cellphones. The other English couple, Harry and Maxine, had gone off to play tennis.

'Bloody silly,' Harry had said before they went, 'when you think that the whole thing could have been so easily prevented.'

'It could have got really nasty too,' Maxine had added and Harry had nodded in her direction, his eyes glazing over as he looked at the breakfast buffet. 'If you're going up, get us another blueberry muffin, love.'

'Alzheimer's,' Missy was saying again, 'it can be so harrowing for the family. Even though it's hard, you have to get them in a nursing home, otherwise they just take over your world, it's tragic.'

'It is tragic,' Beverly agreed, 'it's something that I dread, losing my mind.'

'The rest you can get fixed, but not your mind,' Missy added with a smile.

'So that's the story,' Annemieke concluded, using her hands to signal the finale.

'Well, good for your husband and that young guy for finding her,' Beverly began.

'Sure,' said Missy, taking a sip of the decaffeinated coffee that had just been placed in front of her. 'I can't do too much stimulation,' she had explained, rolling the final word off her tongue as though it was an extremely dangerous euphemism.

'Well, I'm proud of my husband,' said Annemieke, folding her napkin, 'my Jan. His own health is not strong. He has been very brave. To lose a night's sleep is a big sacrifice for him, sleep is hard to get with his illness. I hope that George appreciates him.'

'He has insomnia? It's just an awful thing to live with,' Missy said.

Annemieke fixed her eyes upon her.

'He is dying of cancer. He has just a few weeks left, they say.'

'Oh my God.'

'Oh my God.'

Annemieke stood up and gave a crooked half-smile. She looked into the gardens beyond the windows and took a deep breath. 'This is our last vacation,' she said.

23

Charlotte was a very tall woman, confident and long-limbed. She wore her hair pulled back from her face. She was laughing in response to something Adam had said as she strode ahead of them, through the wire front gate, fending off the children, waving a hand in front of her face to fan herself. It was hot early in the day; her home was on a hilltop plateau, on a grassless plot opposite sugar cane fields.

'Dorothy,' she cried as she entered the house and she might have been calling a child that had been at a sleepover party to let her know her parents had come.

Dorothy was holding a mug of tea, her smile flickering as she moved into the light of the porch. George put a single arm round her and hugged her to him, tea and all.

'Don't have a go at me about it, George,' she said, her voice muffled by his body so that only he could hear her. 'Just don't say anything for once, please. Just this once.'

'All right, all right,' he was saying, 'it's all right now. Everything's going to be all right. You gave me a scare, a terrible scare. I thought I might not see you again.'

'No such luck,' said Dorothy, pulling away from him and setting her tea down. She put both hands up around his face and kissed him on the lips.

'I don't want to lose you, even if you are a bleeding nuisance.' The others looked away.

Charlotte had picked up her own cup of tea and gestured to the two men, 'Want some?' They shook their heads. They were standing in the scrub of the front yard, a small girl was holding out a dog-chewed yellow ball to Jan, which he took at last. It was dripping wet. The long-eared mutt was looking at Jan with a leer, drool hanging off its mouth, tail mustering a slight wag. Two boys appeared from behind the front door and came out to see what Jan was going to do with it.

'I think she wants you to play catch,' said Adam, trying not to laugh.

'Sure, sure,' said Jan, holding the ball by a thumb and a fingertip.

24

'We've got to stop meeting like this,' wheezed Bill Moloney, lowering himself into the Jacuzzi with winces and expletives, on account of the heat of the water.

She had expected him and she might also have expected him to say something like that. Annemieke took one damp magazine page away from the next and came to an image of a woman feigning sleep in a deck chair, dressed in a gabardine long-skirted coat and lace-up boots. It was time to start thinking about the autumn clothing season. This autumn she would do as they suggested, start with the essentials – of which there were many.

'Good magazine?'

She nodded.

'They found the old lady then?'

She nodded again and said nothing. Let him suffer.

'Goo-ood,' he said, stretching the word as he put his face back to take in the sun. He was wearing skiing glasses, with mirror lenses in a black rubber frame, taping his rugby-damaged ears to his head. 'Actually I did hear about it. That manager chappy told me this morning when I had my breakfast. Thank the Lord, eh?'

'Thank my husband and the young man. They were out all night. While the rest of the men in this place slept in their beds.'

'Did you not get much sleep yourself?' he asked, sitting forward.

She saw herself in miniature in the mirrors of his lenses.

'No,' she said, 'not really, no.'

'Well, I'm sorry to hear that. And with your husband being so ill like, it's no wonder you're upset. But I suppose he wanted to go.'

'Yes, of course.'

'I've been thinking about what you told me the other day and I wanted to say how sorry I am. I know you think I'm a big fat eejit . . .'

'What is that?'

'A fool, a moron, an imbecile . . .'

'Yes, yes, I understand, Your accent, it's hard to follow.'

'I'm from Ireland originally. The North. Lived a long time in South Africa though so it's a mess. It's all mongrel. What was I saying?'

'That you're a big fat imbecile.'

He laughed out loud, a great whoop of a laugh, and she smiled.

'Now will you stop that!' he remonstrated, 'I said no such thing. I said that you *think* that's what I am. Listen, I've got things I need to say to you. They're important. I have to say them.' He removed his glasses with an effort and where they had been the skin was white and covered in tiny bubbles of sweat. His eyes were pale blue, large and surrounded with tiny blond lashes that blinked impotently. He laid the sunglasses behind him and turned to her with both of his hands pressed together, the supplicant, his fingers touching his nose.

In the background, she saw that Beverly was leaning forward on her sun lounger.

'Listen to me,' he said, 'friend to friend. Brother to sister. I know how it is. I was you. I am you. When a person comes up against the brick wall of his or her self, the self they don't like and they can't change themselves or swap themselves for something better, what they do is they swap their partner. Not just once, but lots of times. That's what adultery is, it's a dead end. Now I know, because I did it. What I want to know is what you're going to do when he dies and you have to face the fact that it's not him, it's you, you don't like?'

Annemieke said nothing, but her chest rose and she sighed heavily as she tried to master her annoyance.

'Look, this amateur psychology . . .'

'Let me go on,' he said.

'How typical of a man to fail to see the obvious alternative! That it is possible that a woman has the same attitude to sex as a man.'

'Look, when it comes to fantasy action in the sack I'm hardly your prime candidate. Tell me, was it my love handles, my hairy back or my three chins you were attracted to?'

Annemieke looked at him steadily.

'I am not looking for help.'

'But you are. You are married and yet you had an intimate experience with a complete stranger. That's like shouting, "Here, over here!"'

'You are extremely old-fashioned, Mr Moloney. You are almost a romantic.'

'No, you're the romantic!' he said, raising his voice, then lowering it when she put an admonitory finger to her lips. Beverly was now sitting at the pool edge with her back to them, but in hearing distance.

'What I am,' he said in a hoarse whisper, going painstakingly slowly over his words, and now she remembered his accent from some film she had seen about terrorists, 'is a recovering alcoholic with his own set of rules for staying sober, who turned himself around because of his wife dying. That's realism. The romantic is the one who believes that another person can set them free. I don't because I know they can't. She couldn't do it for me. She knew it, I knew it. There's not one other human being on this earth that can save you. But that's what you think, that's why you do it.'

She shook her head.

'Otherwise, why not masturbate?'

'Don't get personal with me.'

'I apologize,' he said, sitting further back, his tone altered now, his voice level, 'but it's not your man's fault that he couldn't change your life, couldn't change you. You ought to know that. Given that he's dying. For his sake and for yours. You might want to forgive each other.'

'As you said, you're in no position to preach.'

'No,' he laughed roundly, 'I'm the opportunist, walking towards the noise of the party, caught in God's headlights. I'm just stuck really and that's the truth.'

She smiled weakly as she sat up to help herself to a sip of her lime and soda through a straw, 'You have a way with words.'

After a moment or two he picked up his glasses from the edge of the Jacuzzi, hauled himself out of the tub and launched into the swimming pool with a belly-flopping dive, soaking the newspapers of the American group and causing Harry to shout out, 'Easy!'

She watched him perform a series of lengths of the pool with determination and energy, taking great bestial breaths of water as he turned at each end.

25

Reluctant to expose Dorothy to the general public, George suggested he go to the bar to bring them back a pizza.

He'd left Dorothy up on the balcony all on her own, reading. A women's book. Historical romance, he thought it was termed, 'Fanny Fuss-a-lot' or what-have-you; all trumped-up emotion and unnecessary anxiety. Bored, he himself had picked up one or two of them, she'd given him the nod saying, 'It's historical,' but they had different ideas of what history was. 'See,' he'd said, 'with History, you've got this that happens, then that, important people, and someone makes a mistake and tries to cover it up, someone else gets the wrong end of the stick, and an incident happens, like a war. Then a country somewhere gets another new name, one of those that's had several already. That's History. Not some young girl getting herself up the duff by the young Master.'

Dorothy had argued with him that there was a kind of history – what she called 'social history', a new thing, all about normal people. 'Who cares about normal people?' he'd said, 'we got enough to worry about without worrying about normal people, some folks we don't know, people who don't matter.' She'd got the idea from the granddaughter. He'd tried to put her right but she'd got funny about it. She'd gone on about how *she* liked it anyway.

When she was quite sure that he was gone, she relaxed, put her book in her lap and closed her eyes. Inside her eyelids, she saw two pools of yellow like egg yolk.

'Do your worst, sun, there's bugger all left of me for you,'

Dorothy said. She pulled her skirt up over her knees, smiling right into the face of the sunshine.

The book was covered in plastic, it was on loan, it was hot in the sun. She smelt it and thought of the countless packed and picnic lunches she'd made for George and the kids and the grandchildren over the years, happy times. She liked the way cheese and tomato tasted after being wrapped together in clingfilm and left in the sun, it took her back, that taste, and as for the smell of a hard-boiled egg that was a day old or so, well it was heavenly! Just a whiff of that eggy smell and she could see George racing here and there with the girls – piggybacks, fishing, kite flying. He was good like that, a doer.

She'd have been better off with a thinker but there you go, you make your bed. When she said to her mum it was him she was going to marry the old girl had said, 'I'll tell you what my own mother said to me, "You make your bed and you have to lie on it."' It hadn't made any sense until it was too late. Nobody can tell you nothing when you're young. Nowadays, anyone could tell her anything and she could see they had a point. 'You get so much more open-minded as you get older,' she thought. Her own mind was as open as a sieve and sometime soon the holes were going to win out over the mesh. She couldn't hang on to a thought for long, even the bigger things were dropping through. Memories or statistics, dates and numbers, which were more important? That her mother hit her with the ladle when she burnt the breakfast porridge, or that they lived at number 42 Seaview Avenue, Bexhill-on-Sea, TN40 6BI? What about the phone number, was that more valuable than the memory of George's face, sitting at the back of the coach with the cow shit on the back of his trousers, after a day trip to the countryside, the day they had their first kiss? What did she need more?

Dorothy shrugged at the sun and pulled in the book, closer to her chest.

George had always been jealous in a funny pernickety way. Not a romantic way. He'd tried to stop her reading. He couldn't stand it. He nagged her, stood over her, couldn't let her be. He'd always have a reason why what she was doing was stupid. He reasoned her out of everything. She'd got so much hidden in that house of theirs even she couldn't find it. They'd think she was a senile old goat when they came to clear out after she died. Books, letters, chocolate bars, bits and pieces. She longed to be alone, to be private.

'I'm good and ready,' she said aloud.

The truth was he couldn't bear her being elsewhere, when she could be listening to him. Once he'd used to get narked if she went into town, or had her head in a book, and now neither of them knew where she went from time to time. Only Him upstairs knew where she was heading, bit by bit. Being shipped over in pieces.

She looked at her old Timex watch. Twelve-fifteen. He'd be back soon.

'Don't go out,' he'd said, and the sod had put her shoes up on the bathroom cabinet where she couldn't reach them.

26

Each day at the resort was fair, to the same specifications, part God-given, part man-managed. The sun shone, a breeze blew, the flowers bloomed, the pool was clean. Breakfast was laid out, beds changed, tiles mopped, cutlery cleaned, splats of dinner wiped from floors, splashes of sticky drinks rubbed off the bar, garbage to be emptied and removed and piled into the hidden stinking containers where the flies went mad in ecstasy, but these things happened before the main act or offstage. Some hundred men and women came together to make it all perfect for the forty or so people that inhabited this little paradise for a week, and they did so every week, even in the off season when there might be just half the number. Burns was required to provide the service required for physical stasis.

'The main thing about good service, is that it's so good you don't know it's happening. That's my theory,' Steve Burns had said to his staff at one of the first weekly team meetings. It wasn't his theory, in a proprietary sense, but it was an organizing notion that he adhered to with some conviction. He had his own individual interpretation. His overly thick-framed glasses spoke of that. Every time he put them on, he knew who he was. He looked like a 1960s scientist. It was quite a popular look with musicians, students, that sort of crowd.

The staff gave service that tended towards the morose.

'You can't teach it,' he thought to himself; that dry, witty, evasive manner of the restaurant and hotel world's staffing *crème de la crème*. It was a European thing. A throwback to

1930s Europe – arch eyebrows, a brittle laugh, the implication that superiority was not completely conferred by the arrangement of paid services.

He was watching Benjamin, one of his barmen, bending down to pass the Dutch lady a drink at the Jacuzzi. He looked miserable.

'Engage with them a little bit,' he said to Benjamin as the man walked back to the bar with his empty tray. He stepped inside the bar with him, 'Watch how I do it.'

The American crowd were already hanging about the bar, by eleven-thirty, looking for the 'lite' drinks they had on drip-feed throughout the day. Diet this and diet that. Had they any idea what the chemicals in that stuff were doing to their systems? They seemed anxious, and were jostling slightly, sharing what they knew of the story of the recovery of the old lady.

'You'd do better with a decent drink in you,' said Steve, grinning at the tall blond man who had remarked that he knew the chairman. 'Let me get you a beer or a nice glass of wine. On the house.'

'No, thanks,' said Jason abruptly, adjusting the waistband of his swimming shorts and folding his arms across his chest. 'Your problem's solved, then.'

'What's that? Diet Cokes, three. The old girl? The lost sheep? Yes, yes, on their way back with her now I expect.'

'Must be a relief.'

'Sure. Ice and a slice? All round?'

Jason nodded. 'Uh-huh, uh-huh,' he said as if counting, as if keeping his temper. 'Minimum effort, too. Didn't even lose a night's sleep.'

Steve looked awkward. Of course he slept, what was he supposed to do, pace up and down?

'There wasn't much else I could do, Sir, beyond what I did,' he smiled briefly.

'You know the Danish guy's a bit of a hero.'

'Who? Oh, yes. Dutch. And our employee, young Adam.'

'Did you know the man is seriously unwell?' Jason picked up one of the drinks and showed it to his wife who got up from her poolside lounge chair and came over. 'The Danish guy, I mean. He's sick. And he spent the night looking for one of your guests.'

'I didn't know that, Sir. No.'

'He's a hero.' Jason took a sip of his drink and squinted at Steve. 'Some folks go the extra yard.'

'Yes,' said Steve, helping himself to a glass of water.

'He deserves some sort of a thank you from your hotel.'

'It's sort of hard to believe that with everything that went on last night, you're just carrying on as normal round here. I think people feel, well, they want to see some sort of acknowledgment, you know,' his wife interjected, coolly.

'Well, I will personally make sure he and his wife get nothing but the best attention from our staff, you can be assured of that, Sir.'

'Like you assured me you were *personally* going to find the wife.' Missy squeezed Jason's arm and gave him what might have been either a reproachful look or a coquettish invitation to an afternoon in bed. It was hard to tell.

'I hear you, loud and clear.' This was what he'd been taught. Make sure they know you have heard them, then hopefully they'll fuck off.

'Did you know the old lady's got Alzheimer's ?' said Missy.

'Oh really?' said Steve, 'I didn't know that.' The stupid old git! To have brought his wife to their resort when he knew she was likely to do a runner at any moment! Why hadn't he been told?

'So you'll give them some sort of recognition then, a party or a gathering?' the wife went on.

'I was planning to have a party actually, after dinner tonight,' he said, as the American couple walked off, the man with a hand on his wife's bare arse. It was only when she turned around to walk off that it become apparent she was wearing nothing more than a thong.

Steve looked at Benjamin. Benjamin grinned, then apologized.

27

After lunch at the bar and an afternoon with his eyes closed, lying by the pool, the events of the night seemed unreal. Jan was uncomfortable but too weary to do anything about it. He had exhausted himself. His head stuck to the canvas cover of the lounger mattress. He moved it left and right feeling the sun strike him with great golden slaps whichever way he turned. He saw, again, George and Dorothy standing together on Charlotte's porch.

'I don't understand anything,' he said to himself, 'except that everyone seems closer to knowing anything than I am.' He sat forwards on his chair, dropping his feet into the flip-flop shoes that were either side of him. He watched the beads of sweat run across his chest and down the central canal, ending as a small pool in his belly button.

Opposite him, a Chinese woman was spreading a towel on to a vacant sun lounger. He had not seen her before. She was wearing a structured black swimming costume. Before she sat down she stood with a hair clip between her teeth, pulling her shoulder-length black hair back from her face to fix it in a ponytail. She bent forwards like an athlete, straight from the waist, and took a paperback from her rather ostentatious handbag; it had an unwieldy gold logo dangling from the zipper, large enough to cover half of the face of the bag and yet when it fell over, she looked down but did not move to stand it back up. Reclining, she raised one knee, and felt for her sunglasses, which were, like her bag, black and gold. Before she put them on, she noticed something and went to wipe them on the end of her towel and as she did so, she saw him looking at her and she gave him a broad smile, showing some teeth.

He went for a swim, principally so that he could look at her without being seen. His head dipped in and out of the water. With each glimpse, his feeling grew that there was something Hollywood about her. Her smile had made him think of the screen goddesses captured on the newsreels he'd seen as a child in the cinema at Brugge. They would raise a hand to the crowds from the steps of a steam train – polite, patient, sure of themselves.

Back on his lounger, he saw that Annemieke had left the Jacuzzi and gone off to their room for a late-afternoon siesta. She had complained all morning about her fatigue. She wanted to be fresh for supper. She didn't want to get too much sun. She was determined to look after herself this holiday, she said.

With his eyes closed, he was in a void. His senses were unoccupied but his mind wandered after them, as if manufacturing dreams, patching memories together. In them, he was a free man, no wife, no children, no history, just himself. He rounded a corner on a summer's evening in a big city, Brussels, Paris, London, even New York, and came upon himself and the Chinese woman together at an outside table, near to a noisy kitchen extractor unit on the wall outside. He felt weightless, he was all heightened perception. He could dance with his feet planted, choose to say anything, choose truth or choose concealment. Becoming strange to himself was pure joy; it was she who owned the new person. Her regard created him. If she liked what she saw then he would live. His heart lurched suddenly like a ship banging into a harbour wall. The two of them were squeezed between other couples, tables askew on cobbles. Elbows were pressing down to preserve some sort of balance between the faces that confronted each other. He saw people drinking things they didn't mean to (it was Saturday night), and saying things they couldn't afford (it was late). He wished he hadn't taken notice of them. It was their eyes now through which he saw himself, the middle-aged stoic with a stern face strung out on a new addiction, high on his self-created problem.

What is sweeter than a problem one makes because one's other problems are too familiar?

Looking again at the scene, he saw that his body was turning, and in his expression he saw the bleak moment in which one realizes one needs help, if only from a waiter. Something was missing, could it be that merely a drink would set things right? His hand twitched but he would not raise it. The waiter came and the evening began in earnest. The Chinese starlet was silent, as impenetrable as a poster. Her bag was new and expensive, so were her shoes and dress. Her worn-in lipstick was the only indication of there being a chance of a discount. And the compliment he'd chosen to pay her was priceless. It was one that you only gave to one or two people in your lifetime. No, he could never afford it! His Catholic upbringing would not let him ditch Annemieke, no matter what the circumstances. It was ridiculous to spend so much time on this woman, to talk with painful candour about love.

As soon as he'd done so, he'd regretted it.

She had faded, she was fictitious, she might as well not be there. She barely lived now. Her eyes were moving slowly across new territory, just gained, she was assessing it quietly. She did not smile.

He opened his eyes and saw the Chinese woman, who was lying flat on her back, with a book dangling from one hand.

Perhaps what he should have said to her was, 'I am alone. Forget everything else. I am coming to you for help.'

But he knew that one person's truth – even when they know it, even if it is with their last breath that they say it – is for another person nothing much more than an imposition.

28

Dorothy had sensed George's anxiety about their going to dinner that evening; even as he washed she knew he was giving himself a pep talk in the bathroom. He came out and gave a big resounding clap of his hands, it had made her jump. Being an old lady was not as hard as being an old man. She could be old but George must ever be the man. He didn't say a word all the way down to dinner, kept his teeth gritted. Like the good fellow he was, he pulled her hand on to his arm and placed his other hand over it.

'I shan't get into talking about it,' he'd said to her after lunch, 'people will want to know. Some were concerned, I expect. But some are just bloody nosy. So we shall just carry on as if nothing had happened.'

'Is that what you and I will do as well?' she'd asked him. He'd nodded, absorbed by his worries.

They'd taken a table and for some reason an American couple had joined them. They'd started off with some nonsense about her 'adventure' and being 'so happy at the way it had worked out' and progressed to the husband knowing the chairman of the group. After a few glasses they'd told them how poorly they thought the manager had handled it all. Jason dealt with what he perceived to be the most serious injury, George's ego, and Missy with Dorothy's feelings. With her jabbering on, Dorothy couldn't hear what the men were saying. She would have liked to know what it had been like without her, like witnessing your own funeral. She was rather thrilled to hear of her George organizing things, to think of him on his own, putting his best foot forward. That was what she wanted to hear, but the woman went on and on.

She was attractive, the woman. But Dorothy felt it was rude of her to be half-naked, with her breasts almost exposed, nipples quite visible through a pale white smock. What was it her London Jewish friends used to say? Chopped liver. That was how Dorothy felt and she resented it now even as she had when she was young and fresh-faced.

Other people had come up to them, with nice things to say, and she could cope with them but not with the American woman. She was ashamed of her animal hatred. The only difference between herself as a young woman and herself now was that she could see her own hatred plainly for what it was, she didn't have to invent other names for it or find faults with the woman that weren't there. Even so, she felt miserable.

Other Americans came up to talk to them, propelled by their good intentions. Talked about other English people they knew or a town in England they or their friends had visited, and all the time their eyes moved like servants' hands, moving over a mess and making it into something tidy; forming an opinion for later.

'I think that events like these, near-misses, are very fortunate. They help us to know what's important,' Missy said. 'We had a really difficult time with Jason's niece. She had started to take drugs, her parents felt so helpless, you know, but we managed to reach out to her at the right time and we got her back. The pain, the worry, I told Jason, it's for a reason, it makes you value what you have. The pain, the worry,' she took a sip from her wineglass and exhaled heavily to suggest she was familiar with both, 'awful things. But you have to deal with them. There are so many people in denial. Pitiful.'

What she said was reasonable, she said things that were measured and well-concluded, they were not ragged, nor did she allude to things that were beyond her scope. She settled where she was and deemed it the universe. You couldn't dislike her, or you oughtn't to, but she said things harshly and finally.

'My own father was an alcoholic who left us. He came back of course when I was first married to Jason, wanting to be friends. That was pretty pitiful.'

Dorothy had never heard the word 'pitiful' used the way the American woman used it. How awful, to reduce the charitable emotion of pity to the equivalent of disgust. It is not the British who have the stiff upper lips any more, she thought, looking at George's bristled profile in the elevator after they left the dance, it's the Americans. She found them proud and complete. Other people suffered openly; like fish held up in the air, lips with hooks in them, gasping.

'All right, love?' said George as the doors opened.

'Oh yes,' she said.

'Tired?'

'Yes.'

'Don't want to go down to the disco then? It's in your honour, you know.'

'Oh no,' she said seriously, 'it's not for me, it's for them. They're young.'

'Good supper,' he said, putting the card in the lock and waiting for the lights to change.

'Yes.' She slipped her feet out of the shoes and felt the cool marble tiles on her poor hot feet.

'Nice people,' he said, moving towards the balcony.

'Yes, very nice,' she said, and she saw his shoulders relax at last. He opened the double doors and breathed in the night air.

29

Downstairs, Steve Burns was busy. It had taken a considerable amount of work to get the music and lights set up in the second restaurant and ballroom. They hadn't been able to find the amplifier. It turned out that Abner had taken it home for the weekend. Burns was going round on foot, with his hand around his mouth, shouting in the ears of various guests, explaining that it was all in honour of the previous night's happy conclusion.

Faces to the dance floor, the Americans nodded as they heard him, one by one. Jason replied, with formal graciousness, that it was a 'good idea'. Steve was pleased. He had considered, at this high point of the evening, whether he oughtn't to lead the old girl herself out on to the dance floor, but it emerged that the pair of them had gone off to bed. Let's hope he keeps the chain on the door, thought Burns.

Jan grimaced when the manager slapped his back for the third time as he passed by their table at the door to the dance hall. Burns had said nothing but stopped once to give him an exaggerated thumbs up, or else he winked and mouthed 'Good man'. When Adam walked through the doors, Burns rushed to him and led him into the room by the elbow as though he was bringing in the comic turn. He stood him next to Jan and gave a short clap of his hands.

Jan put his hands around his mouth and leaned in to Annemieke, who bent her head to hear him, 'Is the man drunk?'

She turned to him and cupped his ear, 'I think he's trying to say well done.'

Jan frowned and indicated that he was going to get them both a drink.

Annemieke had been watching the young black lover and his elderly cargo, moving about the dance floor. With his careful hip movements and a firm grip on the woman's upper arms, the young man looked as if he was carrying a wardrobe over a rope bridge.

Although the music that Steve Burns had chosen, revived 1970s and 1980s hits largely British in origin, demanded solitary movement, the couples from Europe and America were determined to sway with each other, forcibly if they had to. Many of them resorted to swing-type movements, holding hands temporarily until one or the other deemed it time to break away and spin on his or her heels or shake and shudder at the hips, fingers clicking like castanets.

Still, their children were not there.

Harry and Maxine performed a tango and the Americans pointed them out to each other with fond smiles. Jason had his hand round his wife's middle, his fingers dipping underneath her waistband.

Bill Moloney was using one arm as a support for his mammoth figure, hand against wall. A woman was sheltered underneath.

Annemieke averted her eyes and finished the dregs of the drink she'd been meaning to leave.

She looked back at the old woman and the black man. She thought of them in bed together, the young man servicing the old creature. She herself was going to take hormone replacement therapy, as soon as she felt the first hot flushes of the menopause. She had said to her doctor, I will not be rewarded for my duties as woman by becoming a man. I will fight my nature if I have to.

'I suppose she says she likes the company,' she said to

Adam, in a half-shout, pointing out the old woman. Adam grinned.

Bill Moloney was offering his woman his hand, wiping his brow with a napkin. She couldn't wait to see him dancing! The woman was Asian, prettily turned out, petite, elegant even. She accepted graciously, as if being asked to dance by the Prince and not the frog. With her right hand in his left they moved comfortably to the music. They were fortunate that the song that was playing was slower than the previous ones.

Jan had been displaced in the queue for drinks a couple of times and when one of the Americans forcibly pointed out that he needed to be served, he declined with a shake of his head and stood waiting still. She wondered to what principle he was deferring. She was thirsty. She turned towards Adam. She pulled on his loose shirt and he lowered his head.

'I am abandoned,' she said, 'I want to dance.'

He obliged, raising his brow and putting his beer bottle aside. She walked out on to the dance floor, right into the middle and he stood opposite her, moving with ease, his shoulders and hips in time with the music, his eyes half-closed. She mirrored him for a short while, with a slightly faster pace and jogging style motions with her forearms.

She felt awkward. Where was Jan? Whenever she needed him he was elsewhere. He was moving back from the bar now, a drink in each hand, but had stopped halfway to talk. She could see the other person smiling politely as Jan questioned them with the slow and excessively considerate manner of elderly royalty.

When Moloney's back, sports-jacketed and vast, came into her view she reached out and put a hand on his arm. He turned his head round to see her and smiled. The Chinese-looking woman smiled also, as if she were about to make a new friend.

Annemieke leaned in to him, so that he could hear.

'I know why you said those things this afternoon.'

'Oh yes?'

'You want to get into my pants one more time,' she said.

'Is that so?'

'Yes.'

'Would it make you feel good if that was the truth?'

She shook her head knowingly, wagged a finger at him.

'You know him, do you?' said Adam, leaning in to her.

'He made a pass at me,' she said. 'Why is it that Americans can't dance?' Jason and Missy were standing opposite their friends, shuffling their feet, drinks in hand, conferring a little, with serious faces, as if they didn't really have time to dance. Catching her look, Jason lifted his head, and called out, 'Where's Jan?'

'Oh, saving someone,' she called back, laughing.

'Join us?'

'Certainly,' she nodded, heading towards them, leaving Adam where he was.

30

The next morning and for the next few days, the sun shone and the air conditioning system ran, and all was well. Yet everyone seemed to be suffering from impatience – the crisis had awakened their appetites for events and as successful, busy people, they were unable to quieten it now it had followed them here. Rest and recuperation would no longer suffice.

Annemieke attributed her dissatisfaction to drink. The morning after the party found her sweating out a hangover as privately as possible with a headscarf around her hair, a large bottle of mineral water at her side and a sarong creased and screwed up around her midriff, having tossed and turned on her sun-lounger for an hour. Jan was having a massage.

'Why do men get women and women get women? For massages. Why can't women get men?' she'd said, putting on her shoulder bag as she left breakfast.

'Have a nice morning,' he said, placing a single cigarette on his saucer, alongside his coffee cup.

They'd had a good evening at the bar the night before, everyone had wanted to speak to them. The little crisis had stirred a sense of camaraderie that she meant to enjoy while it lasted. Jan, who was usually so holier-than-thou when it came to such things, allowed her to have her sway, standing back, drinking and blinking like a child who'd just discovered fizzy soda. He was relaxing, she'd noticed. He'd had a good nap in the afternoon.

'You look happy to be alive,' she said to herself, looking at him.

There was a sudden weight on the end of her sun-bed and

sure that Jan could not be through with his massage, she assumed that Mr Moloney was paying her a visit.

It was Adam. He was eating a Mars bar, and seemed happy just to sit there, looking past her at the work that was being done on the new spa building. He nodded at it.

'Look at that.'

'Oh hello,' she said, pulling her sarong from under the damp weight of her rear. Was she mother or woman? She sat up.

'They're making a right mess of my tiles,' he said, and turning her head she saw a Caribbean man behind a wheel-barrow, pushing it over the entrance steps, through the double doors that were being held open.

'George's tiles, I mean,' he grinned, and took another bite of his Mars bar. She pulled the back of the sun-lounger up to match her seated position and watched him while he ate. Only young people know how to eat, she thought. People like her were never hungry, they never ate properly.

She saw a symphony of muscles, sinew and bone at work beneath his throat. Below the hollows of his cheeks and the cud-massaging stretches of his lips, with the chin firm, there were two great exclamation marks that stretched from nostril diagonally to either side of his mouth, a double expression of pleasure. His hair was pushed back behind his ears. Even his ears were at work, moving too. With a swallow, he was done. Alerted by a sudden crash and shout from the new building, he raised his head like a dog pricking up its ears.

'You should have something decent to eat,' she said to him.

'Does me,' he said with a young man's pride in imaginary virtues, 'don't need much. Mars bar, can of coke and me tabs. Cigarettes,' he said.

'It won't always be that way.'

'Well, I'm twenty-six,' he said, with a smile, 'going on thirteen. I hope.'

'I don't feel any different to the way I did at eighteen,' she said, stretching one leg.

He looked at her; smiled vaguely and looked across at the building again, wincing as another crashing noise was hailed by a round of blame.

'They're making a right mess of it,' he said.

Still lying, she pulled her feet up the lounger, raising her knees to give him room to sit. She picked up her book.

'Well, best not to look,' he said, 'Jan in bed?'

'No, he's getting a massage.'

'Lucky sod, not the old naughty is it?'

'I don't think he'd understand the offer. Jan's like a professor, or an academic. It's all happening up here,' she said tapping the side of her head with the book, 'not down there.'

Adam raised his eyebrows, 'Harsh words.'

She opened her book again.

'Leaves you in a bind. You're the one that needs the massage then.'

'That's right,' she said, looking at him over the top of her book.

He stood up and stretched and she saw that his stomach ducked beneath his shorts, leaving space at the front of the waistband, space for a modest hand.

'Oh go away,' she said.

31

That afternoon, the sun was hotter than ever and only the Americans remained by the pool. Jan and Annemieke had lunch with George and Dorothy inside, agreed to look at making a trip together, perhaps a boat ride, and then the four of them walked along the corridor that led to the main building. George held Jan back a little as they were leaving, to tell him that he was thinking he ought to call England and mention the incident to their daughters, but he was concerned he would be betraying Dorothy, selling her out. Jan assured him that he would be doing the right thing. Annemieke and Dorothy were at the turquoise and silver jewellery in a display window outside the dining room when the men rejoined them.

Back in their room, Jan took his book out on to the balcony and wound down the canvas rolling shade to cover the area, while Annemieke took her clothes off and lay on the cool sheets of the bed with the fan turning above her. She was bored.

She flicked through the TV channels with the sound muted. She parted her legs to allow the breeze to move between them. She came across two channels with Adult Viewing. She looked down at her nipples and her pudenda and spread her legs further.

Jan came into the room and she didn't cover herself up. He looked at her twice, went to the bathroom, and she heard him zip up and return, padding softly past her.

'Jan,' she said as he passed her by, 'Don't you want to have sex? It's been a while.'

'No.' He stopped and held on to the doorframe as though he might choose to stay and say something, then he turned again.

'Jan,' she said, 'is it the cancer?'

He came back inside and removed his reading glasses. His eyes were small.

'I don't think so.'

'Is it me?'

He rubbed his brow with the back of the hand that held the spectacles; light and wire-framed, they flailed, limbs akimbo.

'It is us.'

She closed her legs.

'Do I revolt you?'

'No,' he stopped, 'no, you are attractive, Annemieke,' he laughed. 'Is that what you want me to tell you? You want *me* to tell you this, now?'

'You weren't interested even before the cancer,' she said, looking straight at him, 'I sometimes think it happened even before we met. You should have been a cleric or a scholar.'

'Yes,' he agreed, 'I might have been happier. Maybe. Do we want to talk about this now?'

'Would you like to talk about it another time?'

'No.'

'So, let's talk about it now. Shall I tell you my theory?'

He looked at her body now and thought of the washcloths in their bathroom that crossed her nether regions and that she left for days. Washed and dried many times they had a low, rough pile, crisp after drying on the radiator, like poppadoms. He hated them, saw them as an indication that she was so active bodily that she must wash this way, in between showers. He had always hated them being around for the boys to see or even use by mistake.

'My theory,' she went on, 'is that you have a feminine attitude to sex and I have a masculine.'

'This is what you think.' He looked away, across the other balconies curving into his view, considered briefly that it was doubtful that George and Dorothy were discussing such things. He envied George the peace he felt he must have.

'Yes. Because for you there has to be trust, you need to feel safe to have sex.'

He rested his glasses on the side table by the door and stepped inside to sit in the armchair there, facing her still.

'Whereas you have a masculine attitude.'

'Yes,' she said, sitting up slightly, arching her back.

Her mother had been the same. Both of them had adored the chauvinistic, philandering grandfather, rumoured to have sired some ten children, of whom only four were legitimate. What instruction had her mother given her in being a woman? Annemieke's mother hated being a woman.

They were silent.

'You don't hold it against me?' She cocked her head.

'Do you need me to forgive you?'

She looked away for a moment and when she looked back at him her lip was trembling and her chin was momentarily flaccid.

'Perhaps,' she said. She reached her arms out to him and he went to her. He held her head against his chest, comforting her, saying, 'Come now, don't start, it is not all your fault, don't cry over it now.'

He held her face between his hands and looked at her squarely.

'We didn't know, we never did know – not in the beginning, nor in the middle, nor now – what to do about each other, but we have stayed together.'

She nodded. As he rose he caught sight of her Chinese shawl over the ottoman at the end of the bed and he took a deep breath.

'Haven't you ever wanted someone else during the last few years? I thought that was why you liked going on your own to those countries like Belize.'

'I did spend a night in a whorehouse once. In Belize City actually. You're going to laugh. It was quite by accident and it was horrible. Remember my trip to Central America? I passed through Belize on my way to Guatemala. Belize City is absolutely amoral. It is how I imagine hell to be. At night-time, the darkness is darker than anywhere else in the world. You would swear there were no stars; there is no moon, no street lamps either. The people fall upon you, for your money.'

He took a bottle of beer from the fridge and showed it to her, she declined, so he opened it for himself.

'When I came by bus from Mexico into Belize City at midnight I was mobbed. I managed to duck into a taxicab and two other tourists followed me. We told the driver the name of a guesthouse from the guidebook. He laughed, telling us it was impossible, but started to drive anyway. He asked us for money and I told him there would be no money until we got to the hotel. The other two with me were young, students, a couple. The driver went up and down streets, as though marking time. Outside there were small groups of men, waiting. Eventually he stopped, in the middle of a street, not even close to the kerb. I looked out of the window. It was obvious that he had brought us to a brothel. Two girls sat long-faced on the veranda of the white colonial house and seeing our car arrive, they went inside and returned with the Madam.

' "Here," said the driver, stopping his car and turning off his lights. He asked us for a sum of money. I refused. The driver simply waited, as dark as the dark. I couldn't see even the glimmer of his eyes. And then the doors to our car were opened by a group of men and a sliver of light entered the car – a knife blade. I tried to stand up. A hand from outside came through we gave them our money, we were left to walk. Along we went, each with a backpack, trying to attempt some sort of good humour. We were in this together. There had been nothing heroic in their attempt to rob us and nothing heroic in our handing over our money. It was as mundane as shopping. I remember the disappointment as we sat to drink a beer in a Korean bar. We tried to find common ground and failed. But you see you can't apply good nature or reason to a desperate place. When everything is bad, how can anything be good? Especially in the night time.

'We asked the owner where we could stay and he pointed upstairs. He had rooms. We should pay first. I had some traveller's cheques, and I asked that they let me pay for the rooms. They thanked me fairly coolly actually, as though this were some sort of recompense for my being older than them. I can tell you, I felt pretty envious of them as I stepped past their door down the hallway to my own room. They were safe, being together. In my room, alone, there was no working light; there was no lock. Tied dogs howled and barked through the night and I sat vigilant, fully clothed, with my neck on the side of my backpack.

'From the opposite room came the animal noises of pain. A woman moaned and screamed and whined and begged and behind her noises was the regular thud of the machine of a big man. Some women like to make a fuss, I thought to myself. Some women like to be hurt. Some men too. But I think that such an arrangement was unlikely in a brothel in Belize. I didn't know what to do. I sat for a while. And then I walked across the hallway and knocked on the door. The machine ceased. A woman's voice answered.

'"Is everything all right?" I asked. "Go away," came her answer. So I returned to the room to sit on the bed and I listened until the sounds ceased. I felt a fool. A damn fool. I was a fool. I've never been so foolish. Maybe that's how you see me.

'When the sun came up I got up to leave. I went to the bathroom to pee and saw blood on the floor. I could piss anywhere in this country, I could piss in the street, I could piss on the bar floor, I could piss in a bank. I would not piss into someone's blood. Then I heard panicking voices at the door down the hall, the Korean owner angry and afraid, the sound of another man, then heavy footsteps running and the Korean calling out for his wife. In the city I went to the bank, got some money, took a boat out to the Cayes and told myself that the previous night was done with, I let it be obliterated by the sunshine of the islands.

'But I was wrong. It stayed with me. I'd had a brush with evil, alone in that room hearing two people mesh pain with pleasure to make something false. I understand that sex can be bought or sold. But something base about the noise in the dark threw me – for good. That was, what, four years ago, that trip? It was about then that I gave myself over to bad luck, to cancer. I'm still sitting in that room, Annemieke. Still sitting there like an idiot.'

'Do you think he killed her?'

'I don't know. It was like I was without a moral compass there. Or maybe, I was afraid. '

They hadn't spoken like this to each other for many years, the two of them. She looked at her husband. He sat up at the end of the bed with his creased forehead and bagged eyes, his long nose pointing down to the hands that were at rest together between his legs.

'Why didn't you tell me about this before?'

His face flickered for a moment, then fell.

'Part of giving up.'

The fan was turning, turning, turning above them and she thought suddenly of the blades on the front of the aeroplane. As they stepped down on to the Caribbean tarmac and walked end of the bed with his creased forehead and bagged eyes, his long nose pointing down to the hands that were at rest together between his legs.

'Why didn't you tell me about this before?'

His face flickered for a moment, then fell.

'Part of giving up, I suppose.'

The fan was turning, turning, turning above them and she thought suddenly of the blades on the front of the aeroplane. As they stepped down on to the Caribbean tarmac and walked towards the airport building, she'd looked back to see the plane bereft, the noise of its engines fading, the rotors slowing tragically, slicing nothing, mired in the butter heat, coming to a standstill.

'Has it put you off sex?'

He laughed. 'No. I don't think so.'

'But it's put you off me.'

'No.'

'You want a safe place.'

'Yes.'

'Do you remember what I said to you on our first holiday together, when we were in the sea, trying to make love in the sea?'

'Yes,' he said, 'we have talked too much.'

In the Mediterranean, with the exaltation of a young woman whose lover fitted hers exactly, she had reared up in his arms as he lifted her on to him and said, 'I will destroy you.' Later, back in the hotel room, she had said that she didn't know why she had said that. He had replied that she was merely showing off.

32

At dinner that night, Bill Moloney was seated with the Chinese lady. Jan, Annemieke, George and Dorothy were all together again, with the men reasonably animated, teasing each other and drinking good wine, and the women otherwise occupied.

The dining room filled early that night. Bill came over to their table and with a hand on each of the men's chairs asked them if they'd like to join him on a jaunt the next day.

'We need a change of scene,' he said. He wanted to drive up to the north of the island, take a look about, see if there was much to be seen. He'd get a picnic packed for the beach. He had room in the car.

'For all of us?' Annemieke asked with raised eyebrows, taking her wineglass towards her mouth. She looked across at the Chinese lady, 'all of us and your lady friend?'

'Laurie? She's not coming. She's here to unwind. She's got a big Public Relations company in Hong Kong, needs to relax.'

Dorothy looked across at the woman called Laurie, who had laid her cutlery either side of the plate and was smiling across at them, brightly. She gave a small wave and Dorothy returned it.

'Is she married?' she asked.

'Divorced.'

'Oh.' Dorothy waved again, 'that's nice.' She saw how beautifully the woman's grey chiffon dress was made, Empire line, and looking below the table she saw matching shoes, 'very nice.'

Jan swallowed and wiped his mouth. He gave the woman a stern smile.

'So are we on?' Bill asked.

George nodded. 'Sounds all right. Plenty of food?'

'Chicken, rolls and sandwiches, salads, a quiche or two and a big Victoria sponge cake, would you believe. One or two tinnies – och, maybe there are twenty-four, I can't recall,' he added, looking at Annemieke with a smile.

'Well I'm no Hong Kong big shot, but I've come here to relax too. So I'll let you three go ahead without me,' she said.

'The chicken,' said George, 'tell them to cook it right, lad. So there's no blood in the meat. I can't take it pink or raw-looking. Turns my guts.'

Bill laughed, 'Fair enough.'

'Fancy having quiche and sponge cake,' said Dorothy raising her eyebrows and stretching her neck. 'Seems a bit queer in the heat.'

'We can pick up some ice cream somewhere.'

'Oh, I had a lovely ice pop the other day when I was out,' she said, 'they're so clever with their ideas for them these days.' Noticing that everyone was quiet or looking elsewhere she paused before saying, 'When I had my funny turn.' George put his hand on hers and gripped it roughly. 'I'm just getting on a bit,' she said, looking at Annemieke, 'the mind gets slack too, you know. First the body, then the mind.'

Annemieke saw that a sliver of prawn skin remained on the old lady's bottom lip, like the empty pocket of a blister.

'Well, you'll have three fine men to treat you like a queen tomorrow,' she said, patting Dorothy's hand.

'You will,' said Jan, and Bill nodded.

George blinked and Jan saw that he put his great plate of a hand on his wife's shoulder and squeezed it briefly, as if it were an unfamiliar action.

With it agreed that they should meet in reception at nine,

Annemieke watched as Bill went back to his table and was all eager attention to the Chinese woman.

'He's a Christian, you know,' said Annemieke with a small smile, 'born again.'

George looked over at Bill. 'No. Not like that American Bible-bashing stuff?'

Annemieke nodded. 'I don't care what people follow but when they start preaching it, then I can't listen.'

'Did he preach to you?' asked Jan.

'Tried to convert me in the hot tub the other day. You'll get it tomorrow, I expect.'

'Oh, I hope not,' said Dorothy, 'it makes me uncomfortable talking about religion. It's not something you should talk about. Like talking about medals. It never seems very modest. There's the ones that do the jawing and the others who do the work.'

'You're right,' said Annemieke, 'you're so right, Dorothy.'

The three of them looked over at Bill again and were quiet.

On their way out, Jason and Missy came over to the table, arm in arm; they were off to the bar and wanted to see if they could offer anyone an after-dinner drink. The English couple declined, and the Belgians accepted. George looked after them as a dog looks at a man with a stick.

'You go and have one,' said Dorothy.

'No.'

'Yes, you have one. I'll be fine.'

'I'll walk you back first, then perhaps I will,' he said, chewing on the one side of his mouth, his eyes glazing over. He no longer heard what the others said, made no replies to their questions, and came back to the conversation only after the dishes were cleared.

33

Steve Burns was busy in reception on Saturday morning with his trousers far too tight. He'd put on weight and his chinos were tight not just around the waist, as it goes with men, but also in the seat. He was reminded of one of his school teachers, who'd contributed to his very acute sense of what was not cool, a man who'd worn too tight maroon Farrah trousers, his arse sashaying rudely between the rows of pupils, his voice drawling sarcasm.

Burns felt like a fruit, handing out leaflets, drawing pencilled circles on maps, reminding the punters of the Saturday night event as they left the hotel. He'd spotted two women of a more mature persuasion, 'Silvers' as they called them in the business, passing comment on him from their huddled position in two cane armchairs, looking at him over their fishing expedition leaflets. He'd asked if he could help them and heard snorts of laughter as he'd walked away. He'd fucking sashayed, he was sure of it, it was the trousers, and then he'd turned round like some Butlin's poof and told them off with a very camp, 'Now, now, ladies, none of that.' It was a loathsome business, at times.

The Yank had been in to discuss with him docking arrangements for his friend's yacht. He was grave and so Burns was grave in response. This was a hundred-footer they were discussing, not a fishing boat. Burns reminded Mr Ryder, Jason, of what he'd advised him the day before – it would be fine. Mr Ryder had nodded patiently, not listening at all.

'I just don't want any problems,' he'd said.

His friend, not Mr Cohen but a mutual friend of theirs, a serious venture capitalist, was going to dock about eleven. He was going to take a few of the guests there out for the day. Mrs De Groot was going, Annemieke.

Burns couldn't believe that Jason would fancy the Dutch woman given he had a highly amenable piece of ass, as the Americans called it, at his obvious disposal, but he was used to all sorts of arrangements taking place on these holidays. He ought to write a book. He'd seen it all, he said to himself, thinking about the old girl and the young black man.

Ryder was all starched up for the day, khaki-shorted legs, a linen shirt brusque about its Polo emblem, his hair a sticky dirty blond, gelled against the elements.

'Should be a good day for some fishing, what can we expect? Marlin?'

'I've no idea, Sir,' he said.

'No idea? How can that be?'

'You fucking prick,' thought Burns, 'you fucking pompous boring fucking nobody, I ought to tell you to shove all hundred foot of that boat up your big American arse.'

'Bluefish, kingfish, I guess. What the locals call dolphin fish, a frying fish.'

The American shook his head, his nostrils dilated, 'I think we'll be throwing those back. Have some things put together for the lunch. My friend has a staff, they'll cater, but I don't like to show up empty-handed. Some shellfish, some chicken, some salads, nothing too crazy. I guess you can do that? Hello, sweets.'

Burns nodded. The wife had arrived, in matching kit, except her shirt was sleeveless and only half-buttoned and she had a polka-dot navy bikini top underneath it. Ryder pulled one strap.

'Just testing,' he said.

'Honey,' she reprimanded him, 'you'll get the knot too tight to undo.'

Burns looked aside, rolling his closed lips together to stop himself from saying anything. When they were close to the door, he allowed himself to call out, 'Don't forget the disco-beach party tonight, Sir, eight o'clock,' and he added, like the sad bastard he surely was, 'clothing optional!' He groaned and kicked the swing doors of the kitchen as he went through and left a shoe polish stain there. If he didn't wipe it off, no one else would.

'Where are those lunches for the Moloney party?'

'Nearly done,' said Brian, the Rastafarian who was cooking that morning. The man's dreadlocks were tied together up above his head. He looked like a leek. He was leaning over a counter top reading the paper's headlines. It was always a football or a cricket headline. This particular issue was devoted, cover-to-cover, to the fact that the English cricket team had been caught smoking dope. 'Shit, man! I never knew your people was into the stuff,' he said, prodding the paper. 'But Adam, he likes a puff. He come hit me up every other day, he likes to take it easy.'

'Just as long as he, you, whoever, doesn't smoke it here, on the premises, I don't give a monkey's, mate. Now what have we got to get rid of? We need to put some stuff together for a group of Yanks. What's going to go off?'

'Got some chicken is high.'

'How high?'

'Not as high as your cricket team.'

'All right, sort that out and some seafood. Lots of it. The rough stuff. And the leftover salads, chuck loads of mayo in, and any old crappy bits hanging about. Let's give our friend Salmonella a run for his money on this one, mate. Make it look good. You know they'll waste most of it anyway.'

'Sure, when we gots Americans staying I know it, them bins is filled from their plates.' The chef shook his head. 'Make me mother cry real tears to see it.' He put an arm on Steve's shoulder. 'Don't you worry, man, I'll see to it.'

'By eleven, if you can, mate,' said Steve, softly, 'and have a beer on me.'

'T'anks, man.'

Well, he said to himself as he went back into the reception area, there was one thing, at least. He, Steve Burns, was not a complete and utter cunt.

34

Dorothy and George had breakfasted as soon as the dining room opened, at seven, dawdled down at the beach for half an hour, then killed time by walking the perimeter of the hotel's buildings. They exclaimed over the garbage skips, watched a cat make its way along the top of a wall, waved to the security cameras and then returned to reception to find they had an hour to wait. They'd gone back to their room so that George could use the toilet again and Dorothy had leafed through the hotel details and checked their homeward bound tickets. Happily, their increasing desire to examine the details of their life coincided with having the time to do it. They had started out liking the big things, schemes and plans, talking in spans of years, and they had ended up content to pore over the minutiae of day-to-day retirement.

Jan came through reception at nine, on his way to breakfast with Annemieke, having taken an early-morning dip in the sea. The elderly couple stood up, then sat down as Jan looked at his watch, patted his stomach and made his excuses.

'I don't often feel hungry, so I'm going to take advantage of it. Maybe an egg,' he said.

They went back to the leaflets they were reading.

'I say,' said Dorothy, 'it's that Chinese lady.'

George looked up, over the rim of his glasses. She was standing by the reception desk, looking through the few papers there, which George knew to be notes on the protection of valuables and warnings about the sea.

'She's dressed up nice,' he said.

Dorothy looked at her husband and then at the woman. She was wearing a skirt and top, with finely beaded straps, and open-toed mules; all coordinated in pale mauve. Her thick dark hair was tied behind her head and she had large-rimmed ornate sunglasses on her little head. When she turned round she waved and came towards them. George laid his brochures on the side table and took off his glasses. He stood up.

'Morning.'

'I'm coming along too,' she smiled, 'Bill talked me into it. I hope you don't mind. Hope it won't make it too uncomfortable.'

'I shouldn't think you'll take up much room,' said Dorothy with a bucket of a grin and a laugh.

'Jolly good,' added George.

'Do you think I need a bathing costume?' she asked, addressing Dorothy.

'I've no idea. Should hope not. I haven't got one myself.'

The woman nodded gravely and they fell silent.

'Hot,' said George eventually, 'hot, today.' The women seized upon this observation and agreed with it.

When Bill Moloney arrived, he was greeted with the familiarity a man of his proportions and generosity accrues so quickly, particularly when he has turned acquaintances into his guests. He was slapped on the back by George, upbraided by Dorothy for being late, then, on saying that he was early, was upbraided for being too early. Laurie smiled at him all the while, holding the handle of her small bag with two hands.

Jan and Annemieke walked in shortly after Bill had shown the others the route he proposed on his driving map. Dorothy recalled what Annemieke had told them about

Bill's religion and was relieved to see that he had brought just the map and his keys; there was no ominous briefcase. It was hard to imagine he was a man of God; he was such a character, larger than life. If Jesus was around these days, we'd never notice him, she'd told George more than once, there was too much else to look at. He might have stood by her at the bus stop and she'd have been distracted by the ad there.

'I'm not coming,' Annemieke said quickly, waving a hand at them, 'just dropping off my husband.'

Jan kissed her on the cheek, 'She's been invited out with the Americans, on their friend's boat.'

'Ooh, wear a life jacket,' said Dorothy quickly, as if she'd just remembered it.

Annemieke gave a half-smile and left them. She was going back to the room to put on her Caroline Herrera shift dress.

'I hope you don't mind if I come along,' said Laurie, once more, looking serious.

Jan looked at her directly, then looked down at the floor, removing his spectacles, and shaking his head.

'No,' he said, shortly, his mouth taut, 'no.'

Dorothy saw Laurie's expression falter as if she thought she might have made a mistake. Laurie looked over to Bill, who was at the reception desk, smoothing the map out before the girl there to double-check a direction. He turned about and gave her a small wave.

'Be right with youse' he said, then he gestured at the basket on the floor by the side of reception. 'That's the lunch,' he grinned, blowing air into his cheeks.

His guests shared exclamations of surprise and pleasure.

'Too hot to eat,' said George, who found himself salivating at the idea of the wrapped barbecued chicken legs.

'You'll manage,' said Dorothy. The others laughed.

George had already proved something of a prodigy at the buffet. ('I don't waste it, I eat what I take,' he'd said in his defence.)

Jan stepped away from the group, his glasses back on his nose, interested in the brochures that they had all read before.

35

They were all glad to get out of the car after an hour's drive, each adding his or her own reason, building a polite consensus of pleasure.

Bill had procured a Bob Marley greatest hits tape for the ride. The rental car bumped along tarmac road and dirt track, reared up behind the yellow or blue buses and slowed down in harmony with Bill's remarks. From a confident sixty miles per hour they could be at a snail's pace within seconds if something crossed his mind, with Bill pointing something out to them, shouting so that he could be heard.

To lean forward would have meant rubbing legs with Laurie who sat in the middle between himself and Dorothy, so Jan merely inclined his head towards the centre so that Bill could see he had his attention. Bill had his sunglasses off and on, jabbing a pork sausage finger at the map that George held like a copilot, and flailing around at the controls when he laughed, causing George to call out, 'Watch it!' and put both hands on the dashboard.

The comedy of the driving, the impeccable sunshine and the appeal of the music with its simple pleas, stirred Jan. He had an overwhelming sense that this entire scene had been directed for his benefit; action, music and message. He wondered whether it was because Annemieke was not there, and he wondered also, slightly ashamedly, whether it was because the Chinese woman was there, next to him.

Bill pulled the car up alongside a lay-by and told them they'd struck lucky. This beach was without any doubt the best kept little secret in the world.

'We'll have ourselves a wee luncheon here, so we will,' he said, hamming up the Irishness and walking around the car with a comic gait, each knee lifted high and to the side.

The women started to murmur together about bathing suits, and Bill hushed them from the boot of the car.

'Now will you stop your blathering on about that little formality, the good Lord gave us what we need to swim with, and for those who feel he didn't give them enough or he gave them too much, there's my own home-grown remedy.'

'I'm not wearing a pair of your underpants,' said Dorothy.

The others laughed. Realizing then that she had made a joke, she went on hurriedly as though she had a lozenge in her mouth that she would never taste again, 'Well, I'm not, even if they are clean.'

'No chance of any of our underpants being clean after that drive,' said George. Jan recalled his grandfather saying that the English liked to joke about underpants. He'd not believed him. He smiled now at Laurie, thinking of his grandfather, at the kitchen table, shaking his head, tears of laughter in his eyes, telling one of the jokes he had to tell about the First World War. A man who'd emerged with his humour intact, who had only good things to say about his fellows. Jan had thought once that it was his experience that had taught him such endurance and dignity, but now he knew it had been a choice. The hull of his character had been hewn from strong materials, and steered with a knowing eye.

'So what's the remedy, Bill?' he asked.

'About five bottles of wine and two cases of beer.'

'It'll need more than that to get me in the nude,' said Dorothy.

'It didn't use to take more than a half of shandy,' said George.

'Who's going to drive back?' asked Laurie.

They looked at each other.

'Now, by my reckoning,' said Bill, squinting up at the sky, 'seeing's how the sun is overhead and the temperature is up in the nineties and I'm sweating like a bastard, I'll be passing the beer through my system at a rate of one point seven five pints an hour. That allows me three bottles an hour, say six in total before we go on.'

'It can only be an improvement,' George said in a stage whisper to the others as they followed their host down on to the beach.

'Perhaps we ought to ask him to drink nine,' said Jan and was surprised when the others laughed loudly. He adjusted his earnest expression.

When they had made a mess of the several drumsticks of chicken, forked through the white wet salads, used each other's napkins and plastic beer mugs indiscriminately, they lay on blankets and towels underneath a tree and started to talk about paradise.

'It's England for me; in the summer you can't beat it. Fresh and lovely,' George said.

'I like to have a breeze,' said Laurie, 'that is paradise for me. It's something we have to make for ourselves in Hong Kong, it's one of the reasons I like to travel.'

'Now, myself, it's good company that makes a paradise. Good chat,' said Bill.

'Didn't Sartre describe that as hell?' said Jan, and blushed as soon as he'd said it.

'Cynical bugger,' said George, shifting one leg with a moan.

'Your man didn't drink enough,' said Bill, 'for sure. I say that with conviction, given that I know absolutely nothing about the poor fellow.'

'Paradise for me is being with family,' said Dorothy, 'nothing's quite right without them.' She was happy fleetingly, as she sat up and looked across the Atlantic Ocean, but her smile went as she said, 'it wouldn't matter where I was or what I had, if I couldn't see them. I think this holiday is very nice, I can see why people take to them, and we've met such lovely people,' she paused, blowing out, her face red from the heat, 'lovely, but I miss my family, and we've been blessed that they seem to feel the same way about us, haven't we, George?'

He nodded and turned his mug upside down. 'Dry,' he said, 'dry.'

Bill leapt to his task and took the top off a fresh bottle. He held out a beer to Jan, and said, with his head moving from side to side, 'Paradise. What is paradise? Somewhere to make us feel good or to make us better people?'

There was an uncomfortable silence and Bill nudged his arm with the beer, saying, 'Here you go, man, while you're thinking it through.'

With three bottles of wine upended and a stack of empty beer bottles, the group lay back and George was nearly asleep when Bill stood up unevenly, shaking sand about him, and rubbing his hands together proclaimed his intention to try the waters. Walking down to the seashore, he removed an article of clothing every few paces until all four of the others sat upright, one after the other,

'He's not . . .'

'He is . . .'

He wriggled out of his Y-fronts and tossed them high in the air behind him before taking to the water with a fine belly flop.

When he came up for air, further out, they applauded him. He raised his hands to acknowledge them and shouted like a boy, 'Whooh-hooh! Bloody fantastic!'

With a grin splitting his face, George stood up and unbuttoned his shirt.

'Not in front of us,' said Dorothy, 'do it like he did, down by the water. Spare us the details.'

George hopped off, grimacing at the heat of the sand on his bare feet, moving like a man half his age until with painful side-to-side movements he managed to get both his shorts and his underpants down to his ankles. His white arse with its red cleft was like the St George cross waving at them and they fell about laughing, hands over their mouths, hands over their eyes, and Bill all the while protesting.

'Not you, mate, the ladies!' And then, 'If you lot think the view back there is bad . . .'

George looked backwards to shout out, 'Bombs away!' and careened into the water, his great legs making much of the waves, kicking up the white of it, crashing through the waves, breaking the barriers between him and Bill. Soon the two of them were bobbing in the water, like brothers, ear-to-ear grins, attempting to salute each other with their toes.

'How is it that the sea can do this to grown men?' said Laurie.

She saw that Dorothy was wiping her face with a napkin.

'Bloody fool of a man,' she was saying, her mouth trembling.

'Shall we join them?' said Laurie, 'I've never skinny-dipped.'

'No?' said Jan, struggling to remember an occasion on which he had.

'I'm not much of a swimmer.'

'Well, I can't swim and I'm a terrible sight,' said Dorothy, 'but if everyone will look the other way while I get in, I'll bloody well do it.'

So Jan went down to the shoreline and organized the men to look away, George protesting he had rights, and they all looked out to sea or up to the road, counting up to twenty, loudly, giving Dorothy time to take to the sea.

'All done!' she said, breathlessly, her head and shoulders wobbling above the water as she tried to steady herself on the shingle.

'Good job, duck,' said George, making his way over to her.

With the majority regarding them from the sea, Jan and Laurie looked at each other.

'I don't think we have a choice,' said Laurie.

'No.' Jan stood up and walked, fully clothed, to the seashore. To the slow hand-clapping of the others he removed his clothes and laid them neatly on the beach until he was wearing merely a pair of boxer shorts. He started to walk into the water. The others began to protest, so he returned and quickly took the shorts off, holding them in front of his genitals until he was submerged, then jettisoning them. Watching his Ralph Lauren polka-dot undershorts travel through the sky and land raggle-taggle on some driftwood, he felt a rush of joy.

'Fuck! This is good,' he said, feeling the water around his penis, and between his cheeks. Tickled, he laughed out loud.

Then Laurie came down the beach with her dress in front of her, her glasses still high on her head, her hair back and her expression stealthy. She dropped the dress and crouched down to take to the water modestly, splashing herself as she went as if to accustom herself to it.

'I've never done this before,' she said as soon as she was in. She bounced up and down on her feet, her hair jumping behind her, her hands dipping in and out of the water sprinkling it like fairy dust at her sides, her mouth open all the while.

Jan stood still, looking at the four of them, to take a

photograph of what he saw with his eyes. Strangers, more or less.

'This is crazy,' said Laurie, splashing him suddenly, 'crazy. I feel so lucky! Don't you feel lucky?'

36

There was no reason why she should not have a new life, why she should not have all the things she could appreciate. There were wealthy men who had ugly wives. An American man would suit her. It would be a fresh start.

She sat at the side of the yacht; chin out to the horizon, feeling the tensile strength in her collarbones and her nipples hard against the flimsy dress. She could reinvent herself. Her boys would fit into the scheme, whatever it was.

The owner of the yacht, Jason's friend, was a hardened man, firmly into his middle age, firm with his opinions. He insisted on this, insisted on that, and as he was the host, the others garrulously concurred with whatever he expressed.

The captain took them out to a place to fish and the men gathered around the toys at the rear at the boat, each pressing the other to take part, keen to see fun happen. She was not used to being relegated to a women's section and was angry that parts of this day were for men only. She was not offered beer after beer as the men were but allowed to help herself from the crate of cold sodas.

The women bored her, discussing some of the more shocking crimes of the times. At lunch they ate the fish the men had caught and the women praised the men. Missy proclaimed Jason's the biggest and they all fell about, taking it in turns to ensure the innuendo had not gone unremarked. Annemieke felt excluded. She sat silent until the owner himself, between mouthfuls, asked her about herself. She intended to set out towards the terrain of her impending widowhood but she prevaricated, with sophisticate modesty, describing herself as nothing more than a bourgeois, but was shanghaied by Missy.

'Not at all! Annemieke is married to a hero. Her husband went out for an entire night to find an old lady, who went missing from the resort.'

With polite interest, secondary to his rapport with luncheon, the owner raised his bushy eyebrows to look in turn at Missy and Annemieke, sucking his fingertips.

'Of course, it turns out the lady has Alzheimer's,' said Jason with head-shaking disbelief. 'Her husband ought to have thought things through before they came away.'

'Can you imagine,' said Missy, her right hand raised, 'the old woman walking, all alone, in the heat, a stranger, going nowhere. It's sad,' she said, looking at her husband with sudden intensity, 'isn't it?'

He squinted at her but apparently saw nothing in it, for he looked distant and shook his head lightly.

'We saw an old man walking along just off the freeway outside of Charlotte once,' Beverly began, 'with a suitcase. We slowed down, Joe and I; I mean nobody walks on the freeway, do they? It was so weird. And with a suitcase. When we asked him what he was doing –'

Her husband cut in, 'He said, "Going home" so we asked him where it was and he wouldn't say a thing, just kept walking.'

'Well,' Beverley went on, opening her mouth and letting it sag, 'we just couldn't drive off, I said to Joe, what if he's just got out of a prison. If we'd seen something on TV or in the papers, afterwards, and seen his face we'd never have forgiven our-selves? You think of Jon-Benet Ramsay, that sort of thing, child abuse, pornography, the Internet . . .'

'No,' said Joe, 'we had to do something. So we called the police and we just kind of trailed him in the Jeep for a ways, until they showed. He kicked up a bit of a fuss, the old-timer, tried to fight them off.'

'You should have seen him, he was all rough shaven and his clothes were awful. Poor man, I mean he was probably just really old. Don't I always say, shoot me if I get like that . . .'

'And I always say, I'm not going to jail for you, darling,' he put his hand on hers.

The other laughed, circulating the coleslaw and potatoes that the Captain had prepared.

'The mentally ill are a real danger . . .' started the owner, 'I'm on the board, don't ask me how, of this institution in Maine, and you wouldn't believe what the folks there have to put up with. The truth is there just aren't enough places to lock these people up. The prisons take some, but the prisons are fit to bursting with drug users. How do we find enough places to stow all the people we cannot reasonably include in our society? This is the conundrum. Our European friends haven't solved it, so it's down to us. It's a big question and something that costs us a great deal of money.' He swung his head from side to side, a dead weight.

'That old fellow, going nowhere, I can't get it out of my head,' said Missy, 'looking for his home . . . it's symbolic,' she said, struggling now. Jason beckoned to the Captain and he refilled all of their glasses, starting with Missy's since Jason indicated he should.

'Maybe he wanted to die there,' said Beverly.

'Maybe,' said Annemieke, taking her chance to speak, 'an animal instinct. Some run away from it, of course. Like Jan.' She looked away, out to sea. There was a small silence.

'Annemieke's husband is, very, very ill,' said Missy.

'I'm sorry,' said the owner, grasping a piece of French bread and tearing it between his teeth. Annemieke looked at him. His skin was tanned, his hair short and well managed, his frame, naked from the waist up, was like a handsome property, but his eyes were dull. She looked down at the corpse of the fish on the table.

She got up to tidy the plates away and was held away by the Captain, who came leaping up from the rear of the boat.

'My job,' he said and so she sat back down, alone with her thoughts; as the others drifted away to their various discussions, Annemieke drifted to memories of her boys as children.

She could recall reading stories to them, a boy either side, soft nubuck-like skin on hers, their lips against her cheek, either side, as she read, the mother's voice ripening in her chest. She thought how every year brought three or four favourite stories that she would be required to read constantly, she could remember them in succession, the Gingerbread Man, the Frog Prince, Rumpelstiltskin. She recalled the King's final demand, 'You spin this straw into gold by the morning and tomorrow you shall be my bride.' 'He was a greedy man,' Marcus would say each time and she would nod. She had joined them there in those certainties, then.

'Would you like to go for a swim?' said the Captain, putting his head up from below, standing on the stairs. 'We're going to be in a good clear place for swimming, just off a bay. In five minutes.' It was about three in the afternoon.

'When will we get back?'

'About five.'

Going on to the roof of the yacht, she saw the Americans stretched out, sunbathing. The owner was sitting next to Missy rubbing oil on to her back.

37

Whenever Jan thought of the Caribbean, he thought of the rich and sticky aquamarine of sea and sky. In Belize he'd lain watching formations of clouds that seemed impossible, maps of countries, giant marlin fish suspended, rapiers on their snouts, clues and signs amidst the ruffles of God's bed skirt. He did not seek answers in the Belgian sky which was a mute grey from day to day. But in the Caribbean where the sea and sky divide the world between them, the land is just a gesture on the part of the sea. The lesson for the day is written up above, for you to follow.

Jan lay on the sand, still naked, with his shorts draped over his privates, one eye open squinting at the sky.

When he sat up he saw Laurie emerge from the water, a steady-footed, dripping diva, making straight for him. His stomach turned with apprehension. She sat down beside him, squeezing the water from her hair behind her head, and he saw out of the corner of his eyes her breasts, soft and damp. He was afraid for himself and he cleared his throat several times.

'This is paradise! Here and now!' shouted Bill from the water, leaping like Neptune.

'He is very true,' said Laurie and Jan frowned momentarily at the peculiarity of her Hong Kong English expression, 'I think there is no heaven, I think it is our job to make one on earth, while we are alive.'

He smiled and kept his face straight ahead, concentrating on Bill as if he were his own child, at risk in the sea. He remembered his daydream about her.

'You are beautiful, Laurie.'

She smiled, cocking her head at first, with her eyes and mouth questioning – then they were steadied by the blossoming of comprehension. Her upper body rose and fell a few times and she did not blink. Before she could say anything he said suddenly, 'Can you help me?' He paused, 'I don't know what I mean by that.'

In front of him, on her knees, she put her fingers about his wrist and turned it over so that the soft skin over his veins was facing upwards. She looked at it, then she brought it to her lips and kissed it.

'Thank you,' he said, feeling the mixture of the sun and the beer collide in his chest.

38

'Well, you have certainly given us some entertainment, Bill. We needed it,' said Jan amiably when a dripping Bill joined them to towel off and put his shorts back on.

'You're right. A tense crowd yesterday. That's why I wanted to get out. They'll be an irritable lot tonight, burnt no doubt too.' He looked up at the sun, and sighed with pleasure as he drained his beer.

'My wife tells me you are a Christian; born again.'

'Now, do I look like a Christian?'

Laurie put her hand up to her brow to shield her eyes against the sun and to see him. 'But anyone may look like a Christian,' she said.

Bill sat down, adjusting his shorts a little as he did so.

'I am a Christian, indeed.'

Jan nodded. 'What does it mean?' he asked, then added, 'I don't mean to be rude. I was raised as a Catholic, so was my wife, but I don't think we'd describe ourselves as Christians.'

'Catholic, Protestant, Muslim . . .' said Bill. 'All of that shite throws me, you see. I have my own relationship . . . I couldn't speak about the way another man believes.'

'But what does it mean to you?'

'I'll tell you.' He stopped for a while, considering the sea. 'It means trying to bring God into the centre of everything I do, to make him present, even now. Sometimes you're so heavy you can't make room or you don't make room and sometimes you're so light, you forget. You fail constantly and that's what I find so cheering, failing all the time. One of the worst.'

Laurie stretched her legs and lifted her face to the sun. Jan leaned forward, agitated and rocking, as if he were hungry.

'How can you know for sure? I never knew, not even as a child.'

'Well, it's different for everyone, isn't it. For me it was a miracle.'

Jan was sad suddenly. A face in a tomato, a cross in a potato, some sort of reported healing at Lourdes, all of the hopes of mothers with ailing children, women who might as well wish as pray.

'My wife, Jerry, now, how do I tell you this,' Bill swallowed, 'let's begin with the truth of the matter. Me, born loser. Jerry, long-suffering, hopeful. Hoping to get me off the booze. Now I can drink and stop at a glass or two, but earlier in my life I could not. I was, and still am, a rotten example of a man. I can say, hand on heart, that beforehand, I'd not done a good thing just because it was a good thing, you know, no strings attached. People had dragged me behind them in their kindness or I'd just been buffeted between people acting in their own best interests, thinking that it was me that had a plan. I went from Belfast as a boy, with my widowed mother, to South Africa, and God love her she dragged me behind her all her life.

'She was a smart woman. She finished her education pregnant with me, raised me and taught English at Queen's University, Belfast, supporting the pair of us on a pittance. When my father died – he was much older than she was – she took up an offer to go to the University of Johannesburg to teach and so I grew up in South Africa, from fifteen years old. She was the bright one, I could barely count the fingers on my fat hands although like most teenagers I thought I was hot stuff.

'She taught all day, the white kids, and in the evenings she went to the township, and taught there, the black kids. She was a good woman, God bless her. Her only weakness was nostalgia for the United Kingdom. In her later years she loved to have magazines with pictures of the Royals in. She didn't drink, apart from the occasional glass, she didn't smoke and if she ever took another man, I never knew of it. I can't remember her saying a clever thing, which you'd think she would being a University professor, but I certainly don't recall her saying a stupid one and that's something in a lifetime. Why, me on the other hand, blabbermouth!

'I worked for a small company installing security gating on windows and doors. I had a bit of luck, there was a lot of call for it in the 1970s when I was starting off, and I copied into a notebook one day the names of the company's suppliers and some of their customers, then, the next year, I started up on my own with money from my mum. Bought a van, had a Nkosa chap help me out for peanuts and went door to door. Tutting and clicking, telling the black maid how those crazy motherfucker Nkosa could get in, if she was Zulu, and if she was Nkosa telling her how the Zulus would kill her in her bed. 'Course she would tell her mistress and give her my card. If they had gating I'd tell them it wasn't enough and if they didn't I'd read them their new religion. Fear, was what we were peddling. I had ten or so teams of guys in vans with my name on driving round and round Sandton. It's a suburb of Jo'burg. You don't see one house that isn't a fortress. My work, most of that.

'Now, I was an alcoholic. I went drinking from my teenage years. Dropped Mum home after she'd done her teaching and went out into the sticks drinking with whoever, Boers, English, I didn't care, and then in my twenties I had the money to be the hero in the place, standing round after round at one crummy place or another. I had a drinks cupboard at work and I'd start the day with a good scotch. I used to keep a bottle of the same stuff in the glove compartment of the car. When I got pulled over by the police, I'd be sitting in the driver's seat, helpful as you like with the bottle in my hands. "Oh, Officer, you gave me a terrible shock, so you did, Sir, I just had to have a wee nip of this stuff." That way they couldn't tell how fresh the smell of booze was. Aye, it worked a few times. Mostly they didn't care.

'I had a love affair with booze. I don't think there is a type of it I haven't tried. Even the stupid shite they make for young women or old girls, chocolate liqueurs and the like. See I tried it all so I could get other people who were harder pressed to love the stuff to find something they did like. I couldn't bear not to have the company. When I got my own house I built a pub bar down one side of the living room. I had the top shelf, the middle shelf too. And mixers on tap. I had a Union Jack over it and pictures of the Queen framed and hanging behind it. Oh, my old mum loved to have a wee sherry sat up at it. And we had parties round it. Expats all of us, former Rhodesians, South African English, all old soaks. We'd get so fucking pissed up, play military marches and pub songs. We'd finish up hanging on to the bar to try to stand for the National Anthem, half-saluting, the men, the women crying.

'I met my girl, Jerry, through a friend who brought her along to the bar. Fresh from Rhodesia and a failed marriage. Forty and fine-looking. I was in my late thirties and a fat fuck. Shite-faced most of the time. Still she moved in with me and helped out at the office. Got me straight with a glass of gin in the morning. I'd be a shaking great jelly of a mess before it. Then she started on about me giving it up. You couldn't blame her. I nearly killed her several times in the ten years we were together. A few times we were driving and I passed out. Once we were in the Drakensberg Mountains and I fell asleep, Jerry grabbed the wheel in time and I woke up and put my foot on the brake, one wheel over the edge of the pass. Jerry wasn't much of a drinker. Thank God one of us wasn't. She used to rant and rage and say I was a godforsaken you name it, she'd go to leave but she'd always come back. Because I needed her, I begged her to come back. She was a wonderful woman but I drove her to distraction. You see she really did want to save me. She shaved all of her lovely long hair off, to make a point like. She took my electric razor and left the hair in a pile on the floor. I went in thinking we was being robbed by a very casual bald-headed fellow, sitting on my sofa looking out to the garden. It was her. I'll never forget that sight. She had streaks of mascara down her face. The maid was sitting in the yard with her broom, not daring to go in there. "Will you stop now," she asked me, "will you stop?" I said to myself, the dear girl's crazy, I shall have to look after her. As is said, I never did a good thing from intention. There was me at the middle of it all. What I needed. Sure I gave her girls some money from time to time, Jerry's daughters that is, but that was to keep her close by. My old mum died and I put a nice grave up for her, showy, like a raised tomb, but that was for me, she'd have hated it.

'I had a heart attack aged forty-six. Struck down still cradling the smooth sides of the love of my life, that bloody bar. You should have seen the state of me. Huge I was, twice the size I am now even, I couldn't fit in a normal car which was fine because I had a luxury one. I couldn't take no more than a few stairs without stopping, wiping the sweat from me and wheezing for breath. She begged me when I came out of the hospital to see it as a warning. She chucked the booze away and converted the pub into a juice bar. God bless her, now will it be a papaya and ginger this morning, my love, says she, or shall we go o.j. and carrot mixed?'

He laughed and laughed and Jan and Laurie started to laugh too. George and Dorothy came back into view; they had been walking in the waves, barefoot, in half-drenched clothes.

Dorothy was holding her skirts up and together, evidently cradling a collection of shells. Bill waved at them.

'Ah, she was a marvel. She was my life,' he sighed and his chest heaved, 'she gave me everything.' He closed his eyes for a moment. 'I went back to the booze. I'm giving you the short version. It's hard enough to bear to tell it short. I went missing for an afternoon here and there. It was only the fact she didn't want to know that kept her from seeing it for a week or so, then she had to face it and we had a fight. I hit her. And the next day when I came to, she was in the bathroom, lying on the floor. The bathroom cabinet door was open, the pill bottle lids were off and she'd done her best, her very best, to make sure she wasn't coming back.'

Jan looked at Bill and seeing that his face was wet with tears that went unwiped, he looked down at his feet.

'Got her pumped,' said Bill, 'pumped her out, they did, but it was just too late. See I'd slept till eleven or so and they tell me she took the pills in the early hours. She knew me, knew I would be unlikely to come round before lunchtime and my reliability as a drunk was the death of her.'

Jan started to speak but Bill put a hand on him to stay him.

'I was in the room with her when she passed away and knowing she was going, with the heartbeat weak on the monitor, hearing her fade, I just sat jabbering on about how I was going to miss her, how I couldn't live without her and so on and then it came to me, what about *her*? You big lump of shite, what about her? And remembering how she had a fondness for the beauty of the words in the Bible I said to myself, "Do something for her." And I picked it up, turned to the Psalms and started to read and then I asked God for his help, not for me, but for her because she believed. I didn't know how to pray so I just spoke, out loud, asked him to love her better than I did. Suddenly the sun came into the room and a shaft of light went across her lower face as though the Lord himself was bending over her kissing her and the light travelled slowly, caressing her body all the way down and I'm looking about myself and the window's a tiny little box and it's grey as you like outside on account of the height of the hospital buildings around. Like a fool, I'm turning, turning to see where the light's coming from and outside I hear this voice, in the hallway of the hospital, a man is walking up and down saying over and over "Jesus Christ" and you can't tell if he's cursing or praising, but it was a voice filled with immanence, like he's hanging on to the Lord's coat-tails. The Lord took her right from me into His arms and she and He made sure I saw it, made sure I knew it.

'It was a miracle,' he said, after a while, 'I was an atheist, and then I was a believer.'

'Ask and you will receive . . .' said Laurie. 'Yes, I remember.'

39

Steve Burns was feeding the fish down at the jetty, waiting for the Americans to come back in. He was also supervising the efforts of his staff to assemble tables for the beach barbecue that evening. The fish were thronging in the water, riding across each other to get at the pieces of white bread, like sardines in a snow-dome.

It was not important that one's ideas were very good or even exceptional, just that one had lots of them and made one or two happen, he thought. He would use this notion at the staff meeting. He turned his back on the fish, letting a hot dog bun fall whole. Take this evening's event, the mere fact that it was taking place was something. The guests seemed to be discontented this week, they couldn't relax. He had to provide entertainment, something that was rarely required. A boy came past him with buckets full of fruit, another followed picking up the pineapples and mangoes that had fallen on to the beach. There was a whole world of difference between an idea and an event. Think, it could have all fallen apart so easily! They had not been able to find sufficient cable to extend to the turntables, so they would use a ghetto blaster instead and pitch this as a sort of teenage cutoffs-and-bare-feet affair. It would appeal to the nostalgia of his greying clientele. Jiving on the beach, necking in the dunes, waking down by the surf; with your wallet gone and someone's knickers in your pocket . . . He grinned, remembering an adolescence he'd never had. His own had been hashed out according to the mood engendered by a bottle of cider in a field and a puff on someone's cigarettes at school or a pint of cocktail and a tab of acid at Poly. He couldn't wait to get the fuck away from it all.

The yacht came up alongside the jetty, the Captain was standing out at the front, with a rope ready to throw to secure it, finally. He motioned that Steve should tie them to the wharf and Steve started to do so but no sooner was he looping the rope when the Captain jumped down and undid what he had done.

'Have a good afternoon?' said Steve, proffering his hand. 'Steve Burns, manager here.'

The Captain looked at him, nodded without interest and jumped back onto the boat. The Americans came forward as if they were very tired, only the Dutch woman seemed ready to disembark. She had a shoulder bag tight under her arm and was frowning at the gap between the boat and the jetty. He held out his hand to her.

'Well, how nice,' she said, suddenly smiling, 'how nice.' Her hand was dry and firm. He thought of the first girl he kissed, whose hands had been the same way and whose mouth had been unyielding. Harriet. He could remember her name even now. He had not liked her. An old soul, an old body, a misery-guts, at fourteen years old.

'You are most welcome,' he said with a flashy smile, his best, seeing Jason and Missy hand-in-hand, behind the woman.

'Ahoy there!'

'Not much in the way of fish,' said Jason, giving Burns an angry look as the man reached for Missy's two hands. With a foot against the side of the boat, his reach over-extended, his balance going, Burns's shoe slipped, he fell forward suddenly and Missy faltered. Her husband caught her by her upper arms and hauled her back.

'Jesus Christ,' he shouted.

Burns righted himself, his hands splayed against the rim of the boat, his cheek pressed to the boat.

'I'm fine, I'm fine,' he said quickly, bent over and walking himself backwards with his hands. 'Don't worry, fine, fine.'

'I don't think he's worried about you,' said the Dutch woman.

Jason was examining his wife. 'Are you okay, baby?' She nodded. 'You fucking idiot, she could have had an accident!'

'I'm so sorry,' said Burns, his jaw aching but steeling himself not to touch it. There was the right thing to do. It was to soldier on, to assist them all off the boat, to make light of it, but it seemed he'd done something for which there were no amends. He thought of the outrage of Harriet's mother when he ate the last piece of cake at her party, having already had one, unaware that it had been reserved for the birthday girl. 'You're such a greedy boy,' she had said, annoyed, 'a horrible greedy pig of a boy.'

He turned on his heel and walked up the beach towards the steps that led to the hotel.

40

Annemieke received Jan into their room with a bitter silence. She asked him if he'd enjoyed himself – with the Chinese lady. He told her he had; that the Chinese lady was charming, as were the others. It had been wonderful. He did not tell her about the skinny-dipping. He asked her how her day had been. She shrugged.

'There's a barbecue party starting at seven-thirty,' she said.

'It won't matter if we're late,' he said, seeing the book on the side table by the French doors, the hotel Bible well concealed by the cover of Jacques Barzun's *From Dawn to Decadence: 500 years of Western Cultural Life*. It was a silly thing, really, but what Bill had said had touched him. He had been trying to read it in order; now he had the idea of reading wherever the pages fell. A sort of Russian roulette in which one hopes to acquire eternal life.

'It will matter to me. I'd like to go. You've had the entire day on the beach whereas I've been on a boat. If I'd known you were all going to the beach I would have come.'

'I don't think it was really planned out. It just happened.' It was either his wistful tone or the fact that he was picking up the book that made her angry.

'You haven't even asked about my day.'

'I did,' he said.

'No you did not.'

It was stupid, he wanted to laugh, but he saw that there was a thorn stuck in her animal side.

'I expect the three of you men had your eyes hanging out

watching the Chinese woman undress.'

He said nothing.

'Lucky for you I didn't come. Is she with Bill or is she unattached?'

'Unattached, I think.'

'Well, you can do as you like, for all I care.'

'How about you, did you find yourself some nice company? Tell me about your day?'

'Well, there's nothing to say,' she said. 'Your wife was the odd one out. Everyone else was in couples. I was like the widow, already.'

'Annemieke.'

He let her shower first, and then while he stood under the jets of water he heard her cries of frustration about the bedroom as she tried to dress. She re-entered the bathroom still in her underwear to remove her lipstick and try another colour. When he put his fingers in his ears he could feel himself being swallowed up by the water; he let it run over his face. Opening his eyes, he saw her standing before him fully clothed, in a shift dress and matching heels.

'The shoes don't go,' she said.

'They look fine. You look good.'

'The shoes don't go. The heels will get stuck in the sand.' She left the bathroom.

'A funny thing happened today,' she said, when he came out. From the bed, she sat, knees crossed, watching him don the usual long-sleeved white shirt and navy knee-length shorts. 'The manager dropped the American's wife, Missy, when he was helping her off the boat.'

'Was she okay?'

'Oh sure. You know how these American women are though, she made a big deal.'

'She was shocked.'

'Not as shocked as Mr Burns. He hit his face on the side of the boat.'

'That must have hurt,' said Jan, sitting down beside her to pull on his socks.

'The American called him a fucking idiot.'

'That's a bit strong.'

Annemieke laughed and put the palm of her hand against his cheek. He was relieved. He sat beside her and put his hand on her knee, holding it there to steady both of them. She was shaking with laughter and he was simply shaking.

41

Annemieke was warmly welcomed back into Bill's party that evening. They ate together, standing, and made quips about the meal being somewhat differently provisioned than the one they'd had earlier. There were knives and forks and glasses and they helped themselves to a buffet of barbecued meats and seafood.

'So much meat, all the time,' said Annemieke, looking at Jan's plate, 'it can't be good for you. I like to eat more simply.'

'It's nice to see you with your clothes on,' said Dorothy to Bill.

'Chipolata anyone?' asked George, brandishing a small sausage on his fork. They laughed.

'Och, it does the job, now,' said Bill.

Annemieke put her plate down ostentatiously.

'I've lost my appetite,' she said, her head turning aside, her eyes half-closed. Jan looked at her and then at Bill. Bill's smile faltered for a moment and Jan watched him recover it only to lose it again. He looked down at his plate to give the man the space to try again.

The Chinese woman spoke. 'How was your boat trip, Annemieke?'

'It wasn't a boat trip. These yachts, they're luxurious, beautifully appointed, beige leather in this case, throughout, and with a small staff. We had a fine lunch. We drank wine and sunbathed. We chatted about this and that. It was very classy. Those yachts are hundreds of thousands of dollars to buy, let alone the cost of the upkeep and the mooring.

Thousands. The staffing and catering! I've been on them before so it wasn't new to me. All the same it is impressive.'

Laurie nodded and started to say, 'In Hong Kong . . .' but she was cut short.

'So did you join in the skinny-dipping?' Annemieke said, her eyes unwavering. The Chinese woman blushed.

'We all did,' she said.

Annemieke looked at Jan, 'Well, well. How energetic of you.'

He knew what she was thinking. The Imaginary Invalid. She looked as if she had been cheated.

''Allo, 'allo,' Adam lurched up alongside them, looking merry. He would insist, he said, on whisking one of the ladies away for a dance.

Laurie allowed herself with good humour to be dragged down to the water's edge where a few people were dancing to the reggae music.

'Someone's had a few,' George said, watching them go. 'Wonder what the boy's been doing today.'

Adam was leaping around in the water, surrounding Laurie, baffling her with his staccato happy movements, whooping and cheering her to join in.

'I'm a bit fucked up actually,' he said when he returned her.

'What've you been drinking, son, your breath smells terrible,' said George, stepping back from him.

'Ah, what haven't I been drinking,' said Adam with a wink.

'No need to shout, I'm not mutton,' said George, disgruntled. Dorothy put her hand on his arm.

Grabbing Annemieke's hand next, Adam took her off to dance and seeing that the Americans were now dancing and there was quite a crowd, she went.

'What's wrong?' Jan asked George, seeing him staring after the boy.

'I don't like to see a man in that state. Out of control like that.'

'Oh, once in a while, a drink or two . . .' said Jan.

'He's got a job here. He's looking for trouble. Did you ever turn up to your office blind drunk?'

Jan shook his head. No, he'd never been there drunk, but he'd been there blind as an earthworm.

The five of them watched Adam career into other dancers, causing a woman to slip into the surf momentarily. She laughed and picked herself up while Adam apologized at great length, hanging on to her for support all the while.

Steve Burns joined their group and exchanged pleasantries with his arms folded over his chest. With his chin slightly elevated, he certainly seemed the master of his domain, and yet Jan could only think of the American calling him a fucking idiot.

Adam was holding on to Annemieke, listening to her while she was saying something. She seemed to be giving him some words of advice. He looked serious and nodded fervently. The two of them headed for the bar on the jetty. Jan watched as Annemieke took a drag from Adam's cigarette and knocked back a drink in a small glass. She was laughing too hard.

'Oh dear,' Jan said, 'and now we have a problem.' Two more drinks were put in front of the pair and promptly swallowed and they were back down by the sea, with Adam steering a volatile course, barging into other dancers.

'Looks like the party's hotting up,' said Burns contentedly. 'Good to see you lot letting your hair down. That's what it's all about.' He smiled. 'Is that Adam?' he asked, squinting in the half-light. The music had changed and Adam was leaping and pogoing in front of Annemieke who was laughing and clapping her hands. Jan knew that this performance was aimed at him. Either side of the couple, people moved away. Adam was now splashing Annemieke with water and her dress was rapidly becoming see-through. Holding her by the wrist, he led her to the bar, where they drank another glass of spirits each, down in one.

George and Dorothy bade the group a good night and Jan watched the old couple make their way up the beach with short and tired footsteps as if their shoes hurt them. He saw George turn back and, meeting his look, nod. Then George shook his head at the bar and Jan swallowed hard. Poor decent George, he too knew what this was all about and he would not stay to see it.

Jan walked over to the bar and stood beside the new teenagers.

'All right, Jan, mate, have a drink,' said Adam, giving him a cursory look, intent all the time on the barman's work. 'That's not a full measure,' he said.

'Are you drinking?' Annemieke asked without looking at her husband.

'No, I'm fine, thanks,' he said.

'Come on, Adam,' she said. Steve Burns came up to them and put a hand on Adam's shoulder.

'Listen,' he said quietly, 'a word. Finish your drink and get yourself off home now.'

'Why's that then?' Adam asked, putting a handful of dollar bills on the bar.

'You're staff, mate. Do I have to remind you? Now finish your drink.'

'*Oh yes, I'm the great pretender* . . .' Adam started to sing. He looked at Steve with his lip curled, his nose like the trigger of a pistol drawn back, and he sneered, 'when you've paid me what you owe me, fair and square, then you can be my boss and I'll be your staff. Until then I'm a paying guest. Mate.'

'You'll be paid, at the end of the month,' Steve Burns looked about him, then moved so that his back would obscure their conversation from Jan. 'Look,' he said in low tones, 'why don't you just fuck right off now, and I'll do what I can to square you up early, as a favour.'

'I don't like being called staff. I'm having a night off,' Adam replied and then he sauntered down to the beach, lighting another cigarette as he went.

Burns exchanged looks with Jan. 'Just a misunderstanding,' he said with a brief smile, 'he wants to be paid before everyone else. I told him the way our system worked when he took the job. What can I do?' he asked, and it seemed to Jan that he really was asking him.

'He's had a lot to drink,' said Jan. 'It's never worth talking to a man in that condition. They don't remember.' Jan was surprised to see that Adam was the kind of man who become nasty when he drank. He could hear Adam repeating, in high-pitched tones, ''E's a fucking idiot, he is,' looking at Burns with a hot face, his hands in fists.

'If I'd known he was a boozer I wouldn't have hired him. Bloody liability.' Burns looked down to the water's edge for a long moment. Jan followed his gaze. He felt Burns look back at the dancers but he himself continued to stare out to sea.

'Oh, fuck me! No!'

Jan turned, prepared himself for the worst, expecting to see Annemieke in an embrace with her young dancing companion, but his wife was standing aside. She was swaying at the knees in a semblance of musical appreciation while Adam was dancing cheek to cheek with the American's wife. The young man's hands were falling below her waist as they moved about to 'Careless Whisper' together, his nose in her hair, his body propped by hers. Suddenly his hands were firmly on her arse and his tongue must have been in her ear or licking her neck for she recoiled as if she'd been burnt and let out a little cry of 'No!' Jason was down the beach in seconds and although his punch was badly thrown it was sufficient to knock Adam off his balance.

Adam was down on his knees in the surf like a man looking for his glasses, saying, 'Calm down, calm down, keep your hair on,' over and over again as he tried to stand. Jan and Burns ran down to the shore and Jan held Adam while Burns held Jason.

'Get off of me,' said Jason, shrugging Burns off easily. He turned on him, 'What kind of a place are you running here with your staff molesting your guests?'

'I asked him to leave.'

'And he sure listened to you.' Jason stood quivering. Physically maladroit, with the pinched nose and sucked-in cheeks of a scientist or a computer programmer, it was only his thick reddish blond hair and his new clothes that gave Jason the appearance of being a wealthy Wasp. His body went awry when upset; at this moment he looked like a question mark. In those rare old-fashioned moments when a man is supposed to be a man, thought Jan, one has the chance to see his true character, as if by X-ray. It was compelling. He was not alone; looking round he saw that everyone was transfixed.

Relaxing his jaw muscles with an effort, Jason took his wife by the hand and said to Burns, 'I'll talk to you in the morning. You'd better find us another hotel for tomorrow night.' They moved through the dancers, who were almost immobile. The music continued. At one point Jason turned back, a single fisted arm flailing, like a vestigial reaction; the rest of his body continued along with his wife.

Looking over to the boy who was putting CDs on the ghetto blaster, Burns saw that he had his eyes closed and was mouthing the words to the song.

Peculiarly enough, he realized that he was as embarrassed as if it was he who'd thrown the hapless punch and trembled like Shirley Temple in front of the crowd. Try as he might to renounce the American, consoling himself internally with words like 'prick', he couldn't seem to shake the sense that they were the same person. One and the same, divided by circumstance, by luck.

42

Because they seldom slept more than an hour or two after dawn, George considered it a weakness tantamount to deviancy to 'loll about in bed'. On Sunday morning, he called their eldest daughter, the one who was keeping an eye on the place. With five hours' time difference on her side he expected her to be halfway through her day.

Dorothy was taking her first cup of tea, in bed, resting the saucer on her bosom. She had her teeth in, but no glasses. She looked lost in thought.

'Bloody still in bed,' George was saying to her, his hand over the receiver, but Dorothy didn't seem to hear. 'I say, Carol's still lolling about in her bed. At ten-thirty of a morning, no wonder she never gets anything done. Shouldn't wonder if the geraniums are parched. I told her, morning and evening at this time of year.

'Yes, still here,' he went on into the phone. 'You sorted yourself out now have you? Put the dog out. Poor bleeder, surprised it hasn't piddled everywhere. Fancy keeping a dog in till ten-thirty. Its bowels must be in a right state.' George winced, looking towards the toilet door.

'Yes, lovely,' he sounded as though he was making a grudging concession. 'We're having a lovely time, but we're coming home soon, you know. Shan't want to see them flowers dead. Of course I worry, so does your mother. Yes, she's fine.' George looked at her, she was lying stock-still, unblinking; he thought for a moment she'd gone.

'Dorothy,' he said sharply, 'are you with us?' Dorothy looked at him; her expression didn't change.

'When are they coming round?' she said, 'I'll put on a joint for lunch.'

'What are you on about?' he said. 'Hang on, Carol duck, your mother's talking.'

Dorothy's mouth began to move anxiously, 'I can't remember if I did the shopping. Have we got any spuds?'

'Pull yourself together, for Pete's sake,' George said, then, into the phone, 'We'll be home Saturday. Not long now. We'll see you then.' And he put the phone down.

'What are you talking about?' he asked, standing. She looked at him with a frightened expression, like a rabbit cornered. He felt the heat of anger rise in him.

'I was only saying, I didn't know what we'd got to cook for lunch, for the girls.'

'We're on our bleeding holidays, woman, we're in the Caribbean. We ain't got to cook lunch. The girls ain't coming round here.'

Dorothy's mouth continued to move but no words came out. With no one else there, he knew he had options, he could comfort her, he could shout at her, he could do anything he wanted. No one would see him, whatever he did, not even Dorothy, for she was not there either.

He stood in front of her bed, like a colossus.

'Come on,' he said, 'come on my old sweet, my old love, you've got to try a bit harder.'

43

With the work on the new annex complete, the terrace area in front of it was no longer roped off and so the dining tables and chairs that had previously comprised the outdoor seating there were reinstated. The residents could begin their day with breakfast by the pool. This was granted, edict-like, via posted bulletins on the restaurant double doors and the news was received with interest. Burns helped out on Sundays himself and he noted the chirruping excitement of the clusters of breakfasters with pleasure. He ought to think up something 'new' every mid-week, it need only be a rearrangement of seating.

What creatures of habit human beings are that they find the mere act of eating a customary meal in a different location a great treat, Jan thought, standing at a remove from the residents who had filled the outdoor tables, looking for Bill. They can tolerate the curtailment of all sorts of freedom, so long as they have petty diversions. There was never a day that he woke and said, today I will choose liberty above all else, or justice, hedonism or even new experiences. No, he chose coffee or tea, albeit very good brands, and sometimes he screwed with the proper order of things and threw in a cube of sugar. Hospitals, prisons and schools – these institutions were crammed with human desire, desire that had been thwarted by other forces, immured and immolated. He and many more men and women like him were empty buildings.

Suddenly his eyes came into focus and he saw that Laurie was looking at him, holding a croissant over her mouth in the shape of a smile. He laughed. There was a seat next to her with an empty cup and saucer and a space between a knife and fork. He had only to fit in.

At the same table were the rest of the crew. 'Morning, son,' said George, looking up at him, then back down at his breakfast. A sinister expression on his face, George was penetrating the interior of a tiny jam jar with a large knife.

'Hallo there,' said Dorothy brightly, wiping her mouth. There were tiny flakes of croissant in the small cracks around her lips.

'How's the missus?' asked Bill, popping a triangle of egg-soaked toast into his mouth. Jan looked at him for a second, saw the tongue reach out to take whatever egg remained in the sides of the mouth, saw the beginnings of sweat on the man's brow, even at this early hour.

'She is sleeping,' he said.

'Sleeping it off?' asked George, turning the jam jar upside down and leaving it in the middle of his plate.

'Why, yes, she is as a matter of fact,' said Jan.

George looked at him quickly, 'You look fit.'

'Why shouldn't I?'

There was a silence.

'No reason, son,' said George.

'So you are joining Mr Moloney's Mystery Tours again, aren't you?' asked Laurie.

'No mystery today. I'm going to church. There's a wee church, one of the first built outside the main town, all white, wooden, a real little gem, up on the northeast and I'm looking forward to the service. Anyone who wants is welcome to come with me. We'll have to get cracking though, we should be on the road within a half-hour or so.'

'Well, I think I am ready,' said Jan, rather formally. He looked at Laurie, watching the slender sides of her neck move as she drank her orange juice. 'I'll finish my breakfast and meet you all in reception if you like?'

'Jolly good,' said George, 'we've got to pop back to the room. I've got to see a man about a dog. Can't get on with the day till I've got it out the way.' He winced as he rose and helped Dorothy up.

'Gently,' she said as he pulled at her, holding her underneath her arms.

'Well, get a move on then,' he said.

'All right, all right,' she was saying as they went off towards the hibiscus alley.

'Pardon!' they heard George say loudly and the three of them exchanged glances and fell about laughing, Laurie folding her napkin and putting it on her plate, saying, 'Poor man.'

Bill leaned forward, waggling his knife at them. 'He's a martyr to his digestive tract, that much he told me this morning when the breakfast was being served, warned me not to mess with the onions, told me he can trace a lot of discomfort to those villainous vegetables.'

Just before they left, Annemieke joined them for a black coffee and a croissant. She waived the menu from the waiter, 'I won't be eating anything cooked, have you noticed there is no staff? I wonder if it's not Burns himself cooking,' she said, lifting her dark sunglasses and raising an eyebrow. Sitting back in her seat, she peeled layers off her croissant. 'I've been to better places.'

'Well, we didn't pay for it,' said Jan.

'That's not the point, Jan. For a businessman, you often miss the point, financially.'

Bill and Laurie began picking up their breakfast things.

'So where is your team off to, today, Mr Moloney?'

'Will you not be joining us, Annemieke?'

'Oh God no,' she said with a little laugh, 'excuse me, no. I don't get much holiday time and I don't like group tours. I'll be at the pool, reading, relaxing . . .'

'Ach well, you've got it all worked out.'

'Yes.'

'How satisfying.'

'Yes.'

'We're going to a little church, it's three or four centuries old,' said Laurie, 'one of the first here.'

'Well, when you're from Europe, churches they don't seem quite so appealing, every town has one that dates back a thousand years or so. And I'm not religious. Neither is my husband. When you see what's been done in the name of religion around the world, it makes it hard to believe in a God.'

'When I see what man has done to man, that's exactly why I believe in God,' said Bill. He sat back in his chair and smiled at her. 'Given the real depths to which mankind can sink, isn't it just amazing that the human race has survived at all?'

Jan looked up at Bill from his plate, chewing, his mouth moving, his eyes still.

'See, he's going to convert you this morning, Jan-tche,' his wife went on, crossing her legs. 'A little "*mea culpa*", some holy water and you'll be absolved, but then you'll have to live the exemplary life that Mr Moloney lives.'

Bill moved his chair back, making a sudden scraping noise, 'Well now, I've already done most of the work. I got the four of them baptized yesterday, so I did. In the sea. Your man's born again.'

44

On a triangular lot of ground, next to a desolate roundabout and opposite one or two shops, a picture-book white church complete with steeple seemed to be on a cliff. In fact the land the other side of the church dropped slowly away to more of the sugar plantations through which they had driven to get there.

They took a quick walking tour of the cemetery behind the church across cracked paving tiles, taking in the plastic flowers in waterless jars, the gothic white marble tombs and bread-slice gravestones with their sombre Victorian names – Ernestine, Archibald and Arnold – and the next generation's sentimental diminutives, Nettie, Archie or Arnie.

The church offered some relief from the heat and the group followed Bill up the aisle and sat side by side in a pew near the front. The Reverend was an elderly white man with an amiable manner and a habit of screwing up his eyes, a relief from his short-sightedness. The congregation was black for the most part, and the service, Bill told them, pretty standard for a Presbyterian church. They were amused, though, to hear the agreement of the congregation grunted and spoken freely during the sermon and prayers.

'Yes, Sir,' a neighbour of theirs felt bound to say every few moments, 'mm-hmm.'

Jan recalled going to see the priest of the church in which they chose to marry, just outside Brugge. Perhaps that was the last time either of them had participated in any sort of religious discussion. The meeting was a mandatory precursor to their getting married in the church. An old fellow had been pleased to offer them tea and take them through the service. He'd then thought, though celibate himself, to share some thoughts with them, some observations. He considered, he said, that along the road of married life they would meet obstacles that hindered their path; he had asked their permission to call these obstructions, 'elephants'. The analogy reeked of use. Jan had tried hard to listen. He knew from the set of Annemieke's mouth what she was thinking and he had held her hand; they were thick as thieves in those days. There would be big elephants and small elephants, he told them, and the point was to distinguish between the two and find a way around them, hand in hand. Even – or perhaps especially – as a relatively unsophisticated uneducated man in his late twenties, this had struck Jan as useless advice. Still, they'd been grateful that it had been so easy. It seemed that the best one could expect from any religious interaction was vague benevolence. They were relieved.

Stepping outside and taking to the little Ford car that Jan drove in those days, they had gone to Brugge for a beer. In those days, beer tasted wonderful and the drunker they became the more she made him laugh and she had been able to make him laugh till his eyes watered. She was the opposite of his conscience, she was the wicked sense of humour he lacked but had sensed since childhood was vital equipment for the good life.

Now, catching the drift of the sermon, rousing himself from his reverie, he was able to understand that the old vicar rummaged in his own bag of memories, recounting tales from his youth in an industrial town in England, then chanced a small conceptual leap and begged the people facing him to be stoic in the face of adversity. Then he'd read a passage from one of Paul's letters and finished by sharing some good news he'd gathered from his congregation concerning the birth of twins and the cricket score.

George was very pleased that when the Reverend came up the aisle shaking hands left and right, he had received a firm grasp and a quick chat. The two of them exchanged birth-places and then regiments, shook hands again and George agreed on all of their behalves to join the old boy for a cup of tea afterwards. He turned to the others and told them what they'd just seen take place. 'He came right up to me, singled me out, as if he knew me, and would you believe he was in North Africa too during the war?' They'd nodded. 'He asked me back for a cuppa. Well, we're all invited, of course. Nice old boy.

'Poor devil looks like he's on his last legs,' he said to Dorothy, turning to watch the Reverend leave. Dorothy remarked that although he walked with a slight hunching of the back he went at a better pace than either of them. 'You always have to gainsay me,' George grumbled.

As Bill, Dorothy and George stepped into the meeting room just off the entry hall, Laurie turned around to say to Jan, who was standing behind her,

'Let's you and I go outside.'

45

By lunchtime on Sunday, the sun was stretched, angry, shaking. Steve Burns stank. He'd been at the frying pans, dabbing damp on home fries, adding more and more vegetable oil to the pan, sending frozen potatoes to a sizzling hell. Brian, the Rastafarian, had kept up a monologue about the cost of living in a country like theirs.

'We livin' in place with two economies, man. Gots to be cheap labour for the man to make a profit, gots to be expensive in da shops on account of the nothing which we make here ourselves. Man can't live like that. No matter how much he love his country. Gots to fly, fly away.'

Steve had agreed with him without much interest. Money was just a score, that was all, the mark of your ingenuity. And luck. There was no point in complaining. He stacked emptied eggshells, half on half, with a sense of satisfaction. Over a hundred empties. As long as the chickens kept popping them out of their arses, as long as people sat with their knife and fork at the ready for an egg on toast, neither the chicken nor the egg was important, nor which came first, just the appetite of man. That was all that counted. He took an icing blade to the frying pan and scraped away at the debris, emptying a bird's nest of it into the sink, ignoring Brian's cry of distress, and starting a new batch of the oil and potatoes.

'Brian, keep an eye on this lot. Season it for me,' he said and he went out with an open steel tureen of the home fries. In the heat, the sweat dripped from his face into the platter. Salt on salt. He needed a drink, so he stepped down to the Hibiscus Bar and sat there to enjoy a cold beer.

In three or four months' time he'd have built up a Sunday staff. There was no way a manager should be in the kitchen. It looked bad. But he was so keen to report higher profit margins that quarter, he'd have cleaned the toilets himself too if needs be. This was a crazy place to turn a profit. The costs! The only way to make money was to savagely overcharge the punters. Emma was right; he'd have to start 'churning' them, pushing them into additional activities, the profitable ones. It was no good them lazing about, sedated on booze, dead-weight at the pool. It was no good him being their mum, finding the missing ones, keeping them from fighting over each other's toys. He should be more like their personal banker, providing a return of fun, enlightenment, whatever it was they were after directly proportionate to their investments.

He felt a prod on his back and turned round to find himself facing his nemesis. Jason.

'Morning,' he said, 'join me for a beer? Oh, I thought you were off? Can I help with the cases?'

'Not now,' said Jason, looking at the clock. 'We've got an issue.'

Well, fuck me, thought Burns, what a surprise. Did a day go by that this man did not have an issue?

'The Danish lady, she's coming out with us for a brunch cruise.'

His wife put a long-fingered hand on Jason's shoulder. Saronged cannily to reveal an entire long leg and wearing another string bikini top, she interrupted to say, 'Another one of your guests has gone missing.'

'Just a minute, I'm about to explain,' Jason said to her abruptly, as if she were staff. 'She's not picking up, the Danish lady, Mrs De G., her phone's off the hook.'

'Perhaps she doesn't want to go?' he smiled, lifting his shoulders. 'Perhaps she's avoiding you. Perhaps she needs some privacy.' He took a swig of his beer while he still could. He had a feeling it would be a short-lived sensation, the gaseous bitterness and mind-muffling torpor.

'No, she wanted to go, she was enthusiastic last night.'

Wasn't she though, thought Burns. 'Not to put too fine a point on it, but she had drunk a lot last night, perhaps she's feeling a little ropey this morning.'

'Sure, it's possible. But your barman told us he'd seen her this morning, at the bar here, having a drink.'

Benjamin, the barman, smiled nervously and shrugged, 'It's the truth.'

'And then she went off with your buddy, the one who likes to mess with the female guests when he's not doing the floors and toilets.'

'He tell her he gonna give her help home, she come over all sick looking,' said Benjamin, wiping the inside of a glass.

'It's really none of our business,' said Burns, signalling with a flick of his head that Benjamin should desist.

Benjamin stood still. He had a smile like an angel; in its warmth his tomato cheeks ripened. His eyes closed for a moment behind his glasses. Only the spectacles broke the sleek beauty of his face. 'They drank maybe two, maybe three Bloody Marys each one of them. Asking me for doubles to go in. I'm putting a little touch of sherry in these days. This is what makes a good Bloody Mary great.'

'So what do you think, Burns? Maybe even you can add two and two together?'

'I can, Sir, but I'm not keen to do so. I like to uphold the privacy of my clientele.'

'Yes. I'm sure Mr and Mrs Davis were glad of their privacy the night the old woman was lost.'

How had this man become his keeper? The beer shook in Burns's glass.

'Any-who . . .' said Missy as if to start a new subject. She flashed a dollar smile at each of them in turn, stepping between them. 'Let's just leave them to it, Jason, I'm sure Mrs De Groot can handle herself.'

'I don't think so,' said Jason. 'She's weak right now. She's easy prey. Her husband is dying . . .'

'Dying,' Burns repeated, looking peeved, his eyes elsewhere.

'He's got terminal cancer. Weeks to live. Maybe days, she told us, no one knows. He pops morphine by the handful every morning . . .'

Burns swallowed, 'I had no idea.'

'Yeah, she's a target, you know. Easy meat.'

'Where is her husband?'

'He's gone out for the day,' said Missy, 'with Mr Moloney and Mr and Mrs Davis, to church.'

'I see.'

'I think we ought to know that she's safe before we leave for the day, sweets,' said Jason, turning to his wife, who nodded and raised her hands in submission.

'It can't hurt,' she said.

Burns looked at the many pendants that hung in the soft valley of her chest, like rock-climbers attached to thin golden ropes. He glanced down at Jason's wrist and saw the man was wearing the very Rolex that he had promised to buy himself one day, when he had the money. He nodded. His beer was all gone.

'No, it can't hurt,' he sighed, relinquishing the empty glass.

46

'So run me through this one more time,' said Adam, holding down the 'close doors' button on the elevator as they entered it. 'You are going to pay me for sex.'

'Yes.'

'A hundred and fifty dollars.'

'Yes.'

'Okay.' Hunching his brow he felt his ponytail lift. The elevator stopped and the doors opened, 'But no, no, no, no, no,' he said, shaking his head and putting out his arm to stop her getting out, 'this is a wind-up!'

She was holding out her room card.

'Do you want to do this or not?' she asked.

'You're nuts,' he said.

'Why? To pay for sex or to pay for sex with you? For the latter, yes, you may have a point. We shall see,' a wild devilment shone in her eyes, 'I have never done this before,' she said, 'but I'm sure the less we speak about it, the better it is. For me.'

'A-non-y-mity,' he said, enunciating the word she had stressed at the bar as they sank their Bloody Marys.

'I want anonymity,' she'd said, 'but more importantly I want to be in charge. I want to have sex with someone that I don't know very well, and I want to order it the way I like.'

'O-kay,' he said slowly.

'I'm entitled to a change. I have always had to have sex with people I knew.'

He feared that she was going to get garrulous. And he struggled with himself, thinking, you sad bitch, on the one hand, but he also thought, this is a story, this is something to tell, she is a real character. There weren't enough weirdos in the world. And he saw too that he could also use this story with other more attractive younger women, to some advantage. He could make it a sort of confession, could claim to have been a male prostitute, women liked that kind of thing. So he started to laugh along with her. They would both be other people, desirable to themselves.

'All right,' he said, 'your wish is my command,' and he stood behind her as she opened the door and he glanced up and down the corridor.

When they were inside the room, he was a little depressed to see items of Jan's about the place, a heavy book on the coffee table, a pair of khaki shorts on the back of a chair.

'I shall go into the bathroom,' she said, 'and have a quick shower, then I would like you to do the same.'

'Fair enough,' he smiled, taking the elastic band from around his hair. She looked at him critically.

'Okay,' she said, 'okay,' and then she slipped into the bathroom.

He looked at himself in the mirror and gave an apish grin in order to remind himself of who he was. Jauntily, he stepped out to the balcony to have a cigarette. It crossed his mind that he ought not to smoke, now the clock was ticking, he was on someone else's time. 'Ah, bollocks to it,' he said, propping himself up on the railing, with one foot swinging, the other supporting him. He squinted down below to the rhodo-dendrons in the shade and tipped little bits of ash downwards. Jan's book, open, resting upside down on the glass table near the balcony, looked like the roof to a Roman temple. Stepping forward, but keeping his cigarette-holding hand outside, he peeped down to read the back of it: *500 years of Western Cultural Life* the cover read. He nodded. 'Good choice,' he said to himself. He noticed that the cover hung over the sides of the book, and with a single finger he poked the cover back, to make it neat. As soon as he did that, he caused the excess cover on the other side of the book to dimple and scuff a little, so with both hands, the cigarette gingerly held between two fingers, he attempted to turn it over and straighten it up. As soon as he turned it, he saw that the print was bold and black and minute and the pages almost transparent. 'A Bible. How weird is that?' Fumbling with the weight of it, he dropped some ash on to the page and leapt outside to blow it off the pages. It had made a mark, smudged the print, but it had not burnt. 'Bollocks,' he said to himself, closing the Bible, with the cover just about attached to it. He flung it back on the table as soon as he heard the bathroom door open.

Annemieke was wearing a white towelling robe. Her hair was dry. She's probably just given her muff a wash, he thought.

'Your turn,' she said, indicating the bathroom, and in he went, passing her between the bed and the dresser, saying, 'Sorry,' as he almost bumped against her and hearing her make some faint noise in return.

In the mirror of the bedroom, Annemieke opened her mouth wide to check her teeth. She raised her arms to check that her armpits were smooth, and then she dropped her robe to look at her body. Glancing back up at her face, she saw she had the hang-mouth expression of a carp, her lips flaccid and glum. She shook it off and assumed a haughty air. She rubbed a hand across her breasts and stood sturdily with her feet apart. 'I can have whatever I want,' she said, and then she went to the balcony, naked, stood there briefly and pulled the curtains to.

'Should I wash my hair?' Adam called from the bathroom.

'As you like,' she replied, hearing her voice ringing out in the empty room.

'Shall I use the hotel shampoo or yours?'

'I don't care,' she said.

'Shall I do my teeth?'

'Of course,' she said, about to mount the bed on all fours, wanting to stretch her back and legs a little.

'Which one?'

'What?'

'Which toothbrush?'

'Mine.'

'Which is that?'

'Oh, for God's sake,' she said to herself, as she pushed her arms out in front of her, lowering her chest and head to the bed. She sat up, 'I don't care. It doesn't matter.'

'All right, all right,' he said with comic inflection.

A German would have been perfect, she said to herself, all performance, no personality. A BMW. Let's hope this man's not a Mini Cooper. She turned her head to look in the mirror past her rear. 'I'm like Cleopatra,' she said to herself, 'like a queen.' Reaching across the bed, she took the phone off the hook.

Adam emerged with dark wet curls, and a towel around his waist. He ran a hand through his hair to stop the dripping on his face and chest. Here was the moment of truth, he told himself with forced bravado, dropping the towel.

'Well,' said Annemieke, a single eyebrow aloft, 'we can work on it.'

'Can I have a drink?'

'Yes. Open some wine. There are some half bottles in the fridge.'

She watched him walk over to the fridge, and bending over, select a bottle. At first he exposed his rear insouciantly and she saw the slightly spotty cheeks and the dark furrow between them. The muscles in his flanks twitched once or twice as he lowered his knees.

'Red or white?'

'Red.'

'Okay. Here's the fellow.' All of this jolly repartee was to make him feel more at ease but it made her feel uncomfortable. They were not what the English called 'mates'.

'So, pour me a glass, take some for yourself, and then come over here and let's get started.'

He glanced at her quickly in the mirror and saw the decline of the skin from her cheeks to her neck, the ragged skin tone of her upper chest. Her breasts were ample but looked elsewhere for their interest, they settled down low, ready for a bedtime story. Her stomach had runways of activity and although she was not out of shape, nor was she fat, there was something about her that failed to rouse him. He absolutely forbade himself to think about his mother. Or Jan. He could place himself in his mind's eye at a party or in a bar, telling the story. 'So did you get it up, then?' 'Well, it was a bit hit and miss but I came through.' Or, 'Well, after I nearly set fire to her old man's Bible, I fiddled about with the corkscrew, then I made my excuses and left.' Then for some reason, just as he whipped the cork from the bottle, he thought of George's wife Dorothy. He recalled the same facial expression — disappointment, underscored many times.

Was this what women wanted? Was this really any sort of recompense? Or was she, as she said, like a man? No chance of a stiffy now. He barged into the chair with the shorts over it.

'Come over here,' she said, shifting on the bed. She looked a proper hausfrau with a frown and her nose like a chewed toffee.

He drank back his own glass and handed the other to her. Standing on her left side, his penis hung down like a bell pull, she could use it to summon room service.

She sipped her wine noisily and handed him the glass to put down.

'You sure you want to go through with it?' he asked, putting his own glass alongside hers on the bedside table, then added, 'Hang on; there's a noise out there. Maybe it's Jan?'

Her chest rose and she said, 'I want you to give me oral sex now.'

A great tidal wave of laughter rose in his chest and he slapped his hand to his face, covering his mouth, dragging down the skin below his eyes. Opening his eyes again to look at her he discerned fear in her eyes and he knew what this was all about – hope.

All right. He would go along with it. God help the pair of them. The money would come in handy. He could get his next flight with it. Move on. He went to the end of the bed and knelt there, looking up at her as she parted her legs. He squinted upwards with an appraising eye like a chimney sweep and cleared his throat, twice, before starting to kiss her lower legs gently and ruefully as he made his ascent. Fortunately she smelt of soap. It could have been anyone. Not Jan's wife, not his mum, not Dorothy . . .

He pretended a sudden fit of delight at the discovery of her lower thighs and threw himself into kissing them, making the appreciative noises of a dinner guest. Her legs spread further apart and her mons pubis loomed before him, a dead end. Hastily, he felt down between his own legs to see if he couldn't give himself a bit of a hand, and was comforted by the warmth and familiarity of the connection made. With his other hand, he began to stroke and tap her pubic hair and his mouth continued to kiss her thigh but, unable to think straight, he kissed the same place repeatedly.

Annemieke was anxious; she was beginning to feel unlovely. With a sudden jerking action she opened her legs further.

He could ignore it no longer. Adam fell upon her and did his manly best, his spare hand still at work below. 'It's not her, it's someone else,' he was telling himself, but the smell of her took him elsewhere, not to previous girlfriends, nor to anywhere else organic, but to the smell of the Bible he'd opened.

Annemieke lay quite still, as if she were at the spa, and he supposed he should continue until she told him otherwise. He had no idea whether she was enjoying herself; her pubic mound rose a little, at one point, and then lowered again. He kept at it in a reasonably conservative way. When, at last, he had a hard-on, he held on to it firmly. Suddenly her back arched and she started to mumble something about 'wanting it', he felt a shudder through his cheeks as she pushed his face against her, both hands on the back of his head, and then she said to him, 'That's it.'

He understood. He rose on his knees and entered her, the back of his hand wiping his mouth, and he didn't look at her until he was in full rhythm. She was silent. When he looked down she had her head way back, she'd thrown the pillow aside, and her tits moved sullenly and out of time but her body seemed grateful enough, and yes, at last, it could have been anybody. But just for safety's sake, he kept in mind Charlotte, the tall, endlessly-legged, perpetually amused young Caribbean mother.

When he came, he sighed with relief and slumped a little but did not fall on top of her into an embrace and opening his eyes after a moment he saw her looking at him.

'Get off me now,' she said, looking aside.

'What's the matter?' he said, whisking himself aside, his tongue touching the tip of a hair between his teeth.

She didn't answer. Oh Jesus, he said to himself, removing the hair surreptitiously. He'd been here before. He knew what it meant.

There was a sudden noise at the door, a card was inserted and removed from the lock and the door shook a little.

'That's Jan,' said Adam.

'No,' she said, 'it can't be.'

The door scuffed and stuck on the carpet but eventually gave way and she heard a voice saying, 'Hello? Hello? Anyone at home?'

47

When Laurie laughed, she laughed hard and bright, her teeth exposed, 'Har, har, har!' They were sitting on the stairs of the church, side by side.

Jan had been to Hong Kong with Annemieke and had been repulsed by the Cantonese with their spittle hawking, their brutal way of addressing each other, their constant stewing of all the worst smells in the world. He had felt as if he bathed in the steam of a bubbling pot of congee when they toured the streets. When he thought of Hong Kong, he recalled the fetid smell of the dried shrimps, little maggoty orange things, loaded into baskets and left in the carbon monoxide air of the streets outside the stores. He'd not been well at the time, having just come out the other side of some chemotherapy, nausea had been constantly at the back of his throat. While he was in recovery from early surgery on his chest, she'd come to his bedside, flicked through some women's magazines she'd brought with her and pointed out an article which explained that pain was formally described in hospitals on a scale of one to ten, with ten, the worst, being described as that of labour. He had probably got towards a four, she conceded.

Laurie was still laughing, covering her mouth with her hand. He had made her laugh by offering her his impressions of Hong Kong. But his mind had scuttled crab-like out of the alleyways of Hong Kong and along the hospital corridors of Brugge.

'Where there is dirt, where there is disorder, where there is noise, there is life,' she told him. 'This is a well-known saying among the Cantonese. It is a very colourful people, you are true. We have bad language and we shout it. If we can use a bad word, we do so. One *gweilo*, he asked me to translate a meeting we had with some of his suppliers, he was a client of mine, and I told him what had been said, more or less. He said he recognized a bad word, and I told him they'd said I would be a toothless old bitch sucking white men's dicks before they dropped their prices and that it was well known that my mother got fucked by dogs.'

Again she laughed as hard as a boy.

'I miss Hong Kong,' she said, as if she were confiding in him, 'I came to Europe to forget Hong Kong for a few weeks and then I could not be bothered with Europe so I came to America and then I did not like America so I came here. Now I know I will go back to Hong Kong next. To face the music.'

'What music?'

'This is a British expression,' she said, moving across the space between them to sit next to him. She scratched her knee tentatively, causing a thin white mark.

'I have missed Chinese New Year,' she said, lowering her face on to her hands, her elbows on her thighs. 'Crazy place,' she said in a whisper, *'tchi-sin.'*

They looked across the brick path to the dried grass of the lawn before the church gate, part of a white picket fence. Dust blew in little effete gusts and settled back down. Across the main street, a spring-loaded windowless door opened and a man stood as if about to leave the makeshift bar there, then changed his mind. Suddenly a woman emerged, swaying with evident pain in her hips and went down the wooden stairs to the small store below, opened it up and disappeared inside. She re-emerged with cigarettes and a bottle and went back up the stairs with the same slow discomfort. It was hot and airless.

'I left my husband, you see,' said Laurie, 'and I started a

relationship with an Australian, a client of mine. But my children, who are at secondary school, they would not speak to me and they stayed with their father. Hong Kong is very conservative and we bring our children up to be the same, to fit in, to work hard, to honour their parents, so this is not strange. My parents also would not speak to me; my mother, she closed the door in my face. Soon, all the things that made me love that man seemed to be like nothing at all. I crashed my car driving down from The Peak one night. I was hurt and went to hospital. After that I ordered my plane tickets for Europe and as soon as I was able to walk I left for the airport.'

'Oh,' he said. 'What are you going to do when you get back?'

'Maybe I won't go back.'

'But you seem to miss it so much.'

'True. But I don't know if I can go back. Because the people I love,' she paused, 'are not able to love me. Nobody, not him, the Australian, not my husband, not the children, not the parents, nobody came to the hospital. The Australian, you see, Brett his name was, horrible name, I had just finished my relationship with him and was moving out. So that's why he did not come. But the others could have come.'

'But Laurie, perhaps they knew that you were fine or perhaps they were told not to visit because you were not well . . .'

She shook her head and looked at him momentarily, then the pupils of her eyes rose up to the sky like dark kites.

'No,' she said.

'They are angry with you but if you say sorry, they will forgive you.'

She nodded without conviction.

'That's conditional.'

'That's all there is, conditional love.'

'Why did you ask me for help?'

He was sitting with a hand around each kneecap. She placed

a hand on each of his. He didn't move, he wanted to be touched, to be held in one place, he wanted to submit to someone else's life, their needs.

'That kind of hope doesn't die,' he admitted, 'not really, no matter what your mind tells you. Or your experience. That's the human conundrum.' He looked away, across to the store, and saw the heavy old woman accompanying a suited old man out to his car. He could hardly walk, and his hand kept saluting an invisible friend. She sat him down in the back of the car and he passed out with his legs hanging outside the open door. She brushed herself down and went back inside.

'I know you are dying,' she said.

'Oh.'

'Bill told me this.'

'How does he know?'

'Your wife told him.'

He emitted a breath through his nose, it was almost a cynical sort of laugh, he didn't know whether he was peeved or nervous. More bad news to come, he thought, for sure.

'Do you love your wife?'

'I don't know.'

'Does she love you?'

He shook his head. 'I've no idea.'

'Would you like to go to Paris with me?'

He ran his hand over his face, to give himself time to answer her. 'I would, but it's not possible.'

'Why not, Jan, what have you got to lose . . . ?'

'It's more you I'm thinking of,' he said, 'I take morphine every day now and they say when you do that it is just a matter of time.' He looked down at the church steps upon which they sat and registered the location as a wry thought.

'When time is short, it is easy to love, I'm sure that we can.' He was amazed at her honesty. He looked at her and saw the otherness of her face. Before he'd seen her as a Chinese woman who was unlike her kind, soft and original, now he looked at her again and saw how oriental she was to him with her blunt expression full of candour and sense, she was watching him, gauging him. 'And then when you are gone, I will have been loved. I will have been loved without conditions. You will be able to do that, I think.'

Seeing that his face was in disarray, she pressed her point home, 'This will be a highest love, because you are dying.'

'Oh Laurie,' he blurted out, standing up, shaking the dust of the church steps from him, 'if I wasn't dying or if you didn't know I was ...'

'No,' she said, with a wrinkle forming between her eyebrows, 'this is the way it is meant to be.'

He got up and paced around in a circle, mimicking the lone car that he saw going around the roundabout. He didn't know what to make of this, he felt sore inside, as if he had been taken advantage of. This was sudden, suddenly. If he went along with his faith, faith in the kind of person he had perceived her to be, then he would grasp her real meaning. She was offering him love; she was saying she could love him, after all. He stopped to look at her. She was sat like a teenager, hugging her skirt so as not to show her underwear. She smiled up at him with the canny readiness a young girl offers a schoolteacher in anticipation of good grades.

'Well?'

'Let me think about it. There is so much to think about.'

48

'You could have knocked,' said Adam, securing his towel.

'What is it, what's going on?' Jason was asking from the doorway. He saw Adam's head, 'I knew it . . .' He made to come in but with an arm outstretched Burns said quickly to him,

'I cannot allow you to come in, Mr Ryder.'

'What is it, what is it?' Jason asked again.

Suddenly a great sob rose up from Annemieke and turning to her, both Adam and Burns saw her with the sheets pulled up around her, crying. 'Real tears,' thought Adam. Her shoulders started to shake and her teeth chattered. Both men stood stock-still looking at her. Adam thought of her at the pool with her glasses up and down and her arch looks. Bitch, he thought. Burns turned to look at Adam with savage accusation in his eyes.

'Oh, don't lay it on so thick,' Adam said to her.

'Mrs De Groot,' said Burns, 'you'd better tell me what's going on here. You're very upset and I wouldn't want to jump to any conclusions but this doesn't look like a happy scene . . .'

Jason stepped into the room and stood alongside Burns with his arms folded across his chest.

'It's obvious what's been going on,' he said, turning squarely towards Adam.

'I asked you to remain outside,' said Burns. 'Now, Mrs De Groot . . .'

She nodded quickly and wiped her eyes on the white sheet.

'I don't really know,' she said, 'I had a drink or two, and

Adam offered to see me back to the room, I wasn't feeling well. My husband is very sick.' A new crop of sobs burst forth and Burns rushed to soothe her, saying, 'It's all right,' a few times until she had control of herself enough to go on.

'Anyway, I suppose I went to bed, and the next thing, this man is on top of me.' She screwed up her eyes and wiped her face with her hands, dragging lines of mascara down her face.

'He has raped her!' Jason said.

'Bullshit,' said Adam, 'she asked me to have sex with her . . .'

'So a sexual act has taken place,' said Burns, 'you admit that . . .'

'Oh God!' Annemieke wailed.

'She asked me to,' Adam repeated, feeling tears pricking his own eyes, 'the crazy bitch offered to pay me for sex . . .'

'That's not likely,' said Jason dryly, turning to put a hand on Burns's arm. 'You need to call the police.'

Burns stood still.

'Call the police.'

'No,' Burns said, freeing his arm from Jason's grip. He walked over to the door and closed it gently, then he came back to them, frowning.

'We need clothes on, we need to calm down and we need common sense,' he said, addressing the three of them. 'Then we'll meet in my office and if anyone wants to change their story, that will be fine. This will remain completely confidential.'

'This woman has been raped!' said Jason. He looked at her with disgust. 'She probably needs medical attention,' he added quietly.

'Yes, I suppose so,' said Burns.

'You don't want to get sued . . .' Jason said.

'But a half-hour won't change that.'

'Evidence,' Jason said with a hiss, 'samples, swabs . . .'

'He admits he had sex with her,' Burns pointed out.

'She asked me to,' said Adam once more. 'Why else would I have had sex with her?' Annemieke stopped sniffing and opened her mouth as if to say something. She shut it fast. Slow as molten lava, the hardening of her chin continued over the landscape of her lower face, engulfing her nose first and moving on, forming a single rock-face.

'We'll take a half-hour on it,' said Burns. In a half-hour it might all just go away. He'd have time for a drink. 'Now, not a word to anyone, any of you.' He went to the door to usher out Adam, then stepped into the bathroom to take a robe from it. 'Here, cover yourself up with this, then you'd better grab your clothes.'

'I don't know what your problem is, fellow,' he said as they walked towards the elevator, 'but you like trouble. I don't know what went on in there, but I've got an idea. I saw you two together last night. I'm not running a knocking shop here.' When the elevator doors opened the old lady and her young black beau stepped out. He was carrying a string bag containing newspaper-wrapped souvenirs. 'We'll have a proper English tea down at The Regal, later,' she was saying to him.

Meanwhile Jason was standing back from the bed, his eyes still averted, his mouth turned down at the corners as if it had tasted something sour, 'If you're okay, I'll be going, there's not much a man can do. I can ask Missy to come by if you like.'

'No,' said Annemieke brusquely, 'please do not.'

Jason nodded and made for the door. He'd never liked the woman.

49

The group stopped at a beachfront restaurant on their way back down to the resort, took teas and coffees and some cake and then continued driving down the western coast of the island. They remarked how the local people made use of the vast resource of the sea, washing in the waters daily, clothed. George and Dorothy told them how they'd seen this in first light down at the beach every day.

'Fancy keeping their clothes on,' said Dorothy.

'Och, just because you're a seasoned skinny-dipper,' said Bill, 'you mustn't judge others by your own wantonness, Dorothy.'

'I'm surprised their clothes don't shrink,' she'd gone on. 'Still, I don't suppose they wear woollens much.'

Laurie and Jan had exchanged looks and laughed. Gazing out of the window, watching the local people watching them moving at a snail's pace through a hamlet, Jan considered again what Laurie had said; a higher love, because he was dying. One peculiar comment should not serve to change his opinion of a person. Of what importance was the dying factor, primary or secondary? Did it matter? he *was* after all dying, it was a fact. He was too cynical. It was an offer of love. He might once have been a believer, he might still. He caught Bill's eye in the driving mirror.

Dorothy began to whisper to Laurie, loud enough for them all to hear, 'I say, he was a terrible show-off to the Vicar. Telling him all about *his* war, you know.' She rolled her eyes. Laurie smiled. George, who could not turn around on account of his bad back, sighed.

'I can hear you.'

'He wouldn't let me get a word in edgewise.'

'Give it a rest, dear,' George said, impatiently.

''Course, we all know what he was doing in *his* war. Trying to get off with Italian girls.'

George's neck was immobile, his hands moved to steady himself, one on the window frame, the other on the dashboard. Bill started to speak, 'I'm sure he had your picture . . .'

'I don't think the Vicar liked me,' Dorothy was going on, tapping Laurie's arm. 'Do you know, he didn't give me the time of day, not so much as a how do you do. These men stick together . . .'

Jan was uncomfortable; the car seemed very small suddenly. He heard George sigh once more, this time with anger. Bill put a hand on the old man's arm and gave it a pat.

'I always get left out of everything. But that's our lot, us women, isn't it?' Dorothy went on. Laurie said nothing, she murmured a little, indistinctly, giving sympathy without agreement. Out of the hamlet, the car went at a brisker pace through the countryside and there was a breeze.

'He likes to show off, that's his trouble. Likes the sound of his own voice.' She gave a little false laugh.

It was too much for George, who did his level best to turn in his seat but was constrained by the seat belt. Almost gagging, he spat out, 'Hark who's talking, you silly old cow.'

Jan dipped his head so as not to see. Laurie reached for his hand and squeezed it. He returned the pressure.

'I'll tell you what went on in there. We was having a nice time. The Vicar was talking to you more than half the time. He must have heard you say the same thing three times, about how your girls were both at university. Three times. It was all I could do not to stop you going on like that. Carol was at Southampton umpteen years ago. Jeanette, well, she must have left Bristol in 1971. Every time he and I got to exchange a few words, up you pop with the same load of old codswallop. How you can sit there and say them things about that nice man, I can't fathom. I don't know.'

'That's right,' she said, 'show me up in front of everyone.'

He took a deep breath.

'You show yourself up,' he said grimly, 'don't need me to do it, my dear.'

Laurie interupted, 'Another glorious day, is it ever grey . . .'

'I'll be gone soon enough,' Dorothy went on.

'Yes, all right, we've heard it all before,' said George, making a sudden laborious half-stand and shifting his sitting position.

'Won't be long now.'

'No, won't be long.'

They fell silent. When they reached the resort, Bill pulled up alongside reception and said he'd let them all out there then park the car. Jan stepped round to open the door for Dorothy.

'Oh, thank you, young man,' she said with affected pleasure and from the way she looked at him Jan could not tell whether he was a stranger to her or whether she was playing. Holding her underneath her forearm he took her up the steps. Glancing back, he saw George sitting still, rigid in fact, inside the car and so when Laurie joined them, he proposed they take Dorothy out by the pool for a lemonade.

'It's hard,' Bill said.

'Yes,' George replied, looking ahead of him. 'I'll come with you. To park the car.'

'There's something wrong with her, George.'

'I've got to face up to it, I know that.'

'There's no point in treating her like, well, like she's normal but just being unreasonable. Do you follow me?'

'What would you do, then?' George asked, turning to face

Bill, chewing down on his teeth as Bill had noticed he did when he was in any way emotional, as if he were trying to stop his feelings, to check them.

'I don't know, my friend. You should ask a doctor that when you get home.'

George nodded. 'Get her on some pills, I expect,' he said.

'Maybe.' Bill put the car into first and they moved off around the courtyard towards the parking area.

'It's going to get worse, you know, that's what the doc said.'

'The Lord won't give us more than we can bear, George.'

They pulled into a space and, slowly, George opened his door and using both hands hauled himself out of the car. 'My bloody back,' he said, by way of explanation.

50

'Mr De Groot?' The manager stepped forward from his office, briskly, 'Might I have a word, in private.'

Jan looked surprised and uncertain; he was still holding Dorothy by one arm. He turned to both ladies. 'Can you excuse me for a few minutes?' he asked, directing his question at Laurie.

'Yes, you've been very nice, thank you,' Dorothy piped up, and she and Laurie continued towards the front terraces.

Burns stood, back against his dark wood door, waving Jan inside. He closed the door behind him and offered Jan a seat.

'Mr De Groot,' he said, heading quickly for his own chair, 'we've had a very nasty incident while you were out.'

Jan raised his eyebrows, 'Oh yes?'

Burns licked his lips and gave a half-smile. 'Your wife, Mr De Groot . . .'

'She is all right?'

'Well, no, I suppose not. She has been sexually molested.'

A small smile tugged at one side of Jan's mouth.

'This is not a funny joke, Mr Burns?'

'No. Call me Steve.'

'But what has happened? I thought she was with the Americans today? Was it one of them?' Jan leaned forward and Burns was grateful for the man's self-control. He applied himself to the subject of his wife's assault with an almost academic concentration.

'Yes, certainly. She's fine, first of all. The incident has just occurred. She is in your room. I asked her to come here when she is ready.'

'Is that possible? Is she not hurt?'

'She seems fine,' Burns said, then corrected himself, 'externally, um, physically, I mean. Psychologically I suppose it's another matter . . .'

'Yes, yes,' said Jan. 'Who did this?'

'Adam Watts. A casual employee here. You know him.'

'Yes, I do.' Jan sat back in his chair. He looked at the reproduction explorer maps framed on the walls behind Burns. Maps of Africa, with the edges deliberately burnt and tatty. He thought of the young man with his long dirty blond hair and easy-going smile. 'But I cannot believe that he is capable of such a thing,' Jan said, removing his spectacles and blinking. He wiped the dust of the road from his eyes and put his spectacles in his pocket. He looked very tired indeed. Burns thought of the morphine.

'Would you like a drink, Mr De Groot?'

Jan shook his head.

'And yet my wife says he raped her? How? When?'

'This lunchtime. We walked in on them. You see, Mr Ryder came up to me saying she had failed to join them that morning and the phone was off the hook. He thought it was suspicious and would I check on her, so we went up and I knocked and entered. Anyway it seems as if she had a couple at lunchtime, drinks that is, and he took advantage of her. When she was sleeping.' He added, 'She wasn't feeling well, our barman tells me, and so she went back to her room to sleep, with Adam Watts accompanying her. Perhaps he was just walking her back on account of her feeling a bit rough.'

Jan lowered his head to look down between his feet at the floor.

Burns was looking at him, a pen horizontal to the desk between two forefingers and thumbs. Jan rubbed his brow and gave a long sigh, shaking his head.

'What is one to make of this, Mr Burns?'

Burns hesitated.

'I would understand if you wanted to press charges . . .'

Jan stretched his lips and shook his head again, 'I shouldn't think so, Mr Burns. I should talk with my wife . . .'

There was a knock at the door and a woman's voice said, 'I have Mrs De Groot with me, Sir.'

Burns stood up and wiped his clammy hands on his khaki rear. 'I asked Amanda to go and see how she was doing and bring her here when she was all set. I would like to hear her side of the story.'

'Sure,' said Jan, his head continuing to nod like the bough of a tree under heavy rain. Comforted by his own rhythm, Jan was still nodding when he felt his wife's hands on his shoulders. He rose slowly and embraced her, stroking her hair and feeling the damp through the chest of his shirt. He said nothing, but patted her to the same tempo of his nodding. When they pulled apart from each other, he asked her if she was all right and she shook her head.

'Oh, Jan,' she said, 'I feel so dirty . . .'

Jan hushed her and took her back into his arms, looking at Burns, looking at the maps on the wall, looking at the papers on the desk.

'What are we going to do?' she asked her husband.

'Shhh,' he murmured, and he had in his mind the image of holding a pillow over her face and whispering sweet words as he did so.

Burns blushed. He cleared his throat and gathered the few papers he had on his desk to find a notepad.

'Perhaps we should establish what actually happened first,' he said, chancing upon a pen.

He indicated the other chair and Annemieke took her place alongside her husband.

Thin-lipped, she began. She closed her eyes and took a breath, 'He walked me back to the room. I was feeling shaky . . .'

'Benjamin said the same thing,' Burns added.

'Who?'

'The barman.'

'I felt awful. Headache. And so Adam he offered to walk me back, in case I fainted, you see.'

Jan was looking at his wife attentively, nodding gently still, as if hearing his child make her case to the headmaster, his will pushing the right story forwards.

'I undressed. I supposed he had gone, but you see, I was in such a bad way, I just wanted to get in the bed and be still. You know how it is, Jan. When I have those headaches.'

'Certainly.'

'I must have passed out. With the pain. And when I woke, I've no idea when it was because I didn't look at the clock, he was . . . he was on top of me. He was . . .' Burns gave a wincing flat smile and mouthed an apology to Jan, 'he was inside me. I felt him there and so I told him, "No!" I know I said that. But he didn't stop until he was done. And then you came in, thank God. I am grateful to you, Mr Burns, because I thought he might start again, who knows what could have happened?' She used the tissues balled between her hands to wipe her eyes roughly.

Jan was silent. Annemieke turned to him and said, 'Are you going to sit there and say nothing?'

'What will you have me to say?' he asked, his accent thick as he spoke in the grammar of his own language.

'What would any man say?'

'I don't know.'

'No, I see that. And not for the first time I see that,' she said, her eyes bulging red with tears, her mouth aghast. A great croak of a cry formed across her mouth as a bubble of saliva, stretched taut; it burst and sobs emerged from behind it.

'Mr Watts does not deny that they had sexual intercourse,' Burns said, cringing.

'I see,' said Jan. He went to take his wife's hand but she snatched it back.

'About pressing charges, Mr and Mrs De Groot . . .'

'My own husband will not support me,' Annemieke began, 'I am alone in this matter . . .'

'Annemieke, this is not the case. Do you want to press charges?'

'I want your support . . .'

'I do support you, I have always supported you, all your life . . .'

'And for you to believe me.'

Jan demurred, his head down, and made a small soft sound that was not a clear word.

'Yes,' she went on, the timbre of her voice inconsistent, 'yes, to believe me.'

Burns blushed again. Nobody ought to hear such conversations between a man and wife. There was their whole history before him, making a sad naked procession through his office. He saw in minute detail how their marriage had been, he saw in his mind's eye the imprint that two bodies lying apart left in bed sheets, saw a man's clothes left on the floor, saw a scar in a cupboard door where a screw had come out, a travel bag half-packed on the floor. He could imagine the great events that coupled themselves with details such as these; the christening for which there'd been no cake on account of an unresolved argument about something else entirely, the first day of school of their first child that came and went with no film in the camera, he saw the car bypassing the shops on the wedding anniversary. He heard the drone of the TV that softened all of these blows. He had no idea where their connubial successes lay. Things come together as often as things fall apart, he supposed lamely, the sun must have shone, hands had been held, a joke would have struck both of them at the same time, the children must have said cute things, surely. His own ideas of success, so poignant and vivid to him, were single, individually achieved, though widely appreciated. They were like TV commercials for expensive cars. One day, he promised himself, he would be on an American freeway, his passport and a single bag on the passenger seat, with his foot on the gas of a performance car, he would stop as and when he liked.

'He won't say anything,' the wife declared to no avail. Jan's face was firm. There was no jury. There was Steve Burns. She looked at him suddenly with hatred that it should be him there, in front of them. 'He doesn't believe me.'

'Of course he believes you,' Burns spoke up suddenly, surprised that he should care. 'We'd best not rush in stupidly, that's all. Of course he believes you. We both do.'

Jan looked up at him too. 'We believe you,' Burns repeated.

'They say this is what happens; they say it is like this in all the magazines, but I would never have believed it. It is because I am a woman.' She recalled Jason's expression in the room. 'You consider me unclean. Dirty.'

Jan looked at her. 'No, Annemieke.'

'Yes, I am filthy, used goods, all used up. An old woman who has been violated, I am worthless in your scheme of things. I can no longer make children. I am empty and dry and now I am dirty too . . .'

'No,' both men protested.

'If you knew, if you knew how I'd suffered, what I've been through,' she was shaking the cumbersome words out through the narrow opening of her mouth, she was making no distinction between the men at whom she shook them, 'every month, killing our babies.'

Burns wanted a drink, he felt for the drawer handle of his desk.

'What are you talking about?' Jan asked her, his hands on the desk in front of him.

'The IUD,' she said, 'the coil. I have read in my magazine that it works by making an abortion. I never knew this. Now I understand why every month I felt like killing myself. This thing, they don't tell you how it works. It stops the fertilized egg from embedding itself. Terminations, deaths every month, that is how it works! This is why I have been so unhappy, all the time. So unhappy. My own body was killing. All that life going down the toilet, it goes against a woman's nature, it destroys her, it's an abomination . . .'

She was becoming unhinged, Burns surmised. He quickly took out the bottle and unscrewed the top.

'A nip,' he said, 'she needs a nip.' He went to fetch three paper cups from the water cooler.

'Annemieke, you exaggerate,' Jan said, looking up at Burns.

'We are Catholics, we were born so,' she said, tears spilling off her chin.

'Stop, you are hysterical, you are not well,' Jan held the paper cup to her lip and she took a sip noisily.

'All around me is death and now this,' she said, 'I tell you this, Jan, the greatest sadness of all is that you don't believe me, you deny me, after a lifetime together. We might as well never have been, we have nothing to show for it all.'

'Of course I want to believe you, but what if it is not as you think it is?' He drank his own measure and felt the heat abrasive in his chest, 'what am I to do? We must have some standard of behaviour; or rather I must have,' he concluded.

Burns threw his own double measure to the back of his throat and swallowed.

'Look, let's not get carried away right now, we don't have to say one thing or another,' he said. 'I shall speak to Adam, get his side of things, I'm bound to do that, you know. We'll take it from there. Wherever you want to take it, I mean. Sleep on it, why don't you? We should all sleep on it.'

He ushered them out with soothing noises, offered to send a meal up to their room, closed the door.

He sat back behind his desk and looked at the three empty paper cups, then he poured himself another dose. He thought how the cups looked like hospital cups, the kind one used for the water one took with pills. The husband was dying. It was bad. He reached for the phone and dialled England. He waited to hear his mother enumerate the phone number he had known since he was a child.

51

Jan had a little Valium in his medicine kit. He suggested she take it and that they both sleep. She thanked him formally. She went to take it in the bathroom. It was an eccentricity of hers that she could not bear to be watched taking medicine. If she vomited, she vomited alone and woe betide anyone who tried to comfort her, she would turn on him or either of the boys like a wild animal. Similarly her female functions, he had assumed, had taken place sensibly. She never spoke of them; he saw no ephemera, no wrappings, no debris.

Hysteria, he reflected, sitting in the chair by the balcony, for he would not lie on the bed, derived its meaning from the Greek for 'womb', it was an affliction therefore of the womb-man. He closed his eyes, he was exhausted. She had suggested that her menses had culminated in slaughter for the majority of her fruitful life. He thought of the coil. He had never seen one, but he imagined it to be spring-like. He thought of the helter-skelter on the pier at Blankenberge, saw thousands of little toddlers, fat-legged, arms holding on to the sides, falling into the sea. To one woman it might be nothing, to another it might be everything. We live in the dark; perhaps we do die into the light, he thought.

'Jan.' His wife was lying fully clothed on the bed, holding a small face towel in her hands, crying quietly. 'Do you believe me?'

'Believe,' he repeated, opening one eye. 'Is that really what you need from me?'

She shook her head and dabbed at the corners of her eyes.

She lay on her side and stared fixedly beyond him at the French windows. 'There has to be something to show for the years,' she said. He gave her a murmur as his reply. It meant simply that he'd heard her.

After a while her breathing slowed and she shuddered and closed her eyes. Soon, he heard the soft snores of sedation and he was relieved to be alone again. He was very tired. He had lots to think about, Adam and Dorothy, Laurie and Annemieke, George and Bill, Burns too, but he was exhausted.

He went with heavy steps towards the bed and lay down beside her on the far side. He took off each shoe with the toes of the other foot and brought his knees up behind hers. He put out a tentative hand, splayed and wide, over her lower belly and touched her.

'*Mijn vrouw. . .*'

She stirred a little and licked her lips, then, feeling him close by, she felt down for his hand and put her own on top of his.

52

Neither Jason nor Missy could sleep, despite a bottle of wine shared and a brandy each too. Jason lay on their bed reading various business magazines he'd bought at reception. Missy was in the bathroom, she had been in there for some time and in trying not to listen he found his attention diverted from what he was reading. He heard one or two little coughs and then the flush of the toilet. She came out smelling of her perfume and wearing a neat thin-strapped short nightdress. Her hair was wet and brushed smooth, it looked like caramel sauce, dripping on to her vanilla skin.

'I can't help but think it could have been you,' he said to her, looking up from his magazine. His features were reflective, reasonable, his mind had come straight from an appraisal of the last quarter's domestic performance. He was considering dumping some retail stock.

'Don't,' she said, with a shudder, as she went to the cupboard with her day's clothes, folding them once more.

'That guy needs some time in an American jail, if you ask me.'

'Yes.'

'It makes me think of what Jerry was saying on the yacht. You never know, you can never be secure.'

'It scares me,' she said, sitting beside him, leaning in to him and putting a hand on his stomach. Automatically, he breathed in, then relaxed. He had been overweight as a young man; he was committed to the gym and to a high protein diet. 'Who can you trust?' she asked.

Whether she wanted an answer or not, he felt bound to give one. They had been married for three years; she looked up to him. He found her esteem very stimulating.

'It's complicated,' he said, putting aside his reading material. 'You see, we need to put serious money behind the drive to seek out miscreants and put them away.' (He liked to say 'we' when he talked about his country, just as he liked the financial planning program he had on his computer to be linked to his hand-held.) 'Offenders are dealt with pretty persuasively, I would say. More so than in other countries. We have more people in prisons per capita than in any other country, I think, except maybe Russia. But we shouldn't overburden our resources. Taxes, you see, honey. We are in a difficult position, stuck between the freedom of the economy and the need to secure our society. Of course individual liberty is the highest value,' he caught a glimpse of himself in the mirror now that he was sitting up and saw the firmness of his chin, the lean shape of his face – he was convinced and convincing. 'Yet some people do not deserve to share in it and we have to isolate them. It's a paradox, hon. Our freedom depends on the removal of others' freedom.'

Missy closed her eyes momentarily and sighed. 'I understand that,' she said as if the burden of it all fell on their very shoulders, 'but freedom is just stuff, isn't it? No wonder we all get so depressed.'

'What do you mean?' he said, rising to get himself a drink and some nuts from the minibar. He saw the chocolate bars in there and considered that one, shared, wouldn't hurt. He poured an Irish cream and took out a Snickers bar.

'Well, I was thinking today, about that woman's husband. He's dying. When he's gone, he's gone. Right? I guess she'll think of this vacation. I mean, his legacy, or any of ours, it's so *nothing*, isn't it? She can give his things, jewellery, watches, clothes I guess, to the children if they have any, but when he's gone he's gone. You know what kids are like. I lost my mother's wedding ring. The only bits of him left will be in their memories, hers and the family. And they're not real. People get confused. So why do we make such a big deal of individual economic opportunity when it doesn't last . . .'

She petered out.

'So that we can be free, Missy! To choose the way we live our lives.'

She frowned, she looked sick as though she had a bad stomach.

'I don't know what that means exactly,' she said.

'You'd know if you hadn't got it! That's the problem. You're glad you don't live in China, am I right?'

'Oh sure – I guess I'm just all shook up by this thing. The violence. What if he'd killed her?'

Women were emotional; men were practical, he was glad that it was now quite acceptable to say as much. They had both read *Men are from Mars* . . . and found it very helpful. They'd bought it for each other's parents, last Christmas, as a joke, sort of. He should, and did, interpret what she said as an emotional reaction to the day's events. She was a sensitive person, not in a showy way; she was not artistic, just feminine.

'Come here,' he said, walking towards where she sat at the end of the bed. He put his arms round her and pulled her in to his chest. 'You know, Missy,' he said, sitting beside her, 'I would kill the man that ever came anywhere close to doing a thing like that to you. It's never going to happen, I won't let it. I'm mad as hell that it happened here, on our vacation. Mad as hell that you have to go through this. This whole resort has been a serious disappointment. Next year we'll go to Dad's place in West Palm Beach.'

She didn't mind being a child. She raised sombre, serious

eyes to him and said, 'We'll always have each other, won't we? Nothing can take you away from me. You'll always love me.'

He applied her face to his shoulder and looked over her at the half-eaten Snickers bar on top of the television. He ought to throw it in the trash.

53

George called Jan at seven and asked to meet him for breakfast out by the pool. When Jan arrived, leaving Annemieke still sound asleep in the room, he saw that George was dressed in long trousers and a checked shirt, as opposed to his normal great flapping shorts and colourful shirts. He was sitting in front of a full cup of tea, still, with his head towards the horizon.

'I don't much relish this,' he said when Jan had ordered some coffee to wake himself up with. 'I am a go-between this morning.' He pushed his cup of tea aside.

Jan inclined his head. 'You are?'

'Adam asked me to speak to you.'

'Oh.' The coffee was bitter; as it hit Jan's stomach it turned to bile. He had taken his regular amount of morphine and the pain in his lower back was diminishing, but for some reason his stomach was particularly sensitive today.

'Straight off the bat, I want to tell you this,' George leaned forward and took off his glasses. The paucity of colour around his eyes was shocking, it was as if two cups had been removed from a varnished surface, removing the top coat, 'I think what he done was wrong, no matter what his reasons were. A terrible thing and I no longer consider him a friend, in fact I'd rather have nothing more to do with him and I told him as much last night when he asked me to come to his place as a matter of urgency. I got Bill to give me a lift there, I had to take the missus with me or, well, you know. But I did not share my business with either of them. I said to Bill, straight like, can you do me a favour and ask no questions and he said he could.'

The coffee had done its worst, Jan's mouth was dry, already his tongue tasted like the back of a postage stamp. He took a sip of his water. 'Please tell me what you have to tell me,' he said.

'I spoke with him, in private at seven p.m.,' said George, looking down as if reading from notes. 'He told me, and these are his words, son, that Mrs De Groot asked him to have sex with her and offered him one hundred and fifty dollars, American, to do so.'

George swallowed and took a deep breath. He replaced his glasses and looked at Jan. Jan said nothing.

'I know, mate, I know,' George said, now reaching for his tea and take a noisy sip. He emitted a cursory 'ah,' and went on, 'it don't make sense, none of it. But he says he never forced her. She was what they call a consenting party, he says.' George looked the other way.

Jan blanched.

'I didn't want to come and say this to you. I told him, it ain't right even if it is true. I've always been someone on the side of truth but is it right?' George shook his head, his eyes still averted.

'The truth is important,' said Jan.

'I don't know,' George continued.

'For you, I know that. For me also.'

George shook his head.

'I shall support my wife, George, no matter what happened.'

'That's right.'

Jan got up to go back to the room. 'It's ridiculous really, George, that everything seems to hang on this, for Annemieke and me, our family.'

'I'm sorry to bring this rubbish to you, Jan. I was asked to and I did so. I'm on your side. What he done was wrong, even if what he says is true. I've a good mind to wring his neck myself for putting a decent man like yourself through this.' George was looking up at him with red eyes.

'No,' Jan protested, putting a hand on his shoulder, casting a shadow over him, 'no, my friend, don't get upset about it.'

54

Dorothy was waiting for George in the room. She had something she needed to tell him. She considered writing it down. Now that she had her mind on it she ought to write it and put it somewhere just in case. But she couldn't think where to put it. She wished he'd hurry back.

When she heard the door open she was all ready for him but he spoke first.

'Terrible mess all of this, dear, I don't mind telling you, I feel rotten, all broke up. To have to tell a man what I had to say to that Jan. Well, you wouldn't wish it on your worst enemy.'

So she forgot what she had been going to tell him but she told herself, well it can't have been that important if you've forgotten it, but this thought that used to give her comfort was now hollow like a lie and her heart felt as painful as if it had been raked, for it was possible she had in fact forgotten something vital, something without which they couldn't survive, but in any case they set off for their customary walk on the beach.

They saw a lone swimmer, making his way with strong ample movements back to the shore, and as he approached them he waved.

'Who is it then, love?' George asked, squinting, he needed to have his glasses checked when he got home, his eyesight was worse.

'It's that Bill,' she said.

'Jolly good,' said George, patting her hand. They stood still.

Bill came out of the water with uneasy steps, swaying as the tide was rough that morning.

'Now that takes it out of a fellow,' he said, panting. He leaned forward, his hands on his hips, to catch his breath, 'When are yous leaving?'

'Day after tomorrow, first thing.'

Bill nodded, 'I'm off tomorrow so I thought I ought to make the most of it. I'm going to Ireland to see some friends, maybe for a month or two. Given it will be almost summer it ought to be freezing cold.'

'That's what I miss though, a good nip in the air, a bite to it,' said George.

'Do you mind if we sit? I'm knackered.'

'We'll join you,' said George and the three of them made for a long piece of wood set further back on the beach. George helped Dorothy to a sitting position before lowering himself. The bough creaked and rolled a little but all three of them managed to sit on it, tentatively at first, the men with their calf muscles taut, looking at the sea.

'It'll be nice for you to go home again,' said Dorothy. Bill leaned forward and smiled at her.

'It will.'

'Now home's what I call paradise. Not this. I like what I know,' said George, 'you can have too much of this sun and sea stuff. Good weather all the time, it gives you the pill. What I'm looking forward to is the wind, the rain. Always busy, the weather is at home; always against you, pushing you, nagging you. Like a wife – you might not like it but you need it. You don't get that cosy feeling of being in your own home, here, do you?'

They stared at the sea, churning itself on to the sand, a clean beach, managed by the resort, and a picture-perfect sky, with just a few little clouds like the manes of small white ponies at a canter.

'The family. Warmth, good food, clean beds. A cake coming out of the oven, maybe even a game of cards or Scrabble. Tea don't taste the same here. It's the water, and the milk. And the tea.

'What I like at night is the English silence, no bleeding crickets, just the noise of the house creaking a bit until the morning and then you can hear the outside, all a-twitter.'

'I can always hear our old Robin Redbreast, can't I, George? I can pick him out when we're still in bed having our first cup.'

'Yes, you've got good hearing, duck.'

'I like to listen out for the birds. Hear their news,' Dorothy smiled.

'I've always been an early riser,' George went on. 'See, really I like to rise about five, creep downstairs in the quiet, with the new day all for me. I sit with a mug of tea at the front window, waiting for it all to start. There's your paradise, right there. You know you've got it right. Family, work, you've provided, done the decent thing, you can see it like that when you get up early.'

'Oh yes,' Dorothy agreed, 'that's the main thing.'

'Well, for me, the main thing is good company,' said Bill. 'It used to be that it was Jerry and me with the papers, busy, as though it were our world, reading about this and that in America or Europe. Precious time. Though I didn't know it then.'

They were quiet, sat on the Caribbean beach, each thinking of their departures.

'It's been nice to have someone to talk to. I shall miss you and Jan,' said George.

Bill looked at him, 'So will I,' he said.

'And the ladies,' George added.

'We shan't miss that Annemieke, though,' said Dorothy, making a face.

George raised his eyebrows and muttered, 'Big mouth.'

'She's a handful,' Bill laughed.

'Wicked is the word,' Dorothy went on, 'I'll speak as I find. Her husband on his last legs and her putting it about,' she looked briefly unsure of her terminology but went on. 'Why couldn't she wait?'

Bill flushed. 'What's been going on then?' he asked.

George sighed. 'It's not really for us to say. But seeing's the wife's gone and spilt most of the beans.' He altered the position of his legs. 'Mrs De Groot has accused Adam of raping her. He says, on the other hand, that she wanted to pay him for sex. The upshot is that Jan has to consider whether to press charges or not and so far he hasn't said he will. Adam asked me to put his story to Jan this morning and so I did, against my will I should tell you.'

'God save us,' said Bill.

Dorothy nodded with a serene smile on her face, crossing her legs at the ankle.

'What's the poor man to do?' George asked, taking off his glasses and wiping them on his shirt.

'So what's the truth of it?' Bill asked. George shrugged.

'She's a sly one,' Dorothy said, 'a fox.'

'I don't know,' said George, 'I barely know the lady. Usually the rules are that you take the lady's word, don't you? Jan wouldn't say to me what he knew, if anything. He said he'd stand by his wife, of course.'

'But Adam? He might be a bit of a boozer, but he seems like a decent young man ...'

'Well, he doesn't deny having sex with her and that gets my goat, fancy doing that to Jan,' said George. 'I said to him last night, I said, What was you thinking of? Was you thinking at all? He says he needed the money. I'm through with the lad, I tell you.' George coloured quickly and wiped his glasses again, looking down at his shirt-tails. His lower face seemed to have slipped inches.

Bill said nothing.

'What do you think? You're the Christian. What's the right thing to do?'

'Ach, Christians are the worst for knowing what to do,' Bill said.

'I suppose so, but you know your Bible, don't you?'

'Somewhat,' said Bill.

'Well, you must do, better than me anyway. What's the right thing?'

'Och, Jesus, man, I'm out of my depth here,' said Bill, rising, 'out of my depth. I'd better go and get myself some clothes on. I'll see you both later. Have a nice morning, now.'

The two old people sat watching Bill go, with lurching footsteps on account of the deep sand at the rear of the beach. Making it to the concrete steps, he hauled himself up, step by step, until he gathered a towel from the stand at the top, wrapped it around his waist and made off.

'He got a bit shirty, didn't he?' mused George. 'Do you think he was upset with me?'

'Mmm,' murmured Dorothy then she emitted a sudden little cry and turned to him. He looked at her, alarmed.

'All right?'

'I've just remembered what I've been meaning to say to you,' Dorothy said, reaching for his hand. 'George? I know something's wrong with me, George, and you know it is, don't you?'

George frowned, 'Don't let's talk about that now, leave it till we get home.'

'I'd rather talk about it while I can, George, I might forget it otherwise. I wanted to explain a bit.' He relented and nodded, looking her in the eyes now.

'You see, it's like I go in and out of the dark, George, I can't think straight, I can't remember things. I can feel a sort of silence closing in on me, like I'm going deaf. You know how when you're a kid you begin by picking out letters gradually and then you can read signs, then words and sentences. Well, it's like doing that backwards. It's like tidying up, or putting your money back in your purse, coin by coin, only thing is it seems like you can't choose what you're done with. I feel like I'm cramming the big notes back in, too quick . . .'

He squeezed her hand. 'I know, dear, I'm going to get the doctor to give you something for it when we get home.'

'I don't think that'll help much, George. I say to myself, I'm a bit scared but I'll be all right. I've had a good life . . .'

George squeezed her hand harder, 'No, no, don't start with that stuff, Dorothy, I can't stomach it.'

'It doesn't hurt, George, it's quite nice in a way, the darkness. I don't mind it. It feels like a bit of a rest.'

'Well, you must mind it, you must pull yourself together.'

She was quiet; she looked out at the sea.

'It's a lovely view. We shan't see anything like this again.'

'No.'

'It's you I worry about.'

'Well, concentrate on yourself, will you? You're the one that worries me.'

'We shall have to say our goodbyes one day.'

'We will, dear, but I ain't going to do it every bleeding day. You can't ask that of me. Now, I'm going to have a go at that breakfast buffet, take advantage of it while we're here,' he said, standing awkwardly. 'Come along, dear.' He gave her a hand up and they both groaned and shook themselves.

'We're a fine couple, aren't we?' she said, accepting his arm. 'We used to ice-skate as well!'

'On one occasion, we did,' he said. As they reached the foot of the stairs he took a moment to look back down at the sea, gathered strength from it and, with his wife leaning on him, he began to mount the stairs.

55

Burns wasn't sure where the opportunity was in this problem. He sat at his computer and erased the entire document he'd written on the subject. His mother had listened sympathetically to him and given him her homely thoughts.

'They say bad luck runs in threes . . .'

He asked himself, out loud, like an aspiring actor, 'What is my motivation here?' Did he want Adam in trouble? Not particularly, given that he was staff. Did he want to discredit the Dutch woman? Not particularly, he just wanted her to go away. He felt a little sorry for her poor husband who was supposedly on his way out. The man bore his trials and tribulations well. If it were him, he'd have been out of there. (A car commercial came to mind . . .) There was nothing to be gained either way. He considered that he could do what was right. But values and morals were mutable, they had a currency attached to them. As ever, he was torn between the reticent principles of his mother and the cunning amiability of his father; to offer something of himself which would later cause him resentment, or to be everybody's friend. His dad was a debtor, his mother a creditor. His dad was bought a drink in the public bar, he insisted he would pay it back and probably he meant it. But he didn't.

He supposed friendship was worth having. He knew he was a good person. Probably it was best for everybody if a man was without dogma.

He hated that bloody Jason, though. Prick. He would be all over this, of course. Letters and phone calls to Mark Cohen. He was the type who sent emails in capital letters. He'd be telling him how ineffective the manager was. First he fails to retrieve mad old biddy who goes walkabout, then he lets some hippy staff member grope the wife, and when the same man is accused the next day of raping a client, he sits twiddling his thumbs. Of course, the message would begin with a reminder of their friendship. What was the American equivalent of 'mate'? Buddy. 'Hey Buddy-boy, have you got a problem down here . . .'

He ought to save his own arse. That was the first thing he should do. He'd call in that sad-sack De Groot fellow, find out what the latest was, insist on pressing charges, and then he'd be in good shape with Jason and his buddy. He'd send an email to Cohen, first of all, telling him how he had the company of a friend of his, tell him he'd had a situation and he'd dealt with it firmly.

He would bring in the police. He would brief the staff. He might do both at the same time and issue a statement to the guests. He would not sweep this one under the carpet. He would say, probably he would close the meeting with, 'I will not allow a violation in this hotel to go unpunished. A rapist must face the most serious consequences that the law can bring.'

He called up to the De Groots' room and spoke to Jan. He asked him to come down to his office at his earliest convenience, and said he hoped the wife was feeling better.

There was a knock at his door and the door opened a little; the sweaty Irishman poked his head into the room.

'A word, if you don't mind,' he said, looking nervous.

56

Annemieke would not look at Jan when he went back to the room. He had brought her a croissant and a roll. She turned away, asking him to pull the blinds back down. She was crying, silently, he could tell from her body movements. He knew why. It was not the 'rape'. It was not his lack of support. He suspected she was ashamed. And there was something else. There was him. He was part of all this emotion on her part. It made him feel more tenderly towards her than he had done before. He sat on the end of her bed and said nothing. After some time the phone rang and he went to answer it.

'Certainly I will,' was all that he said, and then he added, 'Fine.'

He went to put his hand on her shoulder but instead put both hands in his pockets and stood by the side of the bed.

'Burns wants to see me. He asks after you. He will want to know what we wish to do.'

She said nothing but sat up, blinking. He swallowed with difficulty for his mouth was very dry.

'Did that young man hurt you? Did something go wrong?'

She shook her head. He let himself out of the door.

As he came into the reception area, he saw Bill coming out of Burns's office. He raised his arm to greet him and was surprised that Bill feigned not to see him and moved with squeaking sneakers across the tiles to go out through the double doors.

57

Jan stood in front of Burns's desk. Burns was busy and his mouth was down-turned, he looked pale and ill. He coughed like a sick man and then cleared his throat.

'Take a seat, Mr De Groot,' Burns said, using the mouse to shut down his computer, not looking at Jan.

'My wife and I, I suppose we will be pressing charges,' Jan said.

'I think we might need another nip of Scotch today, Mr De Groot.'

'No, thank you,' Jan replied.

Burns closed the drawer.

'If you wish to press charges against Adam Watts, then you should do so on your own behest at the local Police Station.'

Jan balked. 'I would prefer that you ask the police to come here and take a statement, if you don't mind.'

'Well, I'm afraid I'd rather not get the resort involved in this affair.'

'Don't talk nonsense, the attack has occurred on your property, committed by a member of your staff.' Jan tried to swallow.

'Would you like a glass of water?'

'Thank you.'

Burns went to the cooler. Poor man, he thought, waiting for the cup to fill. He padded back to the desk. He had taken his shoes off and was barefoot. He gave Jan the cup and perched on the corner of the desk nearest to him.

'Look, I won't beat around the bush, Mr De Groot,' (he

winced at the unfortunate turn of phrase), 'I'll come to the point. There are two stories. Both acknowledge that sex took place.'

Jan nodded and accomplished the swallow that had been eluding him all morning. The night's dose of morphine was drying him out.

'One account denies it was consenting. Your wife's. But there are no witnesses. Obviously. I have reason to believe, well, that she might not be credible, and I prefer not to involve the resort as I don't think we could support her side of the story.'

'What are you talking about?'

'More water?'

'No.'

Burns saw that the inner rims of Jan's eyes were red, they looked sore. His skin was yellow and dry on his face; only the bleaching of the curly hairs on his forearms indicated that he had had any sunshine. He had been good-looking once, in a formal way.

'Let me tell you the honest truth. Another resident here, a guest, came to me this morning and told me that he had had sexual relations with Mrs De Groot in the resort, recently.'

'But this is not true.'

Burns sat back on his chair and raised his eyebrows in surprise. 'Well, I can't think why anyone would make up such a thing. It sort of discredits your wife . . . you can see that, can't you?'

'It is a lie, to protect the young man.'

'I don't think so.'

'What do you mean, you don't think so? Your job is to protect your clients, not to judge what is true or not true.'

'Listen, Mr De Groot,' Burns sat forward, wringing his hands between his knees, looking into the man's eyes, 'it would be much better for you and your wife to let it drop.'

'My wife does not want to let it drop,' Jan bit down on his lip. 'Good God, man, who are you to judge me, to judge us, to look at us and say, this woman is a liar and her man, he is a fool?'

Burns saw that the man's eyes were bulging; his pupils were blurred behind a thickly watery surface.

'I saw the way she was dancing with Adam on Saturday night,' he said.

Jan looked at him, 'She is on holiday. She may dance!'

'That's not what I meant.'

'I am asking you to support us,' said Jan. A sudden flow of tear water to his eyes was costing him dearly; his throat was raw and dry. He coughed and hurt himself.

'I was going to call the police. But the only person apart from the two of them who can add anything is the fellow who told me he'd also had sex with her here. You know what the police would say; they'd say it was a question of character. Even here, for Christ's sake,' Burns insisted, getting up and making his way back to his chair. 'I don't know what went on between them, how do I know? It was probably somewhere between both of their stories. Listen, I don't even like the fellow . . .'

'You have judged us.'

'No,' Burns said, his voice rising, 'not you. Just what happened. I wish it was none of my business.'

'What shall I do?' Jan stood up and covered his face with his hands for a moment, the dark was pure comfort. When he took his hands away he felt the swat of air on his face from the overhead fan and the light from the window behind Burns, it was all too dry and too light.

'You should comfort her, you should get ready to go home.'

'Home?' Jan walked towards the door, nodding. If there was ever any home to go to, this would put paid to what remained. He turned on his heel as he opened the door, he heard the

singsong note of the computer on Burns's desk starting up
again.

'I was young like you once, I thought only in terms of doing
my job. You don't truly see how other people are when you are
young, you are not married, you have no children. It is all
theoretical. But things change.'

Burns stood up straight and opened out the palms of his
hands. 'I am sorry, Mr De Groot, honest to . . .'

'No, you are not. Not really.'

58

That night Jan proposed that they get out of the resort, hire a car or take the bus to have a look round the main town. He sat by the balcony leafing through the hotel compilation of brochures, circling things in pencil, preparing to make a call.

'I don't want to walk through reception with everyone looking at me and whispering.'

'No.' He closed the folder.

'And what if we bumped into *him*?'

'He's been fired. Burns will be taking care of that.'

'I shall stay in the room for the last few days of our final holiday together. I don't mind.'

'You know, I asked him to press charges on your behalf, Annemieke. It is his most serious advice not to do so.'

'Why? Why is it his serious advice?'

'Because it just is, it would be traumatic for you, hard to win,' Jan had said feebly, stepping out on to the balcony. On this occasion she got up from the bed and followed him out there. She looked quickly from him across the vista of the lawns and flowers and back again.

'He doesn't like me. Don't you think that if I was Jason Ryder's wife things would be very different?'

'Well, perhaps she would not be in this situation, Annemieke,' he said, his back against the railing, facing her. He arched his back; it hurt at the base of his spine, when he breathed in it seemed to catch painfully.

Tears sprang to her eyes and she pressed her lips together, gathering herself a moment before saying, 'I knew it would come out. You've always thought so little of me. You've always seen me as little more than a tart who cannot be trusted and should not be given any respect. You know, my mother was mortified when I brought you home. You know what she used to say to me when I called her crying, she said, "Next time marry someone of your own class." And I said, "There will be no next time; I have to make this work." She said to me, "Then for God's sake have affairs, find a man who can make you happy, you deserve to be happy." '

'And so you took her advice.'

'Only when all else failed.'

'That's some fine advice, coming from a mother.'

There was a knock at the door, quiet at first, then insistent. Jan looked at his watch, it was after seven p.m. and the beds had not been turned down. He looked at Annemieke and she waved him past her. He opened the door just enough to look through and was surprised to see Burns standing there. He stepped out of the room, holding the door behind his back.

'What is it?'

Burns took a deep breath.

'Mr De Groot, I came,' he took another breath, 'I came to tell you that I will give you my support, on behalf of the resort, I will call the police in and we can press charges if that is the course you want to take. I've changed my mind, I want to help you.' He raised his eyes from looking at Jan's hand holding on to the door knob and looked the man in the face. He saw there fatigue and despair. He felt sick to his stomach, sick with sorrow, overcome. It felt like being lovesick.

'I thank you,' Jan said, 'but it is no use, I think.' Burns opened his mouth to speak but Jan shook his head, 'and it is not necessary,' he said with a smile, 'nothing good can come of it.'

'For your wife's sake?'

'Nothing good can come of it.'

Burns had the sudden impression, seeing Jan at the door, holding it, of a man holding out against wrongdoing. He understood that this was an insight and was startled, he tried to hold on to it, to make sense of it, but as suddenly as it had come, the understanding was gone.

59

Annemieke would not leave the room the next day. She lay on the bed, mute and unmoving, while he was there. When he left the room, he waited outside for a while and heard the bed creak as she got up from it. He heard the TV emit the small but growing note of electronic euphoria, then he heard the bed creak again followed by the discordant sounds of channels being changed rapidly. When he returned in the late afternoon there was a room service tray outside the door and he saw the plucked twigs that had borne grapes, the rind of a cheese and an empty butter packet. There was a slice of cheesecake that had been robbed of its fruit topping. She was fine.

Jan had gone out on to the pool terrace, taken his shirt off and his shoes and sat on the end of a recliner. There was no one he recognized. He had hoped to see Laurie, hoped not to see any of the Americans; he was able to discern George, stepping out of the new annex. George turned back and with a hand steadying himself on the doorframe, he bent down to inspect the tiles. He came outside rubbing his forefinger on his thumb, saw Jan and tilted his head in recognition, then made towards him.

'Chalky, that grout,' he said, still rubbing fingertip on thumb. He popped his finger in his mouth to clean it and wiped his lips with his big dog's tongue.

'Looking forward to going home? I expect you feel like a bit of a rest, I know I do.'

'To be honest with you, I have been wondering what home I am going back to.'

'Oh. I see.'

'Yes.'

'Not so good then, things with the wife.'

'No.'

'Well, there's your boys at least.'

'They are their mother's sons.'

'My girls have always been most loving.'

'I was not a good father. Young men can be so busy with other things, their own life. I know I was. I used to resent taking them out, used to get irritable with their chatter. We were so eager to get on with our lives.'

'We're all the same, at that age.'

'The war, you know, we grew up with it in our faces and afterwards we were always pushing it back behind us. You know how they say it was the Americans who won the war but not us because afterwards all people wanted was the American lifestyle. Well, that's true, things changed. My people, they are quiet, modest but also perverse in a way. You speak to a Belgian and he'll shake his head about the Nazis and then say to you, "But the French! The First War, that was much worse." They always remember how the French took charge then, the officers were French, the foot soldiers Belgians, "*Avant!*" they'd order and the Belgians, the Flemish speakers, would retreat. But this ill-will is because of pride, and for a modest people like mine to be so encumbered with this. Why? Who in their right minds could go on about the French when you look at what the Nazis did? They brought with them their anti-Semitism, and they took thousands of our men away to work in factories. My own father died in one. But no, the French are awful, my people say.

'Oh, we tidied everything up, as we always do in Belgium, we're used to being invaded and getting back to work. And men like me, we said, the war is all done, that was our fathers' business, let's make some money and make our families rich and let's not think about countries and ideologies. But perhaps we went too far.'

'Well, I've no time for ideologies myself. Real life is being lived while intellectuals are busy putting it into boxes. The wars were different; terrible both of them, but we was right with the Second one, right to fight it. Perhaps you could say we was lucky that the choices were so clear. We had God on our side, I expect. We had to take a stand against evil. We wanted to be with our families, of course we did, but we said that some things were more important than what we wanted.'

'Did you know the Jews were being killed?'

'We didn't get in it for that. Nor for the Polish and all the others. We had to stop the Nazis coming knocking on our front doors.'

Jan shook his head, 'I am really in the dark, you know.'

'You did what you did, mate. You shouldn't have to worry about the war; it was done and dusted before you could do anything about it. There was so much more opportunity about for you lot who was born afterwards. See, that was different with us. We worked, we worked but we couldn't make nothing. We was always selling up stuff. The war changed a lot. People didn't go to church so much, they went drinking. We'd lost the empire and all, but still those years after the war there was the Welfare State and making sure we looked after our own. I'm proud to collect my pension. It's right. I put the time in. I tell you something. We had nothing; nobody had two shillings to rub together. Do you know, most families back then, if they sold up all they had, wouldn't have got no more than a hundred quid for it. Funny, ain't it?'

'My family rose to be ready for when the sun came up, we worked together to maintain the farm. By ten in the evening we were all exhausted – no one asked what we would do next

– we slept, my brothers and I in the one bed and my sister in another. George, all of the people we knew were farmers, like us. They traded amongst themselves in a village of some five thousand people, a complete economy. Only the doctor asked for immediate payment, you know, and sometimes of course he would forgo this. Each year proceeded as it should, holy days and so on. There was the summer's hard work, piles of pancakes at the end of the summer when the harvest was done, the killing and salting of pork for the winter. Each day had its schedule too, the first meal at sunup, the second meal was at nine in the morning, some bread and lard or jam, lunch was at midday, pork and potatoes, and maybe an apple cake, then there was a slice of bread again in the evening with cheese. Twenty, thirty years later it was all gone.'

'A way of life went, didn't it?'

'We had a different life. But I don't think I was really much good at the new ways. Certainly my wife and I would have been better if we had just settled with being a business partnership, in the old way of things. I never really took the time to understand Annemieke or to find a way of getting along with her; I think I saw it as a retirement project.'

'Well, I suppose you made a mess of things, didn't you . . .'

Jan smiled; he now understood that English phrase 'cold comfort'. He was used to receiving tepid advice rather than cold comfort. The way George spoke to him, with a dour gravity, felt fatherly. He took him seriously. Jan had been a lifetime without a father.

'Yes. It is strange, you expect that death will meet you halfway, even now I do. I hoped, coming here, to get a reconciliation with my wife that I could take home with me, share with the boys too. You don't think that death will come when you know that you've made a mess of things.'

'It's your kids what affect you the most. You ought to set

things straight with the boys. Do what you need to do. My girls know how I feel. I shan't go making a song or dance about it before I go. I don't want to say goodbye. I don't want to be sitting with my bags packed, waiting. Makes me a bit nervy.'

'It's been a long-drawn-out anticlimax. I never liked birthdays either. You tell yourself you deserve some finer feelings from those people around you, you ask yourself why they are not kinder to you, you become bitter. This is what has caused my sons to distance themselves from me, I believe, the bitterness.'

George sighed. 'Don't know what to tell you, mate, except I wish for it to come like a bolt out of the blue. And I know it's selfish but I was expecting it would be me first. Now, I don't know. It's like she's gone already; walking and talking, but she's on her way out, you can see that. Anyway, I've decided to write my memoirs. For the kids. Jot down the past before she can do a runner with what's left of it.'

'Good idea,' Jan said, with a smile. 'What about a drink at the bar, my turn?'

George looked at his bare arm as if it bore a watch. 'It's time,' he said. 'We could have a spot of that pizza too.'

'Pizza. A good English dish, I hear, like lasagne.'

'No, it's Italian, son,' said George, going ahead.

60

Sat in the armchair next to slightly parted French doors, Jan made notes in his book. He was noting the effect of the 'holiday', the temporary evacuation. 'The movement is circular,' he wrote, 'it allows for a reconciliation of man's liberal imagination with his conservative constitution.' It appeared to him that the need to holiday was part of the human condition, an agreeable palliative for an ailment mankind barely knows how to complain about; the life we have made.

He watched as Annemieke began packing. George and Dorothy had begun the same day. Bill had already started to stow one or two of his Hawaiian shirts. He no longer put his underpants in a bag to be laundered but let them fester in the corner of the wardrobe, transferring them to the zipped compartment of his suitcase on Monday afternoon for the sake of the room maids. Jason and Missy held out for any final fine dining, keeping the exact number of outfits hanging, but by Tuesday afternoon, Missy was going about the folding of Jason's better shirts with the solicitousness of a new mother.

A couple of days remained, yet the holiday was over for their group. They were marking time, each dragging himself or herself between pool and bar the way a dog turns about itself to settle in the same place.

At dinner and at the bar, at lunchtime and in the evening, Jason turned expectantly to his cellphone, seeking messages where there were none, worrying out loud that the system was at fault. Bill offered to lend him his own and Jason looked at him as if Bill were in some way stealing from him.

Bill stowed the phone back in its leatherette crocodile-look soft case and turned it off. He finished his drinks alone those last nights.

Laurie was spending a couple of days on snorkelling expeditions. She was tired when she came back in the evenings. After a coffee at the bar, and an inquiry regarding their mutual friends, she went to bed, determined, she said, to be in good form for the return journey.

'Where to?' Bill had asked her, as nonchalant as a big ruddy Irishman could be.

She'd shrugged, 'Ah, New York,' she said, 'just for a week or so.'

'That's a fine place to do some thinking,' he'd said.

'Any place is fine for that.'

'How about coming along to Belfast?' he'd said, making it sound like a joke. She gave a single hard fast laugh, the noise of a suitcase being slapped shut.

61

Lying by the pool, face down, his back like a tombstone, Jan remembered the real world. Flanders. The northern fields, apparently still and yet moving when you got close to the earth, put your nose to it. With his eyes closed, he saw the baked mud of the farmyard in the summer, a brown oasis where he had lain as a child in the place the dog had chosen, having pushed the mutt away to listen to the pulse of the land.

The land had been his to take, by the handful, freely. As a child he knew every square kilometre. His was a kingdom of mud that checked the spread of grass. He played in it, wet and dry, knew it by type, from woodland humus-rich or field-dry like a watercolour palette of one colour, ready to be made into paint with a lick. He could hear the music of the earth, the grains of dirt on the narrow ridge of his teeth as he removed mud from under his fingernails.

Now, with the sun burning through his thin hair, he lay, a grown man in a sterile place, and heard again a shout or a laugh from his childhood, the breaking of the icy cracked waters of the pond and the thud of silence that came with each night, sleeping in a room with his brothers and his sister. They, like many others, forsook the church schools in the village and cycled there and back each day, and sometimes at lunchtime too. In a few years, hundreds of years of history were done away with and the state took over education and welfare in Northern Europe and supplanted family, community and church all at once. The modern age overcame them more forcibly and more unexpectedly than any of their many invaders. It was irresistible. The education was free. His brother became a doctor. No one had imagined that a farmer's son could be a doctor. The priest chided parents from the pulpit. But the Catholic Church was losing its grip. Few would choose to pay the weekly stipend of the local church school. Around the same time, electricity came to the village. The agricultural regions were late to it; it must have been the 1950s by the time the whole village had the benefit. At first lights were barely lit and the electric outlet was just here and there, often in places where it was not needed. His mother stood in the new light one evening, by the front door, held a book up to it and then got her chair to sit under it. But she turned it off after a few minutes, shaking her head.

Over the years, walking home from one of the bars in the village he saw more and more lights in the dark – false stars. In his earlier years, the village had lain quiet at night. Slowly at first and then with a momentum that was gathering by the late 1970s came televisions and telephones, and his ageing mother realized that what was far away was in their own home and what had been near, the quiet watching land, was remote.

The modern age had straddled them like a bully. But Jan was obdurate. His core was earthen. He would go back to the land.

He heard the soft sound of someone settling beside him, the slight giving way of the lounger next to his, and he felt a hand on his back, between his shoulder blades where it fitted, like a cup being put on a saucer. He did not stir. After a while he felt the draught as the hand was removed and he felt the absence more than he had felt the touch. He heard the shuffling of shoes being regained and only after a while did his hearing converge upon the sound of footfalls on the tiles, at a distance, going away. He turned his neck slightly and opened one eye to see Laurie making back towards the hotel. He was aware of a quickening of pain in his lower back and thought of the morphine in his room. He closed the eye and replaced his head where it had been, swallowed, and went back to the dark.

62

'I wanted to say goodbye, before I went,' said Bill.

Jan wiped his mouth and did not turn around. They were at breakfast. Opposite him, George put down his knife and fork. George's eyeballs, covered by the opalescent veneer of age, seemed even more fogged that morning. His expression was one of anticipation though; you could read his face like a book. Seeing hope at work behind every muscle in his friend's face, Jan considered what he should do. He had seen Bill coming out of Burns's office. There was no mistaking the man's guilty glance. He had intended to cut Bill. He had prepared for this very moment. But now he got up from the table, nodded and went to shake hands with Bill, to offer a parting.

'Can we speak?' Bill asked, holding the hand still. Jan nodded again and walked outside the breakfast room and across the corridor on to the terrace. 'I should have come to you before now,' said Bill, 'there's something I need to tell you.'

'No,' said Jan, extending his top lip a little and shaking his head. He looked down towards the hibiscus bushes and out towards the sea. The sky was riven with little clouds, like an old page torn at the sides. 'I know what you would like to say to me and I know why you would like to say it, to get things off your chest, but it's uncomfortable for me to listen to that.'

'Shall we have a coffee?' said Bill, shifting from one foot to the other at the side of Jan, his eyes on Jan's face.

'I have already had one.'

Bill let out a small sigh. 'You're right,' he said, 'it's for my sake. I feel just shocking, man. You see, it's as though I've acted against you, not once but twice, and I never meant to do so.'

Jan raised his eyebrows.

'I couldn't see the man go to jail, that's why I spoke to Burns.'

'It would not have come to that.'

'You can't be sure! And we don't know what the police force or the court system is like in this country. But more than that, Jan, I thought I should do what was right, in all conscience. I believe the man to be innocent.'

'Based on what?' Jan said, turning towards Bill. Bill looked away.

'Based on my knowledge of your wife.'

'You know my wife?'

'In a sense.' Bill was scarlet-faced, he was wet at his armpits, wet at the centre of his back.

'Enough to know she is a liar?'

'No, not exactly, but enough to know that she has a certain attitude to . . .'

'Sex. You had sex with my wife.'

'Yes.'

Jan looked away. 'What kind of Christianity is it that you practise?'

Bill looked down and shook his head. 'I didn't know she was married. I didn't know you.'

'You should not have tried to become my friend after doing something like that.'

'But why not? It was done with, it was meaningless. It was over, it would have been forgotten. But Jan, you and I, we became friends. Of course if I'd known you before I would never have done it.'

'Look, I have always known how my wife is.' He gave a short laugh and ran a hand over his face. 'As it happens it is not a complete disappointment, just more bad news. I am disappointed in you, Bill. Everything seems so false to me. There's more to it than you, though, there's what you *stood* for.'

'I know,' Bill said, meeting Jan's eyes.

Jan nodded slowly. 'I'm old and tired, because of the cancer I suppose. It's not about you, really, it's more to do with her, and with me,' he said. He looked up and saw George through the restaurant window watching them from the table. 'I'm not making sense. We're all wrong as far as I can see.'

'I'm sorry, Jan,' said Bill, 'truly I'm sorry, I wish it had never happened.'

Jan thought of Laurie briefly. Nothing had ever landed on his plate, and even if it had, he would have refused it, for having done so. He looked down at Bill's patent leather shoes.

'I didn't think you were an opportunist,' he said.

Bill looked miserable, he was chewing on the insides of his mouth and blinking. He extended his hand, 'Goodbye, Jan.'

63

It was one of the most religious countries to which Bill had ever travelled, and on his way to the airport he took every spire, every triangular shelter, every cross, every graveyard as a reproach. He clenched his eyes shut and when he opened them, the car turned up on to an ascent through sugar cane plantations towards the centre of the island and the sun reached out a finger and touched the interior of the car, the back seat. Tears rolled down Bill's cheeks, and he took a tissue from an ornate holder between the front seats and blew his nose.

A crucifix of dried palm leaves swung from the driving mirror. The driver looked in his mirror, his head jolting from side to side, to the beat of the evenly spaced potholes.

'Hard to leave,' he said.

Bill acknowledged him by lifting his head.

'You going back home? England?'

Bill shook his head, 'Ireland. Close.'

'Then you don't need to be sad. You look like a good man with a good life. Smile. No need for sadness.'

Bill told himself he was a fraud. Sitting there with money in his pocket, a passport too, as if he knew where he was going and had the means to get there. He could feel the suitcase in the trunk of the car as if it was hanging on his back. He felt too big for the car, too small for the world outside. Too stupid. Too wrong.

'I make my own sadness,' he said.

'What's that?' asked the driver.

Bill gave a slight shake of his head and looked out of the

window. There was a small fishing boat down on the beach,
above the shoreline, and it had been graffitied with the words,
'Jesus is beautiful.'

64

She slept with her head back and her mouth wide open, God bless her. She'd never had a lot of what you call feminine grace. Nor had she had what they call feminine wiles, to be fair. George watched her half emerge from her sleep, wipe the corner of her mouth on the paper cover on the headrest and snuffle back into what comfort she had. He shook his head and grinned. When the hostess came by he gave her a nudge and tapped the rim of his beer glass.

'I say, I'm parched, duck,' he said. 'It's the altitude, I expect. I get thirsty.'

'Would you like some water?' she asked, wide-eyed and kindly. He was used to being looked at like that. He could narrow the gap, even at his age, between that look of hers and the look she'd give a young man. He gave her his best smile, as if he were spruced up and aftershaved.

'No, dear, can't bear the stuff. A beer would be just right. And a whisky chaser if you can spare it.' He gave her a heavy wink.

'You sure you ought to?'

'I'm not as old as I look, love. I've had a hard life.'

'Oh yeah?' She poured the beer.

'There's that and I like to travel incognito. I've got a bit of a cosmetic disguise, you see. Underneath the skin's smooth as a baby's.'

'Fancy that.' She handed the beer glass along with the can and started putting ice into a plastic cup when George stopped her.

'No need for that, dear, takes up space, don't it?'

She gave a sigh. 'I suppose I'd better make it a double then.' She handed him a very large Scotch. 'Go on with you then, let's just say my hand slipped.'

'Now there's a thought!' George said, raising both eyebrows at the same time. She gave him one of those closed-mouthed sexy smiles, all secrets and twinkling eyes she was, and with the taste of the beer in his mouth and his hand on the glass of Scotch, he was a happy man.

He had their travel bag on his lap, with all the brochures, vouchers and ticket folios. He started to go through it, wondered if the young lady could use the vouchers. There was a free upgrade with any weekend car rental, a free dessert with any main course and children were included in the adult fares for the boat trips. They'd barely used anything, just the flight tickets. The travel agent itinerary had been unfolded and folded many times, almost daily. There was a plastic wallet for the traveller's cheques. He would be able to put them back in the bank. They'd not needed them. He'd paid for their extras with their bank card. One hundred and forty four pounds. He'd been careful; things were shocking expensive in a place like that. The first time they'd gone abroad on a trip they'd taken a lot of their own refreshments. Kept them on the window ledge of the hotel room as it had been nice and chilly in Ostend. Bought milk and cereal for their breakfasts, brought their own teabags, brought their own spoons. She'd gone and taken their own pillowcases, to make it feel more like home. He hadn't been fussed himself. Food and drink was one thing. He didn't need to take a bleeding teddy bear to cuddle, he told her. He'd explained it to her slowly, 'When you go away, it's a holiday ain't it, you do things different. We needn't do things the same way, at the same time,' but of course they'd ended up taking their lunch every day at one, their tea at four-thirty – sandwich and a bit of cake – a cuppa and a snack at seven and were in bed by nine-thirty. He'd looked out of the window when she was asleep and seen people strolling about round the square, beneath the window he could hear the soles of their shoes tapping upon the medieval cobbles. He'd watched how lightly a man or a woman would take the brass rail of a bar door in their hand and disappear from his view.

Still, they'd always had a bit of money saved up. They'd never been spendthrifts. She got a new wallet once every ten years or so. He'd only ever had three or so in his life. His indulgence was shoes. He bought a good pair every other year. His hands touched the sheets of paper he'd folded and inserted in the wallet, hotel paper upon which he'd started to write down his memoirs. He'd started from where they got married.

When we got married the wedding reception was held at my parents home in Enfield. We had about twenty friends and relatives. We had purchased a home via the Halifax building society with a down payment of £36 on the total price of £636. We had to pay £3.4.0 a month in repayments but our income was only £5 a week. I took a job with a refrigeration company in Turnpike Lane, mostly building cold rooms for butchers. The cold rooms were made of wood, one side covered with ply wood or sheet metal already spray painted white. We turned the hollow side up and cut slabs of cork to fit it, then sent for the man to cover the inside with hot pitch and then we placed cork slabs on this about 2 inches thick, then we put pitch and cork again and placed ply or metal panels on the same and the top and bottom were constructed the same. We put it together on the joinery floor bolting it all with 6 inch coach screws through holes and blocks already placed inside the body of the cold room sides and top. The base was done the same way but had a cement floor with a drain hole towards the rear. These bases were placed on carpenters stools and cemented on them so that Dick the cementer did not have to bend down as he was a portly man. After about a year I asked if it was possible to go outside assembling cold rooms in butchers' shops and I was told it was. I usually received a joint or chops as a tip.

The week after our wedding I was asked to go to Smethwick near Birmingham to refrigerate a moving belt on which baking tins were to be cooled down whilst passing through the freezer which I had to build while the belt was in motion and carrying hot tins. I did get some cakes given to me, mini chocolate rolls. I was there a week then back to my bride.

We couldn't afford a honeymoon what with the purchase of the house. I went to work at a church near Cockfosters. They had run out of money to build the church so we made a false wooden end to go on it. At this time my father was in ill health. He was 66 years of age. He was fading fast with Arterio Sclerosis, hardening of the arteries. He was my mentor, the man who taught me how to behave, and he gave me his love of music and woodwork, it endured a lifetime. One day the wife came to the church. My mate and I were fixing a large wooden cross to the end we were working on. I looked up the hill and saw her waving. I was off that scaffold quick as lightning; you see I dearly loved my father. When he died, my mother insisted on having a horse drawn hearse and carriages as she did not want to be seen to rush him off.

Then followed the war. With not much happening in the building trade, I joined the Enfield Fire Brigade, jumping out of 90 foot towers and rescuing people trapped in bombed buildings, and I used to fit out air raid shelters too, with my building experience. In 1942 I was called up for service in the forces and became a despatch rider in the Royal Signals in Ireland, then in Yorkshire, then Africa, Algeria. After a couple of years there I went to Italy until the war finished and had a marvellous time with my comrades. It was the time of my life.

After the war we decided we wanted an outside life. So we bought a nursery growing tomatoes, chrysanths and vegetables. We was pushed to make a living like that. Very few years at the nursery did we make any sort of profit but I was able to find work to help pay for it, driving mostly.

It was something, not everything. It was a list. He would write it like this for the grandchildren, so they would know how he'd done his part; that was the main thing.

It was about fifteen years after the war, when the elderly relatives that they'd looked after had one by one carked it, that he said to her, come on, let's get us two single beds. He'd been seeing the widow then. There wasn't any point in going on as they were. Might as well have his own space. And her mouth straight and grim as death she didn't raise an eyebrow, just said, 'As you please.' Meaning, you're the boss; which was her way of saying, I'm a slave to you, aren't I? He'd used to try to bring a smile, used to tease her, she had Irish ancestry see, so that was a joke between them for a time, in the early years. Once or twice he'd pinch her bum, come on a bit fresh when they were in the gardens together, he liked to watch her bend down to smell the tomatoes. 'There's a symmetry to that,' he'd say. Home-grown tomatoes. That's a smell you don't forget. Green smelling, with a sort of lovely straw to it, a bit like piddle. Never taste like that from the supermarket. She'd say 'Geddoff' in the years after the war and crack a smile. Then take the smile indoors with her and stick it in her pinny. She never encouraged anything to do with touching. She had her invalid mum to look after who was a right cow and just picked up where she'd left off before they met, making Dorothy's life a bloody misery. He never got mixed up in it. Perhaps he should have.

He looked at Dorothy, her mouth closed now, her head slumped on to her ample bosom. She'd been a smashing cook, from nothing much she could make a spread show up on the table. She was a wonderful mother too, she'd made all their clothes, knitted new sweaters for them every winter. She wasn't like that Dutch woman. She was a good 'un. A pal. He patted her hand, took it in his and smelt it for a minute. Bleach, even after two weeks away. He laughed.

He felt for the traveller's cheques wallet. Inside, there were a very thin couple of notes. He pulled them out. Two hundred quid. He could see that a few cheques had been detached. They'd only spent one hundred by traveller's cheque at the resort – the rest he'd done with their bank card. They'd started off with five. Two missing.

He went to nudge Dorothy, but stopped himself. What had she done with them? Perhaps they'd been nicked. He thought of the woman who'd looked after their room. No, he couldn't see it. Perhaps there'd been a break-in? Dorothy murmured something and when her lips settled they were out of place and ajar. He let her be.

65

'Ryder (junior) is an investor of sorts. He has an income, privately, and he uses it to play the markets mostly. Obvious stuff. I know his father better. Former Chairman of Nabisco. Big gun. Bad guy with a heart of gold. He's kind of somebody. His son isn't. How are your financials shaping up?' Burns filed the email message in his folder titled 'head honcho'. The information we need always seems to come after we need it, he reflected. He perused the financials on the Excel program, considered how the deduction of certain salaries might improve the bottom line, considered – with a quick spin of his chair, feet against the wall – how much work it might add to his lot and on a whim, went back to his email program to check incoming mail. There was a cosy-looking message from Joanne@hotlips.com entitled 'young girls crazy for you' which he deleted, there was a circular joke purporting to offer twenty differences between the sexes from a friend of his working in Birmingham; that was all. When he deleted every one of his mail folders, the keyboard chimed like a fruit machine. He could reverse the procedure. But it felt good to go naked, and he decided to make the entire desktop look as anonymous and enticing as if the machine were new. He dragged up his resignation letter, revised the formal gentlemanly tones of its statements (using much qualification he had explained how he was unsuited to the job) in favour of a more blunt version, and with a final 'hereby' omitted he looked at the two words that remained, 'I resign.' After that, he tidied away his real desktop, putting all the papers stacked in piles into drawers. He went through his in-tray and found a large hotel envelope with his name on it in old person's handwriting, complete with an 'Esq.'.

Opening it he found two smaller envelopes and a note to him. One of the envelopes was addressed to '*Adam Watts Esq.*' and the other to '*Charlotte, on Sugartown Road. (Adam knows the location.)*'.

> Dear Mr. Burns,
>   I should be very grateful if you would see that each of these envelopes gets delivered as soon as possible. With cordial thanks,
>   Mrs. Dorothy Davis.

As neither envelope was sealed, Burns was able to lift the flap and take a quick look at the contents. Inside each one was a traveller's cheque for a hundred pounds. He sat back in his chair and put his bare feet on his desk, crossing them at the ankles. He flexed his toes and smiled. The old girl's savings. Why Watts? he wondered. Perhaps she too owed him for services rendered. He grinned.

'It was like running a knocking shop,' this was what he'd say to the lads back home, over a beer. Running a real knocking shop would be fun, good clean fun, and he could make some money. And do some good, unburden a few sad souls. Now that was worth thinking about. He could do some research on line, starting with Miss Joanna Hotlips. He put one hand on his lap and the other on the mouse. Oddly, from nowhere, came to him the sudden and firm conviction that he should complete his commission for Mrs Davis. Joanna and the thousands like her, suspended in a sort of eternal limbo of apparent sexual surprise, all pursed lips and pink parts, well, they would wait.

66

They went through the darkness of the Caribbean night to the European daytime, the plane urging itself on through the night, hurrying home.

Annemieke was by the window, on her side, turned away from Jan. She considered the economy of her tears; emerging with the timing of hiccoughs, each tear made its way from her left eye, which was above the other, over her nose and fell into her right eye, gathering more mass and momentum before dropping out on to the armrest and beneath the seat. She lay like that for a few hours. No one could see her or hear her. Jan would have thought she was asleep.

They arrived in the morning in Brussels. The weather was typically Northern European, she saw, raising the shade on her window and looking at the miniature world below moving about its business. Landed on the tarmac, she saw the fine drizzle at the window. They went down the stairs to waiting buses. Sunshine can be ignored, forgotten, but rain penetrates. The baggage handlers had their collars up, they went about their business frowning, warding off the weather with efficiency.

Their eldest son, Marcus, was there to meet them and Jan took the front seat while Annemieke sat in the back. After they had answered his questions they turned each of them to their windows, examining the rain, watching fields shake hands with hedges and homes. Two or three times her son looked in the mirror to find her face. She gave him half an answer, no more.

When they were home, and her son had gone to pick up some milk and bread, she excused herself and made a phone call. Then she went back into the kitchen where Jan sat with a cup of lemon tea and told him what arrangements she proposed.

'You were busy those days, locked away in our hotel room,' he said. 'You have managed to create a new life.' They sat opposite each other at the small kitchen table at which they'd taken all their smaller meals for many years, breakfasts, teas, coffees, late-night drinks. 'I suppose there is nothing I can say now in any case.' He rose and went to lie down in the spare room, the one that had been Ben's, while she packed a bag in their bedroom.

'I don't want you to go,' he said, alone in the dark, next door.

When she heard her son in the kitchen she went to him and motioned that he should step outside. She held the door handle all the while she spoke, facing him, with her back to the home, the cold drizzle on her face. She explained that they were going to live apart, that she was going to be with André De Vries. He offered her whatever help she needed and gave her a solemn embrace. His face was drawn and dour, just like his father's.

'This is not a fairy-tale ending, but we must be sensible, I suppose,' he said as they stepped back inside out of the cold, 'we must do as you both wish. It has been hard for you, Mum. Personally I might wish you could have waited to the end;' then reading her face he added, 'but the end, it is true, has been a long time coming. Don't worry, we will all help you through this, both of you,' he added, looking up at the small ledge in their kitchen where she arranged the knick-knacks the family had accumulated in its lifetime. There were the children's handmade clay pots, a stray egg cup, framed photos of the grandparents, a Delft tile from her grandmother's kitchen, a vase the boys had bought her one birthday; the worthless brica-brac of any family. Then he ducked his head – he was over six foot – and stepped through the doorway into the rest of the house, calling softly, 'Father?' although his habit had been to call his father by his first name in recent years.

She heard the low tones of an exchange between them and Jan emerged with his hand on his son's back, ushering the young man out of the house, shaking his head and protesting that he would be fine.

'What did Marcus say to you?' she asked him.

'He said we ought to be happy here and now, we ought to forget about the past. He said nothing else mattered now.'

He turned his back on her with the pretext of going to get a book. In fact his son had embraced him and spoken apologetically. He'd said, 'I am so sorry for all of this. I feel terrible about it. We have all made mistakes, Dad. All of us. No parent is all wrong, no child all right. I hope you know that Ben and I, we love you.'

Jan had replied, 'You are the son; you are allowed to make mistakes. I hope you learn from mine.'

He looked at his son in that room with his mouth opening and closing between thoughts and he saw his own face unlined – cleaner, fresher, more noble, more peaceful. It might have been possible to escape himself, after all, once. He could have moved away from himself the way a foot moves out of a shoe.

67

Half an hour later, Annemieke let herself out of the kitchen door without saying further goodbyes, took their small car, a Renault Clio, and left him with the Audi. It hadn't been hard to pack. She had not taken her good things away with her to the Caribbean, they were fresh and folded in her drawers. She only needed enough for a few days. She was to meet André in the lobby of the Hotel Boudewijn on De Markt, in the centre of Brugge. He was there when she arrived, looking aghast, excited. They asked each other in turn if everything was all right and then they went directly to the room he had arranged; it was one of the best, with a view over the market square and a four-poster bed. There were English toiletries in the bathroom, thick towels and silken sheets and bedspread; there was even a fireplace, and a fire had been lit. She took off her clothes and put on a bathrobe while he watched her from an armchair, sitting in his ironed raincoat, his eyes serious as a cat's. After a bath she put on a La Perla nightgown, light brown with soft cream-coloured lace around the neck of it. She dabbed a spot of Jean Patou's 'Joy' on either wrist. Then she brushed and dried her hair in the bathroom and when she came out she saw that he was in boxer shorts, sitting on the bed, with a glass of champagne in his hand.

'A new life?' he asked, swallowing. She nodded and he took a filled glass from the bedside table and stretched across to hand it to her, holding his stomach in all the while, she saw. He looked her over as she drank. Then he took a deep breath through his nose. He saw that she wore diamonds in her ears, and a wine-coloured lipstick. He closed his eyes for a moment. As he undressed he'd looked at her Louis Vuitton carryall at the foot of the bed, he'd seen the stockings and fluffy slippers, some lingerie, and the soft fabrics of her folded outfits.

All of these things, the hotel room, the toiletries, the champagne, were the tokens of a formal love affair. It was not wrong. These objects served to establish a distance between them that constituted perfection. When he took her into bed alongside him, they would be strangers, allied only by this moment, with no claims upon each other.

'You want me, don't you,' she murmured into his ear as he moved over her. He silenced her by kissing her mouth with vigour.

68

When Jan quit Belgium he went by train from Brugge to Brussels and then on the fast train to Paris. From the train window, Belgium looked like a misplaced section of Eastern Europe, suffering cement raindrops blown over from Polish skies. He saw the small grey huts, beside the train tracks, innocent of purpose as if a board game had been abandoned; beyond them lay a lachrymose landscape, flat, grey. Churches that were never cathedrals despite their size were decked with scaffolding. It was green enough, the countryside, when you got up close to it, there were plenty of leaves, plenty of nettles and brambles. The houses were neat and unobtrusive. The 1960s and 1970s buildings with their conformist aspirations for 'one society' were of geometrically simple shapes, hewn in shades of pastel blue and brown. A wrought-iron balcony here and there hinted at Frenchness, but the windows were stained by acid-rain. Against this sobriety something silly would brush up occasionally. He noticed a rather risqué advertisement, with a double entendre tenuously linking the image of a woman's nipple to a car dealership, and a white delivery truck painted to depict a red-haired character, naked apart from a fig leaf promising that 'Willy Van Den Est' was holding a '*slaapfestival*'.

Aboard the train a group of four men barked and encouraged each other like billy goats, rearing up on their machismo. Their handlebar moustaches would have marked them as homosexual anywhere else in the world. Here, their well-kept women sat together across from them in another four, holding their words, their hands on their bags, practising to be widows.

Jan watched a handsome little girl who was sat alongside her heavyweight mother. The girl blue-eyed, heavy-lidded, solemn but fresh, the mother blown-out, dark-rooted and jaded. This woman sat with her eyes closed to preserve her energy; great ham shanks of arms were stacked atop her breasts. Her head slumped into her chest like a Big Top circus tent being let down.

Something in the stupor of the girl's eyes recalled a little German girl who used to play with his sons, her parents having moved from Hamburg into their suburb of Brugge. Even though she could only have been six or so when he knew her, the little girl unsettled him. She used to come round to their house and say in a frank way, 'I need something,' and her eyes were all of a reverie whilst her mouth proclaimed her need. Was it drink, food, a certain toy? A cookie surely? No, no, no. She would get herself into a state of agitation, with both boys quite lovestruck, and then, finally, she would take a lungful of air, and declare that that was it; she'd only needed air, after all.

He thought of Laurie, who was like the little girl, both in her directness and also her air of being puzzled by the body she had been trapped in, unsure of how to use it. Perhaps that was what made her lovely. When her eyes alighted upon you, for a moment, you thought that it might after all be you that she needed.

'After Madrid, I will be at the Hotel Trois Etoiles in Paris, for two weeks, then I will go back,' Laurie had told him, 'unless . . . well, unless I change my mind.' They had said their goodbyes in reception at the resort. When he saw her coming across the room to him, he had the sudden conviction that in a moment he could change everything, he had felt wild, as if he could choose life over death. When she came up close to him he felt his heart subside and submit, and he had to stand aside, to step around the pair of them, as if there were a tree falling.

He took a second to gather himself and he put out his hands in a gesture of almost avuncular warmth and forced a smile. 'European-style goodbye,' he had said, kissing her firmly on either cheek, taking his time, pressing her arms against her body.

'Goodbye?' she had queried, holding his arms still as he pulled back from her.

The daughter leaned across the table and her eyes considered the landscape that they were leaving behind, then she buried her ponytailed head into the 'M' shape she'd made with her arms on the table, closing off the light from her eyes.

His own children, two boys, adults now, pale and extreme as their mother, they were making respectable livings in this respectable country. That was something. Goodbye to all of them, he thought. Good luck to the girl.

69

There is a small family-run hotel on the Île St Louis in Paris that is less expensive than the big name hotels but nevertheless attempts its own ostentation. The lobby is crammed with delicate objects, vases with lids are placed on spindle-legged tables that shift as one passes, drawing attention to the precarious beauty of things made in the past. With his oversized suitcase, George was obliged to take the elevator to his room on the next floor. In his attempt to avoid the help of the young man from reception and his anxiety regarding the claustrophobic space and iron gating, George lost his temper.

'Just leave us alone, thank you, I can manage!' he instructed his helper.

'But of course, whatever you like, Monsieur,' said the young man with a wry smile.

'France is all right, but the bleeding French know it all, don't they?' said George, on the phone to Jeanette in his room. There was a tap at the door, followed by a few more taps, and George told his daughter to hold on while he went to it. It was the young man again.

'I hope, Sir, you will pardon me for my further assistance but you have left your wallet on the reception desk.'

George took the wallet from the man, nodded and closed the door.

'That was him again. I don't know who he is, do I. Works here. Pain in the neck. Anyway, duck, I'm here safely. The train ride was a real treat. I shall never forget that. Nice English fellow doing the food. They leave you alone, the

English. I like that. How's your mother? You're watching her then? Because she will take off, you know. Keep the door closed. She'll badger you about the keys and how she needs to get home now, but just be firm with her. Just you tell her, "You *are* at home." Keeping on about the bus to Tottenham. No, I'm not winding myself up; no, no, it's bloody hot in here. I'll have to open the windows. You and your sister went to see the residential home this morning, didn't you? Not bad, is it. Still if we all pull together we won't need it. Yes, of course we know it's there. That's a fact, ain't it? It ain't somewhere else, is it? 'Struth. I shan't stick her away while I'm fit and able, duck, let's not have an argument about it. Hold the line, just a moment, I can't take this perishing heat.'

He got up and took his jacket and tie off, then went to the window and threw it open. It was a grey, overcast day. A pigeon presented him with its profile and bobbed its head at him. 'Go on, dirty little bleeder, go on with you,' said George, waving an arm at the bird. He went back to the phone.

'No, it was a bird this time. A pigeon. Look, as I was saying, we can manage. Nobody knows how long for. I'm all right. This break will do me the world of good. You're a good girl to do me the favour. Just watch her for me, will you? I do worry.'

When they had finished speaking, he hung up the phone and lay back on the bed, looking at the mirrored door to the big dark wardrobe in front of him. He could see his two large feet, the shoes newly soled with good leather, and when he hoisted himself up on his elbows he saw the old man's face that occasionally took him by surprise. He looked at his watch. It was five in the afternoon. Jan was going to meet him there around seven and they would go out for supper. He could have a nap. But he didn't suppose he'd be in Paris again, so he raised himself, sluiced some water over his face at the hand basin and pocketed the room keys and his wallet, saying to himself, 'Silly old bugger, all we need is for me to start losing me marbles and all.' He let himself out of the door and went down the thickly carpeted stairs with his body at an angle on account of the narrowness of the stairwell.

He did his best to evade the young man on reception and was nearly out of the front door when the fellow hailed him, 'Monsieur! Monsieur!'

George turned heavily.

'Shall we keep the key here for you? It is normal.'

George went up to the desk and thanked him with gritted teeth.

'Monsieur?'

'What is it now?'

'It is raining. An umbrella?'

'No. I've got a hat, thank you. A hat's good enough,' and George took to the narrow pavement feeling in his pocket for his usual peaked cap and retrieving it with pride. He put it on his head and turned back to the door, pointing it out to the young man, through the glass.

He took a turn along the street upon which the hotel stood. The fine drizzle pleased him. He could see the *bateaux-mouches* through the gaps in the houses, making their way along the Seine with people pressed together inside. Popping his head into a few of the restaurants and bars, he noted one or two open fires, and low lamps, and discovered he had an appetite. He'd have a nice bit of steak for supper. '*Pas de cheval, merci.*' Jeanette had told him was how you said 'no horsemeat'. '*Pas de cheval,*' he said now, dodging a middle-aged woman. There was room on the pavements for only one pedestrian.

From a brightly lit toyshop a young woman emerged with

a stroller and tackled the step down on to the pavement with difficulty. George attempted to help her and she shone a smile on him that had him blush. Her child had a hat over his or her curls and sat with Wellington boots crossed at the heel in comfort and security, holding a wooden giraffe. He walked after them and when they stopped at a small park with a swing and a slide and a single bench, he stopped also and sat watching the mother push the child on the swing. When the child laughed, he laughed out loud himself and so he passed a happy fifteen minutes. The mother took the child out of the swing, coaxing it with a few words; the child made some tentative steps and broke into a short run straight towards George. He put his hands out, as if to catch the child, but it turned back the other way and ran off again. Still he sat with his hands out, his whole focus upon the child, concentrating on it not falling. His head was forward, his tongue on his lower lip, his calves tense. When they went, he got up and retraced his steps to the hotel.

Jan had checked in and was in his room. At his request, the young man placed a call to Mr De Groot's room and George took the receiver from him.

'Hallo, mate, thought you'd never get here. Yes, lovely trip, thanks. Ravenous now. I say, mate, I could eat a horse!' The young man sighed pointedly, George noticed. 'Have a wash up, yes, and we'll see each other down here, say, in half an hour. Splendid!'

He returned the receiver to the man with a terse, 'Thank you,' and made for the stairs. He was on the second or third step when the young man called him again.

'Your key, Monsieur.'

George would have put money on the beggar having waited until he was on the stairs. He took the keys with a snatch.

'Perhaps you can remember them when I'm still at the desk,

next time. I'm an old fellow, you see, it would help me out.'

'*De rien*, Monsieur, you are most welcome,' said the young man, in a cheerful tone, turning back to his logbook.

70

Two doors down from the hotel there was a restaurant with several small rooms, a central open fire, and menu boards posted around the place offering just two or three suggestions. George sniffed a little; 'Seems like they can't be bothered.' Jan suggested that it meant they might do the little they did rather well. 'Oh yes,' said George, 'there's that, of course.' He slathered the crusty white bread with butter and sat eating it, looking about the place and in particular at two young women by the window.

The place filled quickly and the loud conversation and background music obliged them to lean across the table to make themselves heard. Jan ordered a sweet white German wine for George, and a bottle of red too.

'I can't drink the whole lot, mate.'

'I'll be joining you.'

'Seems a lot of wine. Are you expecting company?' George nodded towards the table at the window and raised his eyebrows a few times, 'Eh?'

Jan watched as George ripped open a small sachet of sugar and poured most of it into his wineglass, stirring it round with the handle of his table knife. Catching Jan's look, George shook his head, 'Too sour, all the wines, they make them too sour. Why they can't do a nice sweet one I don't know.' Jan motioned at the waiter and said, *'Beaumes de Venise, s'il vous plaît.'*

'What's that you say?'

'I'll get you a wine you'll like.'

'Not more!'

'Why not?'

'Is it cheap in here then? I thought it looked a bit like someone's front room.'

'Why should we care about money tonight? Besides, I am paying.'

George shook his head, 'Can't let you do that, mate. Your missus, is she all right with you going away on a blokes' weekend, then?'

Jan took a large draught of his wine, nearly finishing the glass. Red wine – like blood. He felt replenished. The heat reached his brain quickly, sedated his anxiety and flooded the chambers of his heart at the same time, he exhaled into a smile.

'Oh, she doesn't mind,' he said, swinging his head, and then pushing his glasses back up the bridge of his nose.

'Jolly good,' said George, 'everything was all right once you got yourselves home, I suppose.'

The waiter brought their main courses, two very handsome steaks accompanied by French fries.

'*Mou-tarde, s'il vous plaît,*' George enunciated heavily, then blushed and stuck his neck out as if expecting a fight.

'When you got home, I was saying . . .'

'There is no place that is home,' said Jan, cocking his head and raising one eyebrow as he picked up his knife and fork.

'What's that? No, it goes, "There's no place *like* home."'

'Yes.'

'It means there's nowhere else as good.'

'How is your wife, dear Dorothy? She doesn't mind you coming away?'

'To see you? 'Course not. No, she's very pleased. It's a break for her too, ain't it? Chance to catch up with the girls. Watch the nonsense she likes on the TV, do her own thing . . .'

'She is well?'

'Oh yes. No better, no worse.'

Jan smiled to see the mustard fringing a few hairs of George's moustache.

'To be honest,' said George, walking his upper body forward on his elbows with knife and fork in either hand like ski poles, 'I was thinking you might have got in touch with that Laurie.'

'Why do you say that?'

George tapped the side of his nose with a forefinger. 'Keep my eyes open, don't I? You was pretty pally the two of you. She's a lovely lady.'

'Yes, that is correct, but it would complicate things too much.'

'I don't know about that. People always talk about things being complicated, don't they? I thought we was supposed to be getting it all easier nowadays. Load of nonsense. Well, it's not too late for you and her. I bet you've got her number.'

'No.'

'Well, you could call that Burns fellow, tell him you've got something of hers you'd like to return,' he gave a salacious grin, 'like her bra.'

Jan set his knife and fork aside and turned his full wineglass about between his fingers. 'I have thought of her, of course.' George nodded as he chewed. He had nearly finished his plate already. He ate like a wolf, hunkered down, slightly aggressive, not taking any chances. Jan thought to himself how it might have been Laurie sitting in George's place, popping a French fry into her perfectly lipsticked mouth, warming him with her flirtations, making his head swim faster than the wine. This adrenaline surged at the thought of it. He had dreamt about her since they came back, more than once. The dreams had spilled over into his daytime, leaving him anxious and heart-sore, as though something important was badly wrong, his mother was dying or his child was in hospital, only he could not recall what the thing was, he just felt troubled. He had felt so close to her in the dream, so bound to her.

George allowed a belch out of his mouth, sideways. It was loud, nevertheless.

'*Pardon, Monsieur*,' insisted one of the ladies at the table near the window. George turned about and gave them a cheery smile and a wave of the hand.

'Seems I'm not the only one with a touch of wind,' he said, taking a big swig of the wine, 'd'you hear her?' It was like taking a big boy out to dinner and giving him too much soda pop and too many doughnuts. 'Well, anyway, you could get her number. I could do it for you. I shall have to get in touch with that Burns fellow because I never got old Bill's number and I should like to give him a call or write to him.'

Jan said nothing.

'Nice fellow. I know you had a bit of a falling out. Never asked why, shan't ask now,' George paused while he applied more mustard to his plate, 'but he was a good sort. I talked to him about poor Dorothy, you know, her failing memory, and he said to me some very interesting things. He said he thought that the memory was like a kind of bank account. A savings account what you can't take out of. He said he thought that at the end of the day, it was the only thing we acquired in our lifetime of any value. Blow the car and the house; it's memory what counts. He said no wonder I was getting a bit upset about Dorothy, it was like she was robbing the bank. Our bank account. So anyway I thought to myself: well I'll just make sure to close the account and keep the loot myself, under the bed, so to speak, and that's when I started writing the memoirs. I've gone right back to when I was born, earliest memories. I've enjoyed it, and I'm bloody glad I'm doing it, because none of us know when we're going to pop our clogs, do we?'

Jan raised an eyebrow and shook his head, laid his knife and fork down beside the small neatly tailored piece of steak that remained alone on his oval plate.

'That's why I'm glad you and your missus are all right. See, you got your history, haven't you? That means something when you're getting on a bit.'

'For sure. Shall we get a dessert or some cheese?'

'Lovely bit of meat. Looked like rubbish but it was tender.' Jan saw that George's plate was clean apart from a smudge of mustard. 'I'm full, mate. I'll have a bit of pudding, though. What've they got?' They ordered a *Napoléon de la maison* for George and a coffee for Jan.

George was on his third glass of the dessert wine that Jan had ordered for him and he'd pushed the sugar basket aside. 'Now that's a good wine. Why can't they make them all that way?' He applied himself to the slice of cake set before him, with gusto, licking the spoon carefully, all of it, up to the handle. 'He liked you.'

'Who?'

'Bill. He really liked you, you know. He said some very nice things about you.'

'Yes. Oh, as you say, he was a good sort. A bit out of control, though.'

'He couldn't half eat, you're right there! Cor dear, he could shovel it down like there was no tomorrow, he could. He told me he got terrible heartburn. Shouldn't wonder. One night after dinner I slipped him a Rennies, brought it down from the room and we sat down and had a nightcap. I shan't forget what he said because I thought it was good. He said there were two types of people in the world – he said someone famous had said it but I can't recall who it was – the righteous who are sinners and the sinners who are righteous. He said he hoped he was in the latter but he probably wasn't because he thought about himself too much. He said that because you thought so little of yourself, God would raise you up. Funny way of putting it but you get the drift. Nice thing to say about a person.'

Jan laughed and put his hand over his mouth. His brow relaxed and he looked across at the open fire, watching the flickering of the flames that was repetitive but never the same. Will I think of fire? Will I think of phrases from certain songs, will I think of Paris? he wondered. What will it be? Will I be here again, feeling this way?

'I couldn't see which category I fell into,' George looked at the smudged glass in his greasy fingers. 'I said to him, well I don't think I'm such a bad old stick, so am I doomed then?'

'What did he say?'

'Said he didn't know. Sod's Law, ain't it?' George shrugged. 'Well, seeing my salvation's hanging in the balance, would it be all right to go on somewhere, do you think? I've always wanted to wander round Pigalle. Pig Alley the Yanks called it in the war, we heard stories of it. Wished we had a Pig Alley in Italy. I'd like to have a stroll down the Champs Elysées too. It's still early, right?'

'Let me pay and we will go there.' Jan signalled at the waiter.

'Do you know what the Jerries called a French breakfast, so I heard, during the war? Do you know? A cigarette and a woman. Dirty sods.' George gave a slow smile of evident admiration. 'I'd like to go to Rome again and all. See what it's like now. There's a few places I wouldn't mind seeing. Got to get on with it. The wife won't do it, though, so I shall have to go on my own. I want to do it while I can.'

'I will come with you.'

'Will you? What, to Rome? Lovely. When are we going then?'

'How about in a couple of weeks' time?'

'Be sensible, mate.'

'Well, I am being sensible.'

'Oh.' George looked down at the plate and, seeing the stem of his glass, finished the small amount in the bottom of it. His mouth had dropped; it was pulled down by the weight of his jaw, submerging.

'Well, we should go while we can,' he said, 'you and me. We should have some fun.' He looked up at Jan and smiled. 'After all it's good of a young chap like you to come with me.'

'It's good of a young chap like you to come with me. I only hope you don't get me into too much trouble.'

'Lovely looking lot, those Italian girls. We'll need some spending money.'

'We will. Why not? We'll have a little flirtation or two. We're good-looking fellows, men of maturity and panache.'

'That's right.'

The waiter put the bill between them on a small saucer and Jan reached for it.

'Fair's fair,' said George, pushing a note across the table and getting up. He leant across to Jan and whispered, ''Ere, how do you say goodnight in French?' He listened with one eye closed, raised a finger and nodded, then went to find his coat and hat, stopping briefly in front of the two ladies to say, with a small bow, '*Bon-soir,* '*dames.*'

71

'*Au revoir, mon Général,*' called the owner of the porn shop.

'Hear that,' said George, 'thinks I'm Monty.'

Jan looked backwards. The man was reclining against the window of his store, his mouth opened by laughter, his eyes creased, surrounded by the garish colours of the silly artefacts of an industry in which souvenir shopping meets physical desire.

'I never thought it would be like that,' said George, settling, like Jan, against the cool leather of the immaculate interior of their taxi.

'It's not as interesting as Amsterdam, you would enjoy Amsterdam.'

'Load of rubbish they sell, don't they? Who buys that stuff? Dirty old men?'

Jan laughed, 'Like you and me.'

George balked, his head back against the seat, his chin straightening.

'Nah.'

They were full of fun. They had shared another bottle of wine at a small café on Montmartre and descended the steps below Sacré Coeur at some pace.

Their taxi driver was an old man, with a few strands of grey hair combed neatly over his mottled head. He had an electric hearing aid which was whirring noisily, Jan noticed as the old fellow jumped out to open the door for them. He spoke and Jan laughed again.

'He asks if you were a General. He heard what the man in the shop said.'

George leaned forward between the seats and smiled at the man.

'In Italy,' he said, 'I was a general nuisance.'

The man nodded seriously, tapping with a flat hand at the side of his head, trying to right whatever was wrong with his hearing equipment. The whirring took on a new higher pitch and the man cursed and swerved.

'*Dites que mon père etait aussi Général,*' he said, turning round to look at Jan, his eyes intent, '*pour la résistance.*'

'He says his father was a General – in the resistance,' said Jan, raising his eyebrows, adding, 'They all say that.' The man said something else and gave a small dry-throated laugh and nod.

'What's he say?'

'He says if we would like to meet some nice girls, he can introduce us. For a fine General like yourself . . .'

'Nah,' said George, looking out the window as the car took its tour of the Place Concorde, 'at my age I'd rather have a whisky mac. I'd have liked to see some French tarts, you know, miniskirts and high heels, red lipstick. I'd have liked that. I didn't think much of Pig Alley though. Those shops.' Jan recalled how the owner of the last store they had gone into had offered George a video tape promising '*Folies Anales*'. George had taken his glasses from the top pocket of his zip-up jacket and inspected it closely. He'd not flinched at the cover shot of an engorged penis directed at a young woman's anus. He looked through his lenses and over his glasses, moving the tape in and out of focus before he handed it back.

'No, ta.'

The owner, clearly amused, had headed off to the section marked 'XXX', returning with two or three other tapes to show to the old man. George was putting his glasses firmly back in his top pocket and shaking his head, 'It ain't a video I need. I know how to do it. You don't forget.'

'Take us up the Champs Elysées,' Jan asked the driver, who nodded, *'jusqu'au soldat inconnu.'* After a few moments of silence, gliding underneath the sparkling lighting of the wide street, Jan began to hum *'Alouette, gentil' alouette'* and George picked up on it to sing the words, Jan joined him and soon they were singing the few lines of the song, with exaggerated emphasis on the 'oh' that precedes the refrain, at the top of their voices. The driver fiddled with his hearing aid, apparently tuning it and exclaiming with irritation.

Jan pointed out the tomb of the unknown soldier under the Arc de Triomphe, and asked George if he'd like to take a wander down the Champs Elysées. George shook his head and patted Jan's knee.

'No, son, I've had a lovely time, you done us proud with the tour, but I'm all done in now. Tired. Let's go home, shall we?'

Jan agreed and had to tap the driver on the shoulder to get him to turn his hearing aid back on so that he could hear their instructions.

72

Jan was sitting on the bed, his legs crossed at the ankle, the window wide open and the lamp over his bed providing just sufficient light for him to read his book. He had restored his book on European civilization to its original cover and was a few pages into the first chapter. He had been in the same place at least three times before. The pain in his back was bad. Pretty soon he should go on to the morphine shunt. They had told him it would give him control over his pain management, they had implied it would give him some sort of freedom. They had spoken about it, his doctors, as if it were a wonderful thing, as if it would give him new life. He need never feel the pain; he need only squeeze the button to top himself up. It was a one-way street; it was the direct route home. He had taken out a capsule of the morphine he had with him and had poured himself a small glass of water from the plastic bottle by his bed when he heard the knock at his door and George's voice saying, 'Sorry to wake you, mate, it's me.'

He went to the door and stood in front of George who had removed his cardigan and shirt and was now wearing a vest with his trousers. His braces hung down at the sides. He looked distressed.

'Just had a call from the oldest daughter. Dorothy had a stroke today. She's all right; she's in hospital overnight, for just a few days they hope. They put her on some medicine to sort her out.'

'Is she okay?'

'She's lost the use of one side of her face, Jeanette says, but that might come back.' George licked his lips and swallowed. 'Can't stay here, though, with her poorly. I shall have to go back tomorrow, mate, first thing.'

'Of course.'

'I'll get another ticket.'

'For the train.'

'Yes. Carol's going to meet me at Ashford.'

'I will come with you to the station.'

'No, mate, I'll be leaving first thing, before six I expect.'

'That's fine.'

'You need your sleep.'

Jan shook his head and smiled, 'No, I am feeling good, George, after our night out. I shall come with you. Make sure I send you off with a cup of tea.'

'All right.' George extended his hand and Jan shook it firmly. 'Sleep well, son.'

'You too.'

He watched George make his way along the narrow corridor, using his hands against the walls to steady him. He saw the thick fold of pink skin that separated the few rows of short white hair at the back of his head from the white cotton of the vest beneath it. He saw that his friend's hands were mottled like the driver's head and that the skin behind his upper arms hung loose, like chicken flesh. When George turned about at the end of the corridor to raise his right hand in a goodnight salute, Jan could not see his eyes, just the dazzling reflection off his glasses from the crystal chandelier wall-lamps.

He went back into his room and looked at the bed with its austere blanket and sheeting tucked around the mattress as though it were nailed in place. He chose the chair by the window and sat down in it and reached for the phone. He was going to call his oldest son, and ask him to meet him at the train station in Brugge the following afternoon. 'Bring Ben,' he would say to him and he would buy them a good dinner and let them go their own ways early. He would see their faces in the candlelight of an inn he knew.

Acknowledgements

I'd like to thank my friend, Germaine Vooghden and also Eric and Lieve Landuyt for help with the Belgium details.

With thanks for reading to Susan Martin, Mirian and Jason Lamberth, Marie Doig, Fiona Burles, Sophie Harman, Babar Javed, Claire Potter, Cliodhna Purcell, Catherine and Paul Lyons, Carol Thiess, Eric Houseknecht and Rob Dunbar. For keeping the animals at bay – thanks to Sandra Walker, Nicole Vilhem, Brigitte Dutouquet and Raymond Guisiano.

With my thanks to the fantastic team at Simon & Schuster, to Rochelle and Nigel.

I am indebted to two talents: Tif Loehnis, my agent and Ben Ball, my editor.

This book is for Bette Waller and Iris Soan, for Jim, Denise and for my parents.

It is also for John. I'm grateful to you, you see . . .